THE WHIRLWIND

THE WHIRLWIND

Alan Savage

This first world edition published in Great Britain 2007 by
SEVERN HOUSE PUBLISHERS LTD of
9–15 High Street, Sutton, Surrey SM1 1DF.
This first world edition published in the USA 2007 by
SEVERN HOUSE PUBLISHERS INC of
595 Madison Avenue, New York, N.Y. 10022.

British Library Cataloguing in Publication Data

Savage, Alan, 1930-
    The whirlwind
    1.   Great Britain. Royal Air Force. Fighter Command - Fiction
    2.   Germany. Luftwaffe - Fiction
    3.   Air pilots, Military - Germany - Family relationships - Fiction
    4.   Air pilots, Military - Great Britain - Family relationships - Fiction
    5.   World War, 1939-1945 - Participation, English - Fiction
    6.   World War, 1939-1945 - Participation, German - Fiction
    7.   Brothers - Fiction
    8.   Domestic fiction
    I.   Title
    823.9'14 [F]

    ISBN-13: 978-0-7278-6474-1   (cased)

All Severn House titles are printed on acid-free paper.

Typeset by Palimpsest Book Production Ltd.,
Grangemouth, Stirlingshire, Scotland.
Printed and bound in Great Britain by
MPG Books Ltd., Bodmin, Cornwall.

This is a novel. Except where they can be historically identified, the characters are invented, and not intended to depict real persons, living or dead.

'They have sown the wind, and they shall reap the whirlwind.'

The Bible
Hosea 8:7

CONTENTS

PART ONE
THE WIND

'When all aloud the wind doth blow.'
William Shakespeare
'Winter' (from *Love's Labour's Lost*)

Bombs

Colonel Max Bayley stepped from the taxi on to the pavement, handed the driver a note, then stood beside his suitcase, gazing at the street. Of medium height, but strongly built, with his uniform as a senior officer in the Fighter Wing of the Luftwaffe fitting him like a glove, he made a handsome figure, just as the tilt of his high-peaked cap, and the Iron Cross along with the Knight's Cross on his tunic indicated that he was very much a fighting pilot – and a successful one at that. All of which made his face, with its rounded features and relaxed expression, somewhat incongruous. Until one looked into his eyes. They were clear and blue, but they had looked on too much death and destruction in the last three years, even though he was not yet twenty-three years old in this late autumn of 1942. He had begun to wonder if he would ever again know true contentment, much less happiness. Now, however, there was some prospect of that on the horizon – supposing he survived for a while longer.

Even Berlin itself was no longer a happy place. When Max remembered the huge, hysterically joyous crowds that had thronged the streets in the summer of 1940, only two years before, celebrating the greatest military success in Germany's history, it seemed like another world. The people who now hurried by on the pavement were anxious, depressed, uncertain, whereas only two years ago there had been no doubts.

The downward spiral – although no one in Germany would dare call it that – had actually begun even before that euphoric summer of 1940 had ended. That there might be difficult times ahead had become apparent in the failure of the Luftwaffe to destroy the RAF in what was known as the Battle of Britain. Few people in Germany had recognized the importance of that. They preferred to follow the example of their Fuehrer and consider it merely an example of British intransigence, which would be sorted out as soon as the more important matter of Soviet Russia had been dealt with. Max Bayley, the son of an English father and a German mother, knew better, just as he doubted that the small matter of Soviet Russia would ever be resolved satisfactorily. And judging by the faces of the Berliners today, most of them were beginning to doubt that too.

'Colonel Bayley, sir!' The doorman was hurrying forward to pick up the suitcase. 'Welcome, sir. It is good to see you again.'

'It is good to be here, Jorge.' Which was no lie, despite the atmosphere of pervading gloom. Max had been introduced to the Hotel Albert by his wealthy cousins, the Bittermans, his mother's family, when he had still been a boy, and over the years had come to regard it almost as a second home. But he had never seen it with sandbags piled round the entrance. 'Have you been hit?'

'Oh, no, sir. But sometimes they come quite close.' Jorge pointed across the street to where workmen were busily filling in a crater. 'That broke a few windows.'

'I'll bet it did.'

'When are you going to destroy the bastards, sir?'

The bastards, Max thought. His half-brother was an RAF pilot, and an ace in his own right, as befitted the two sons of one of Great Britain's premier fighter pilots of the previous war that now seemed so long ago. Although he did not suppose that Johnnie, essentially a Spitfire pilot – even if he was now apparently flying the new-fangled and very long-range Mosquito – had ever actually been over Berlin. And when he thought of what the Luftwaffe had done to London and so many other British cities, not to mention places like Warsaw and Rotterdam, it was difficult to decide who were the real bastards.

But that was not a thought to risk airing to a patriotic German hotel doorman in the heart of Berlin. So Max merely said, 'We're working on it,' and followed Jorge into the lobby.

'Colonel Bayley, sir!' The reception clerk was as unctuous as ever. 'Your room is waiting for you, sir.'

'Thank you, Joachim.'

'And there are messages.' He held out the three envelopes, rolling his eyes as he did so. The envelopes were sealed, but he had undoubtedly read the contents before doing that.

Max nodded and thrust the envelopes into his tunic pocket.

'Will you require a table for dinner, sir?'

'Yes, I will.'

'Ah . . .' Joachim had followed with interest the course of Max's various amours over the years, and even if he knew the Colonel was now married, for the second time, he also remembered that the first marriage had not made *too* much difference to a chaotic private life, at least until it had ended in tragedy.

'I shall be alone, Joachim, at least as far as I know.' Max followed the bellboy up the stairs.

The best thing about the Hotel Albert was that, sandbags on the front door apart, it never changed. All the bedrooms were identical, and therefore Max knew that he could have slept in any one of them on a previous visit. They all contained both nightmares and the sweetest of memories. It was in one of these bedrooms that he had seduced Heidi Stumpff, and in an excess of boyhood passion and gallantry – he had only been twenty – had asked her to marry him.

He recalled how surprised she had been, while sitting naked in his bed. Although he had been warned by his superior officers that, however well-bred and however wealthy her father, Heidi Stumpff had the reputation of being a whore, the thought of possessing all of that fragile blonde beauty had been overwhelming. Equally important, the thought of *not* possessing it, not being able to claim it whenever he wished, had been unacceptable. Besides, like most twenty-year-old boys, he had had no doubt that he could change her into the woman of his dreams, rather than allow her to remain the slut she undoubtedly was.

While Heidi had clearly reflected that if the naïve young man was a bit of a bore, marriage to an already famous fighter pilot, about to receive his first Iron Cross, would be glamorous and would give her reputation a much-needed boost. Besides, as he was currently fighting a war, he would only be around on rare occasions. She had had no intention of changing her lifestyle. That that lifestyle, that insatiable desire for sexual stimulation, would eventually lead her into the arms of a British agent, and thence a Gestapo cell and a hangman's noose, he now saw had been inevitable. At the time he had been distraught, had gone into combat with the sole desire of being shot down and killed, but with every intention of taking as many of the enemy as he could with him, and instead had become one of Germany's most successful surviving aces.

Now, however, he had every possible reason for surviving, and prospering, and being happy. He tipped the boy, took off his tunic, sat at the table, and laid the envelopes in front of him. He slit the first one, took out the two sheets of notepaper, and felt a warm glow sweeping through his body.

> *My darling! We have been separated for two months and already I am desolated. Do not be concerned. The people here are kindness itself. Munich is a lovely city. The Alps look magnificent in the distance. But for Junior, I would look forward to skiing in those mountains in another couple of months. But for the time being I must be patient and dream of you. I suppose you will not be able to tell me why you have been summoned to Berlin, certainly now that I am no longer a serving officer in the Wehrmacht, but I am sure it will be another step forward. Do try to be with me for the birth, but if that is impossible, remember that I love you always. Hilde.*

Max laid down the letter, slowly, leaned back in his chair to stare at the wall, to envisage her face, always somewhat serious save when illuminated by her sudden smile. After so much misery, to be so happy . . . even if he was constantly aware that happiness, in this greatest of conflicts, was a transient emotion. He slit the second envelope.

> *Colonel Bayley. Field-Marshal Milch will see you at ten o'clock, Tuesday, 24 November 1942.*

Tomorrow. That was why he was here. He frowned at the third envelope. The handwriting was familiar, but he found it hard to believe she would wish to contact him after having summarily dismissed him from her life a year ago. But with

Erika von Bitterman Haussmann, nothing was ever final, not for good or for bad. He took out the sheet of paper.

Max! I must see you. I know you are coming to Berlin and will be staying at the Albert. Please telephone me when you arrive. This is most urgent. Erika.

He considered for some moments. His instincts were to tear the paper up and throw it into the wastebasket. But he knew he was not going to do that. He supposed his entire adult life had revolved around Erika. She was his cousin, the daughter of Count Max von Bitterman, his mother's first cousin, and now head of the German family. Both men had been named after the original Count Max von Bitterman, Karolina Bayley's father and Max senior's uncle, the founder of the family fortune. He had first met Erika, then still a teenager although several years older than himself, at his mother's funeral in 1934, and even at that early age – he had been fifteen – had been struck by her flamboyant personality.

That a cousin would seduce him only a few years later had been unthinkable then. But nothing had ever been unthinkable to Erika, and at nineteen, having only just found out the truth of his parentage and position in the family, he was like a ripe apple ready to fall into any arms that could offer him love, warmth, sexual stimulation, and above all, a *place*.

He was not sure when his confusion had been replaced by an ever-growing resentment, directed principally at his father and his brother, but also even at the mother he, and everyone else, had adored.

Karolina von Bitterman, only daughter and thus sole heir to the wealthiest man in Germany, had, like so many other young socialites, determined to do her bit for the Fatherland during the Great War, and had become a nurse. Neither she nor her family could have expected her to fall in love with the badly wounded young British pilot she had tended in a prison hospital. The romance would certainly not have been allowed to develop had Grandpa Max lived. But he had died – perhaps of a broken heart – as the shooting had ended in Germany's total defeat, and Karolina, finding herself a multi-millionairess with a financial empire to manage, had turned away from her German cousins, to their deep resentment, and

married her English patient, transferring all of her preroga-
tives to him.

By then she was already pregnant. There had been the perfect
romantic story. But there had been a skeleton in the closet.
On embarkation leave before going to France in 1917, Mark
Bayley had unknowingly fathered a son. Then he had disappeared, into combat and fame, and a German prison, after
having been reported as missing, believed dead. It had taken
two years for Patricia Pope to discover that her fleeting lover
was actually alive, and by then it had been too late: Mark had
been married, and his wife was pregnant. So Patricia Pope
had abandoned her one-year-old son and committed suicide.

That catastrophic series of events had cast a blight over the
happiness Mother and Father had been enjoying. But Karolina
had solved the problem, as it had been her nature to solve
every problem, by going directly to the root of the matter.
She had insisted on adopting the orphan, and bringing him
up as her own, together with her natural son. No one could
do less than admire her for that. But Karolina, in her determination to compensate for the tragedy that she knew was
haunting her beloved husband's life, had gone beyond any
reasonable expectation. Making no difference between her two
sons, it had followed naturally that the elder, John, should be
regarded as his father's heir, while the younger, Max, took
his place dutifully behind.

Neither son had known anything of the truth until they had
been teenagers. Max had adored his elder brother, been content
to follow him in everything. Until, so suddenly and so tragi-
cally, Mother had died of cancer at the age of thirty-eight.
Then the truth had been revealed. Father had been utterly
devastated by what had happened, but he had also been reassuring, as only Father could be. They were both his sons,
and he wanted only the best for them. But as Max had slowly
taken stock of the situation, so had his resentment grown.

In his more reflective moments he had known he was being
selfishly unreasonable, and going against everything his mother
had wanted. But the facts were there, and irrefutable. John
was heir to the Bitterman – now Bayley – fortune. He would
inherit Hillside, the huge house in which they had both grown
up. He was also now married and a father, so the line continued.
But none of that fortune, or the house, had ever been Bayley

money. The only member of the English family with Bitterman blood in his veins was himself, and yet he would have to spend his entire life in the shadow of his illegitimate brother.

Max knew that but for Erika he would undoubtedly have grown to accept the situation. But then had come that fateful summer of 1938 when Erika had visited her cousins, and wrapped him around her little finger just as she had wrapped her legs around his body. He remembered how disturbed he had been. A cousin blatantly inviting him to bed! But it was an irresistible message for an impressionable nineteen-year-old. He was being robbed of his inheritance. There was nothing anyone could do about that now. But at least in Germany he would be amongst friends as well as relatives. He would have a future of his own, not merely as Bayley Minor – and as the son of a famous pilot, that future, she had promised, would include a career in the Luftwaffe, flying what had then been the finest fighter aircraft in the world: the Messerschmitt 109 E.

Erika had not lied about that, and when he had fled with her to Germany he had had no idea that in little more than a year Great Britain and Germany would be at war, making the break with his English family irreversible. And as Mark Bayley's son, he had indeed prospered. But he had not gone to Germany to achieve fame and fortune. He had gone to marry Erika, and bask for the rest of his life in that exuberant sexuality. Well, the exuberant sexuality was still there, but it had never been his to possess, except on the rare occasions when she felt like bestowing it upon him.

Early on he had realized that he had been utterly and completely duped, that she had not come to England in 1938 to holiday with her English cousins, but simply to destroy the family for her Nazi masters, who equally resented the removal of the Bitterman fortune from their control. But that realization had come too late to reverse the course of his life, for he had already been trumpeted in the British press as the arch traitor. And despite his catastrophic marriage to Erika's best friend, her body had remained at that time the most exciting thing in life for him, far more so than flying.

Until last year, when he had been returned from Russia in disgrace for having assaulted an SS officer, and officially designated as suffering from a mental breakdown owing to too much combat. In despair, and desperate for reassurance, he had instinctively contacted Erika . . . and had been rejected with the coldest contempt. Erika von Bitterman Haussmann, wife of a senior Party member, did not waste her time with failures.

Yet now she seemed desperate to see him. She must know that he had at last met a woman he could love without reservation, and who could equally love him back, even if she probably did not know that Hildegarde was pregnant. But she did sound desperate. And she was his cousin. And besides, it might be interesting to see Erika in trouble, for a change.

He picked up the telephone.

'Yes?'

'Erika?'

'Max! Oh, Max, it is so good to hear your voice. Are you at the Albert?'

'If I were not at the Albert, Erika, I would not have received your note.'

'I will be with you in fifteen minutes.'

'No, you will not.'

'You mean your wife is with you?'

'No, my wife is not with me. But I have only just arrived, and I wish to have a shave and a bath.'

'I can scrub your back.'

'I will meet you in the bar at six o'clock this evening.'

'Six . . . that is four hours away.'

'I am sure the time will pass quickly enough. If you are good, you may stay to dinner.'

There was a brief hesitation. 'Max, I am so sorry about that problem last year.'

'You can tell me about it over dinner.'

Max called Joachim to order another place for dinner, had his bath and a brief nap, dressed in a clean uniform, and entered the bar at five past six. This early in the evening there were only a few customers, but Erika would have stood out in a crowd, even half turned away from him. She wore an off-the-shoulder black evening gown, its deep décolletage leaving no doubt that her breasts were as magnificent as he remembered, just as the clinging material at her hips reminded him of the length and shape of her legs.

The colour of the dress accentuated her own colouring, matched by the long black hair drifting down her back. Even the bold, if slightly coarse, features fitted into the voluptuous whole. Max stood at her shoulder.

'I assume you're drinking champagne.'

'Max!' She swivelled on the stool to throw her arms round him and bring him against her for a kiss on the mouth, watched with jealous appreciation by the other customers as well as the barman. 'It is so good to see you. I am actually drinking cognac.'

'At this hour? Things must be bad.'

She made a face, and pushed her glass across the counter. 'Join me.'

'I'll have a schnapps, Jaime,' Max said.

The barman filled both glasses.

'Your health.' Max brushed his glass against hers. 'Do you wish to talk now, or after dinner?'

'Let's sit over there.' She indicated a corner which was reasonably private, and led him across the room before sitting down and crossing her knees. 'How is married life, second time around?'

'Married life is unbelievably good, second time around.'

'How nice. I heard somewhere that the lady is a serving officer in the army.'

'She was, yes. She is now preparing to be a mother.'

'Good heavens! Congratulations.'

'Thank you. Now tell me how you knew I was coming to Berlin.'

'I have friends.'

'In high places, no doubt. So what is the problem?'

She finished her drink. 'Hans has thrown me out.'

Max was tempted to say congratulations but decided against it; in any event, it would apply to the husband rather than the wife. 'You must have been in bed with someone special. I thought he went along with your peccadilloes?'

'Are you going to get me another drink?'

Max snapped his fingers and the waiter hurried over. 'So?' he asked, when she was again sipping her cognac.

'Does it matter?'

'It obviously mattered to Hans. You don't have to tell me if you'd rather not.'

'It was terrible. He beat him up.'

'Who beat who up?'

'Hans beat Richter up.'

'Good lord!' Max had only met Erika's husband once, and that had been back in 1939, before they were married, and before he had had any idea they were going to be married. He had then been living in a boyishly euphoric dream, flying 109s by day and believing that he was the only man in Erika's life whenever he had a free night. He remembered Hans Haussmann as a large, somewhat bland man, not someone he would have associated with physical violence. He personally disliked him simply because of the shock he had received when, given leave after the enormous victory gained by the Wehrmacht and the Luftwaffe, in May 1940, he had hurried down to Bitterman to ask Cousin Max for permission to marry his daughter, and had been calmly informed that that was an absurd idea as Erika had, a few weeks before, married her childhood sweetheart . . . who also happened to be a wealthy man, someone out of an itinerant fighter pilot's league.

He had come very close to seeking out the happy couple and doing some beating up of his own, but had thought better of it and retuned to see what he could do about the RAF instead. But that had not meant that he had lost Erika, as he had supposed. She had always been there, ready and willing, whenever he was in Berlin on leave, more often than not with her friend Heidi Stumpff, and in their company he had sunk deeper and deeper into the amoral mire that was Nazi Germany.

But those days were behind him now, and if he could have no doubt that Nazi Germany was on a collision course with history, he at least intended to enjoy what was left of it . . . with Hildegarde. So now he merely asked, 'Would I be acquainted with this Richter?'

'I shouldn't think so. He was Hans's chauffeur.'

Max put down his glass to stare at her. 'You went to bed with your husband's chauffeur? For God's sake, Erika . . .'

'He was so big,' she murmured dreamily. 'I think he was even bigger than you, Max.'

'How nice of you to say that. Had I been Hans, I would have beaten you up as well as this Richter character.'

'He did. I will show you the marks, after dinner.'

'I don't think that would be a good idea.'

And at that moment the maitre d' arrived with the menus.

'So what are you doing now?' Max asked as they ate. 'I mean, here in Berlin?'

He knew that the bright lights and social whirl of the city had always been her natural habitat, but that had been as the wife of a prominent Nazi Party member, and when Berlin had still been a place of bright lights. Now that the war had come uncomfortably close, at least in the air, the bright lights and the social whirl were conspicuously absent.

'Most estranged wives,' he went on, 'go home to mother.'

'Bitterman is such a bore,' she pointed out. 'All of Bavaria is a bore. And Mummy is the worst bore of all. All she wants to do is lecture me. I am twenty-seven years old, for Christ's sake. Don't you think I know how to live my own life?'

'The evidence suggests not. So you are . . .'

'Oh, I'm living in the flat. They don't object to that.'

'And doing what? Apart from, I assume, fucking every man you can lay hands on. What happens during the day?'

'I don't get up very early. And I can usually find someone to amuse me.'

'Erika,' he said earnestly. 'There is a war on. It is the greatest war in history. Everyone is doing his or her bit. Except you. You are going to wind up being investigated by the Party.'

'I am Erika von Bitterman Haussmann,' she pointed out coldly. 'I am . . . Oh, for God's sake,' she cried as the wail of the siren cut across the evening.

'Ladies and gentlemen,' the maitre d' called. 'I am sorry, but I must ask you to leave your tables and proceed to the air raid shelter. It is just outside the back door. The staff will assist you.'

'Seems like we'd better do what the man says,' Max suggested, standing up.

'I thought you people were supposed to be keeping the Tommies off our backs,' Erika grumbled as he held her arm to guide her across the room, which had suddenly become an obstacle course of pushed-back chairs and scattered napkins, but almost no panic; the people of Berlin had become used to these increasingly regular incursions.

'So did we,' he agreed.

They emerged into the back yard and he looked up at the sky. It was a dark night, and although it was criss-crossed with searchlight beams he could as yet see no planes. But it was a measure of the increasing confidence of the RAF that to be here this early they must have left England well before dusk, which would have meant their having to fight their way right across Europe. Of course nowadays the Tommies had the support of their new long-range fighter bombers, such as the de Havilland Mosquito, capable of speeds over four hundred miles an hour and with a range of two thousand miles – and Berlin was only seven hundred from London. Perhaps his brother John was up there now. But to get here they would have had to engage his own Wing in Belgium – without him to lead them, he thought with a pardonable excess of personal pride: he was, after all, one of the best they had.

And without him to lead them, they certainly did not appear to have checked the enemy. They reached the entrance to the shelter as the first bombs began to fall.

The interior of the shelter was crowded, but again everyone was very orderly, and the hotel staff were hurrying about spreading blankets and pillows; there were only a few benches and most people had already settled for the floor. Max led Erika to a free spot and sat beside her. 'Anyone would think we were here for the night,' she growled as a maid handed them two blankets and two pillows. 'Don't get me wrong, I do want to spend the night with you, but not on a stone floor and with all these people around.'

'At least it's heated,' he pointed out, preferring not to take up her other remark: the people surrounding them were his best protection.

Down here the noise outside had been somewhat muted, but now there came a very loud crash; the entire shelter trembled and the lights went out. A woman screamed and the alarm was taken up by others. Max scrambled to his feet, and Erika clutched his boot. 'What are you doing? Where are you going?'

'I must try to get some order into these people.'

But as he spoke there was an even louder crash from close at hand, and pieces of plaster came down from the roof. The screams redoubled, and in the darkness there was a general movement to and fro. Max shouted to try to calm them, telling them the raid would be over in a few minutes, but no one took any notice of him.

'What you need to do is fire your pistol,' Erika recommended.

'My pistol is in my bedroom,' he pointed out. 'I do not usually wear it to dinner.'

'Well, then, you had better come back down here beside me and hope we do not get trampled to death.'

He supposed she was right, and her courage was invigorating. He was not aware of being afraid himself, although he supposed to be immolated in a darkened cellar would be comparable to being unable to bail out from a burning cockpit. He had been in a burning cockpit once, and although he had managed to get out, it was an experience he would never forget. But it really would be an absurdity for a fighter ace to die in a darkened cellar. On the other hand, he, and everyone who had any details on the subject, could never forget what had happened to Cologne and Essen only a few months ago, when the RAF had subjected the cities to thousand-bomber raids; the exact amount of damage done had never been made public, but there could be no doubt it had been immense. As someone who had taken part in the bombing raids over London in 1940 – although flying as an escort fighter rather than delivering the destruction himself – he could not help but think of the biblical saying: he who sows the wind will reap the whirlwind.

He sat down again, and Erika snuggled against him, taking his hand and putting it inside her bodice; she never wore underwear. He supposed he should resist her, but the noise and the confusion and the darkness were inducing a desire for intimacy, and this woman had been his first love.

In any event, as he had foreseen, the raid was over fifteen minutes later. The all-clear siren wailed, to be replaced by the clanging of fire-engine bells, and the largely dishevelled diners finally emerged into the night air.

'I suppose our dinner is good and cold,' someone remarked.

'Where did you intend to eat?' asked his partner.

They stared at the blazing hotel, over which hoses were in vain aiming jets of water.

'Shit!' Max muttered.

'I wonder if my apartment has been hit,' Erika said. 'Come on home with me, and I'll scramble you an egg.'

'The Field-Marshal will see you in a moment, Herr Colonel.' The secretary, a tall young woman, despite the traumas of the night, was as spic as could be, in her white shirt, black tie and blouse, black stockings and shoes. She was regarding Max with some suspicion; his uniform was distinctly crushed, his boots were unpolished, and worst of all he was wearing neither cap nor belts. On the other hand, her diary indicated that he was expected. 'Do sit down.'

'Thank you.' Max merely smiled at her as he took a chair; he had had to run a gauntlet of stares while making his way through the Air Ministry building. But he could not subdue a feeling of euphoria, combined, of course, with guilt. In the year that he had been married to Hilde, he had never even looked at another woman. There had been no need. Hildegarde had provided everything any man could possibly want when it came to sex. But as she had slightly old-fashioned views on several subjects, sex had suddenly ceased when her pregnancy had begun to show. In addition to that, he had felt it would be safer to remove her from the active war zone that the skies over Belgium had become in recent months, and which often encompassed the land beneath those skies as well. Hence Munich. But that meant that he had not even had her company for the past couple of months, except for a weekend visit. Add to that the flowing adrenalin caused, even in a veteran like himself, by the air raid, and the fact that it was not possible for even a monk to spend a night alone in an apartment with Erika Haussmann and not succumb to her charms, and there were all of his reasons and excuses neatly lined up. But who were they to be used to convince? This was not an episode he ever intended Hildegarde to learn about.

'The Field-Marshal is ready for you, Herr Colonel.' The secretary was holding the door for him.

Max stepped inside and stood to attention. 'Heil Hitler!'

'Heil Hitler! Max, how are you?' Erhard Milch was a heavily built man with strong features and dark hair brushed straight back from his forehead. He had known Max for several years, and had been his friend since that famous day immediately after the Dunkirk evacuation, when he had urged Goering to undertake an immediate airborne invasion of England while the British Army was shattered and the British people unprepared to withstand a blitzkrieg. And Max, that day acting as his pilot, had supported him. Goering had dismissed the idea as a fantasy, perhaps rightly, and Milch's career had gone into temporary decline, but he was now back as Operational Commander of the Luftwaffe, and he had never forgotten Max's support on that fateful day. Max could not doubt that his position as the Field-Marshal's favourite pilot had protected him time and again, particularly on the occasions when he had reacted violently to the more vicious aspects of Nazi philosophy, just as it had been responsible for his rapid promotion.

But now Milch was frowning as he took Max's hand; his grip was firm. 'Are you all right?'

'I must apologize for my appearance, Herr Field-Marshal. I was at the Albert last night.'

'My God! Of course. You always stay there.'

'Yes, sir. I'm afraid my gear went up with the hotel. I will of course replace it, but I overslept this morning and felt that my appointment with you should take priority.'

'But you *are* all right? You were not hurt?'

'No, sir. I was not actually in the hotel when it was hit.'

'Thank God for that. But come and sit down.' He seated himself behind his desk. 'So where did you sleep? The Albert was hit before midnight.'

'I found alternative accommodation, sir.'

Milch scratched his nose. He knew that his protégé had a penchant for peccadilloes, but he also had acted as promoter of Max's marriage to Hildegarde Gruner. He decided not to pursue the matter, at least directly. 'Hildegarde is well?'

'As far as I know, sir. I have not seen her for six weeks.'

Milch raised his eyebrows.

'I thought it safer for her not to stay in Ostend during this stage of her pregnancy. But I hear from her regularly, and she seems happy enough.'

'But missing you, no doubt,' Milch suggested pointedly.

'As I am missing her, sir,' Max countered, refusing to lower his eyes.

'So she is at Bitterman, is she?'

'Ah . . . no, sir. She is in a hotel, in Munich.'

Milch frowned. 'But Bitterman is your home. And it is only fifty-odd kilometres from Munich.'

'With respect, sir, it is not *my* home. It is my cousin's home and . . . well, I am not sure they would welcome Hildegarde.'

Milch regarded him for several seconds. 'Do you really believe that it is their home and not yours? It is the family home.'

Max was mystified. 'Yes, sir. And my cousin Max is head of the family. He and his wife have lived there ever since my mother died.' With their daughter, he reflected.

'You have discussed this with Count von Bitterman, have you?'

'Well, no sir. It is not my place to do so. Max and Oriane were very good to me when I first returned to Germany, and indeed, ever since. It's just that, well, they are a little snobbish, and Hildegarde is not . . . well . . .'

'Sufficiently aristocratic for them?'

'I would not wish to embarrass either her or them, sir.'

'Hmm. I think you need to have a serious chat with your cousin, Max, and straighten out a few things.'

'Sir?'

'You are obviously unaware of it, but Bitterman belongs to you, not to him.'

'*Sir?*'

'I have looked into this matter, because . . . well, I am interested in you, in your future. You do know that your mother was the only child of the original Count von Bitterman? And that he left his entire estate to her?'

'I do know that, sir. But when she left Germany, the title and all her property here went to the next male descendant, my cousin.'

'No, no, Max. Admittedly when your mother took up residence in England, you were a babe in arms. But you are still the next male heir. In fact, it is specifically stated in your grandfather's will that the inheritance he bequeathed to his daughter was to pass, on her death, to her eldest son. You're her only son.'

Max stared at him in consternation. 'She never told me of this.'

'Well, you were only fifteen when she died, were you not?

And she could not have expected to die so young. I imagine she did not wish, at that stage, to introduce a discordant note into her marriage.'

The penny slowly started to drop. 'But if what you say is true, sir, then . . .'

'Exactly. Apart from the Bitterman estate here in Germany, you are entitled to everything your father now has in England. It is of course possible that your mother never intended that you should inherit . . .'

Possible, Max thought, bitterly.

'. . . because that might have broken her marriage. We shall never know. And of course there is no way of your mounting a legal challenge at this moment in an English court. But after the war, well, you will have a lot to do. However, as we are still fighting the war we must put your domestic affairs on the back burner for the moment. I'm sorry I haven't been able to get down to Ostend recently, but I have been rather busy. How are things along the Channel coast? Are the Americans making a big difference?'

Max tried to concentrate. What he had just been told was too immense to be taken in at one gulp, as it were. He grinned. 'Only in our tally of kills, sir. They come over in daylight, in great swathes. Oh, these Flying Fortresses, as they call themselves, are very well armed, but they are quite slow, and without fighter escorts they really are sitting ducks.'

'So it seems . . .' Milch glanced at the file on his desk. 'And you now total more than a hundred. That makes you our leading living ace, apart from Hartmann. And soon you will be surpassing even Marseille's hundred and fifty-eight, God rest his soul.'

'I have been lucky, sir. And I do expect the Yanks to improve their tactics, or at least abandon this suicidal daylight raiding and take up night bombing, like the RAF.'

'And how is the RAF doing?'

'They are being a nuisance, as always. They come over most nights, and although our radar seeks them out they are of course more difficult to hit in the dark. And more often than not they have fighter support.'

'The Mosquitoes,' Milch said thoughtfully.

'Yes, sir. I really am sorry that we have not had more success against them, but they are so damned fast . . .'

'Quite. We will get to them eventually. Your brother flies a Mosquito, does he not?'

'Yes, sir. And when I engaged him, over Cologne, in May, he shot me down.'

'How do you feel about that?'

'Frustrated. When this war started, I believed that I was flying the better machine. Now the boot is on the other foot.'

'Are you certain of that? Aren't you now flying the ME 210?'

'Yes, sir.'

'Is it not the best machine you have ever flown? It is certainly an improvement on the Gustav, with its tendency to explode. You know that Marseille was flying a Gustav when his engine blew up? Just as happened to you in Russia last year. You managed to get out. He didn't.'

'As I say, I was lucky. As regards range, and fire-power, and reliability, and speed, the 210 is perhaps the best plane I have flown. But when it comes to manoeuvrability . . . I must confess I sometimes yearn for the old 109 E.'

'The 109 E is a museum piece, Max. These new Spitfire Mark Fours would eat a 109 E for breakfast.'

'Oh, undoubtedly, sir. But, well, only a couple of weeks ago a squadron of my 210s ran into a squadron of Spitfires over England, and two of us were shot down.'

'I read the report,' Milch agreed. 'It was put down to the pilots' lack of experience.'

'I agree that was a factor, sir. The point is that the 210 is not good enough to redress the balance in the air. As for going into combat against the Mosquito, it really is out of its class.'

'Perhaps. But only temporarily. We have some outstanding new models and ideas on the drawing board. However, I agree that we need to get hold of the Mosquito's secrets. As we don't seem able to shoot one down, we are having to use other methods.'

'Sir?'

Milch nodded. 'Spying is a dirty business. But it is sometimes necessary, and thank God it is the business of the Abwehr, not us. We are approaching the problem from another point of view. As I said, our research people are working on a variety of new machines that will be more than a match for the Tommies. But for the time being, you feel that our people are coping with the situation?'

'On the whole, yes. We couldn't do anything about Essen. Or Cologne. Have you any first-hand reports on what happened in Cologne?'

'I have,' Milch said. 'It was not half as bad as the Tommies are claiming. Oh, about five thousand houses were destroyed, and some five thousand people were killed. Those are not unacceptable figures. And, as you say, there is not a lot we can do while they are prepared to send over a thousand planes at a time when our resources – both our planes and our experienced pilots – are tied up in Russia. That is our number one priority. Once that business is settled we can start dealing with the Tommies and the Yanks.'

'And that will be over this year, won't it, sir?'

'It isn't over yet, Max, and we are into another winter.'

'Yes, but surely now we have the Volga . . .'

'Max, we do not *have* the Volga. We have managed to reach the river. That is all.'

'Yes, but now we hold Stalingrad, we control the river, surely.'

'We do not *hold* Stalingrad, Max.'

Max stared at him. 'The papers . . .'

'Surely you, of all people, know better than to believe what you read in the newspapers.'

'But . . .'

'The Sixth Amy has reached Stalingrad, and actually does control at least half the city, but the Russians are defending it house by house, cellar by cellar. Some people are saying that they are fighting so hard because the city bears Stalin's name. A more realistic judgement would be that they know as well as we do that should we gain control of the city, and thus also control the river crossing, we would be well on the way to splitting European Russia in two.'

He paused, and Max swallowed. It was the suggestion of doubt, the use of the words '*should* we gain control' instead of '*when* we gain control' that was bothering him.

'Now the situation has taken a turn for the worse,' Milch went on. 'You understand that what I am about to tell you is in the most complete confidence.'

'Yes, sir.'

'It is possible to suppose,' Milch said, 'that we have tried, as usual, to do too much. The plan for this summer was for

Manstein to complete the drive for the Caucasus oilfields,
while Paulus drove through the centre, occupied Stalingrad,
secured the river crossing, and prepared to split European
Russia in two. But war, as they say, is an option of difficulties. We need to accomplish both of those objectives in order
to eliminate Soviet Russia as an enemy, but it was always
known that such drives deep into the Russian heartland would
result in exposed flanks, which would have to be protected.
Unfortunately, after the heavy casualties we suffered last year,
we lacked the manpower to do this protecting ourselves, so
we gave the task to our allies: the Romanians on the northern
flank, the Italians on the southern.

'It is not my intention to denigrate these people, who are
undoubtedly gallant soldiers in themselves. But at the same
time we must accept the fact that these armies lack the histor-
ical infrastructure and traditions of ours, just as they lack the
discipline and determination that German soldiers possess.
Frankly, this was not considered a vital matter, as it was
assumed by OKW that the Russians equally lacked the
resources and the determination to mount any kind of counter-
attack. It was therefore felt that the flank guards would have
nothing more to do than repel occasional raids. Well, not for
the first time we have been wrong in our judgement of Soviet
capabilities. Last week they launched a massive counter-attack
to the north of Stalingrad, and we have learned that the
Romanians have collapsed. The Russians are streaming across
Paulus's lines of communication, and they are also attacking
the Italians in the south.'

'My God!' Max said. 'If they were to meet . . .'

'Paulus would be cut off.'

'But surely he can pull out, fight his way through to safety!
He has an entire army corps.'

'Certainly he could do that. Unfortunately . . .' Milch paused
again to stare at Max, to leave him in no doubt that he knew
the importance of what he was about to say. 'The Fuehrer has
determined to hold on to Stalingrad, no matter what.'

Max stared at him in turn. 'But that is . . .'

Milch held up a finger. 'Please do not say it, Max. The
Fuehrer is of the opinion that it could be disastrous for the
reputation of the Wehrmacht for the Sixth Army to, as it
were, cut and run. He also feels that the Army can hold its

ground and survive until relieved. Some of us may not agree. We may remember that only a few months ago General Auchinleck chose to abandon Tobruk behind the advancing Afrika Corps, feeling that it would only be isolated for a few weeks while he regrouped and then counter-attacked. Well, he was proved wrong, as Field-Marshal Rommel took Tobruk in a fortnight. That mistaken decision, as you may know, has cost Auchinleck his job.'

'Yes, sir. But if the reports of what happened at El Alamein are correct, haven't the British won a battle and regained Tobruk just the same?'

'That is perfectly true, and we must hope that the same thing will happen at Stalingrad. Manstein is being recalled, with the bulk of his forces, from the Caucasus to relieve the situation. I'm sure you will agree that Manstein is a class above any Britisher as a general, and that the German soldier is a class above the Tommy.' He paused, awaiting a comment.

'Ah . . . I'm sure you're right, sir.' Max knew he had not managed to keep the doubt from his voice.

'However,' the Field-Marshal went on, 'there can be no doubt that the task will be an immense one, certainly with another winter on its way. So it may take a little time. For that time the troops in Stalingrad will almost certainly be cut off, and they will have to stand siege. Of course they can do this. Paulus has a quarter of a million men under his command, and that is more than sufficient to defeat any Russian force sent against him. However, to defeat the enemy an army needs two things: the food to sustain itself and the ammunition to fire. Paulus has estimated that he requires eight hundred tons of supplies per day.'

Yet again he paused to stare at Max, who was beginning to get an inkling of why he had been summoned here so peremptorily. 'Can it be done, sir?'

'Reich-Marshal Goering has promised the Fuehrer that it will be done. The air fleet is being assembled now. Of course it will mean a drain on our resources, and we shall have to act on the defensive in the west until we have won in the east. However, it should not take very long. It *cannot* take very long,' he added, almost as an aside. 'So, you understand what I am talking about.'

'The transport fleet will have to be protected.'

Milch nodded. 'Have you any reservations about returning to Russia?'

'I have no reservations about going anywhere that I am sent, sir.'

'As I had expected. But I must warn you, Max, that things are slightly different now. The Ivans have got new planes and many more of them. I am not saying they are as good as ours, but they are a lot better than the biplanes you were shooting up at will a year ago. You will also be operating in conditions that will make Norway last winter seem like a summer holiday camp. On the other hand, quite a few of your old comrades are still there, and they will be able to advise you how to cope. I am appointing Colonel Langholm as your chief of staff. Does that please you?'

'It pleases me very much, sir.' Gunther Langholm was his oldest friend in the Luftwaffe. They had trained together before the war, had flown together over France in 1940 and then in the Battle of Britain, and they had flown together again during the heady days of the summer of 1941, when all Russia had lain at their feet. Gunther, as his second-in-command, had taken over his Wing following Max's disgrace for striking the SS officer. But . . . 'Did you say chief of staff, Herr Field-Marshal? May I ask who will be commanding the fleet?'

'Why, you will, Max; that is why you will need a chief of staff. I am promoting you to general.'

Max gazed at him in amazement

'Oh, I know there will be criticism of your appointment. You are only just coming up to twenty-three years old, and with your disciplinary record you are not . . . What do they say in England? Everyone's cup of tea? But did not Don Juan of Austria command the Christian fleet to victory over the Turks at Lepanto when he was twenty-five? You are our finest fighting airman, and you are the man for this job. Because that flow of supplies to the Sixth Amy has got to be maintained. Understood?'

'Understood, sir.' Max's head was spinning.

'So, off you go and get yourself measured for a new uniform. And get a new hat as well. You have three days' leave to go down to Munich and see your wife, but I want you to be in Kiev on Sunday.'

'Yes, sir.' Max stood up. He had not yet properly assimilated what he had just been told. A millionaire and a general in the same morning! Hilde would be so proud. He wondered if Dad would also be proud, at least of the promotion, when the news got to England. And Johnnie? There were no twenty-three-year-old air-commodores in the RAF. Things like that just did not happen in the carefully organized and totally hide-bound British services.

'Thank you, Max,' Milch said. 'I know you have a lot to do.'

'Yes, sir. Heil Hitler.' Max saluted, turned to the door, and checked; thinking of Johnnie had suddenly reminded him of something. 'Excuse me, sir. This Abwehr plan to obtain the secrets of the Mosquito. Would they involve my brother?'

'Because he is your brother? I have no idea how these people's minds work. Nor do I wish to. You should not either. You have a job to do, Max. I look forward to your success.'

A Voice from the Past

Rufus, the huge black Newfoundland, had been running in front of the pushchair, casting to left and right of the path as he searched for rabbit warrens. Now he suddenly stopped, head thrust forward and tail extending in a straight line.

'What have you got there, Rufe?' Jolinda Bayley asked. She was pushing the chair, in which Little Mark was dozing, but now she too stopped to peer into the copse that lay ahead of them.

It was a magnificent early winter's afternoon in the south of England. From the crest of the Downs it was possible to see the Channel sparkling in the sunlight, and in the comparative warmth and peacefulness of the scene it was very easy to become somnolent, as the baby had done. But Jolinda reflected that it was only half a mile to the house and a refreshing cup of tea: over the two years of her marriage to John Bayley she had become very anglicized in her habits.

This did not bother her, because she actually was half-English and had dual nationality. Her father was an Air-Vice-Marshal in the RAF, and while her very American – and long-divorced – mother had thrown up her hands in horror at the concept of her only daughter deciding to rejoin him in England and to volunteer for the Women's Auxiliary Air Force, Mom had spent her life throwing up her hands in horror at Jolinda's various escapades. *She* had never regretted it for a moment, and even less so since she had drifted into the orbit of John Bayley, son of Air-Vice-Marshal Cecil Hargreaves' best and oldest friend.

Out of which had come both the ring on her finger and the adorable blob of humanity at her feet. And a great deal of happiness as well, even if she often felt frustrated at her inability to get as far into Johnnie's head, his psyche, as her essentially positive nature required. The cause, she knew, was a combination of Johnnie's somewhat uncertain background, about which he was reluctant to speak, and the war, the things he had experienced, about which she felt he would like to speak, but could not until it was all over. Then she might finally learn the truth of what had happened in France the previous year, when John had been shot down but had managed to evade capture and get back to England after several months on the run. He had explained that he had been forbidden to discuss it because of course he had only got out with the aid of the French Resistance movement, and a single careless word could cause the arrest and probable execution of many devoted people.

As if any word spoken in the privacy of their own bed could ever get back to Germany! But Johnnie was a stickler for obeying rules. And the fact was that the number of words spoken in the privacy of their own bed had dwindled sadly over the past year. When she had first joined the WAAF, she had, thanks to the machinations of her then Air-Commodore father, been posted to the station that had housed John's Spitfire squadron, situated only a bicycle ride away from Hillside House. Thus when they had married, and she had moved in with Johnnie's father and stepmother, they had been able to get home together several nights a week. But since he had been transferred from Spitfires to Mosquitoes, which flew out of Hatfield in Hertfordshire, he was only able to be with her perhaps once a month . . . Not that she supposed it would have made too much difference even if he had still been based just up the road: Mosquitoes were essentially night fighters.

Jolinda was therefore in the unenviable position of being an untouchable grass widow. She might be a mother, but she knew she was still a most attractive woman, who enjoyed congenial male company. She had no intention of ever cheating on John, but just to be offered a drink from time to time would be nice . . . But all of her male acquaintances were airmen, and there was no pilot in the RAF who would dare look twice at the wife of the country's most famous fighter ace.

She would have been more patient had she not known, deep in her heart, that *something* had happened during those months they had been separated. She could not even guess at what it might have been, but Johnnie had returned from France a changed man. He was as passionate as ever, and as loving as ever, but too often his eyes had a faraway look. He was remembering something, or someone, and she did not know what, or who, it was.

Rufus growled, and a man stepped from the trees in front of them. 'Well, hi,' he said. 'Is that dog safe?'

Jolinda regarded him closely. She was not the least afraid at being accosted by a stranger. For one thing, his accent and his form of address told her that he was a fellow American, although why that should be immediately reassuring she had no idea. But she was not in the habit of being afraid of people. She was a tall, strong young woman, her full figure oddly set off by her delicately attractive features – an inheritance from her father. As she was not on duty, and in fact was wearing slacks and a couple of loose jumpers, her long tawny-yellow hair also loose, restrained only by a ribbon on the nape of her neck, no stranger could possibly guess that she was actually a serving soldier. But in any event, no one could ever be afraid of anything when in the company of Rufus. 'He won't attack you, if that's what's bothering you,' she said. 'Unless I tell him to, of course. Shall I do that?'

'That sure would be unkind. Say, you're the Yank.'

'However did you guess? But you expected me to be. Tell me how you knew that.'

She was studying him as she spoke. Even more reassuring than his accent was the fact that he was wearing the uniform and side cap of a GI, with a sergeant's stripes on his sleeve. He was not very old – she did not think he had more than a year or so on her twenty-five – and, was in fact an inch or two the shorter although very powerfully built, and if not handsome, he had pleasantly rounded features. She ruffled Rufus's head reassuringly.

'Well, I'm down here on a furlough, see, and I got talking in the . . . what do you call it?'

'That depends on what *it* is,' Jolinda pointed out. 'But I suspect you're talking about a pub.'

'That's right. Pub. Ain't that quaint.'

'It means public house,' Jolinda explained. 'Which means a bar open to the public.'

'It sure was a bar. Had a funny name.'

'The Wellington Arms,' Jolinda suggested, guessing that he must have been in the village.

'You got it. Well, I got talking to the chick behind the bar, and she spotted I was a Yank . . .'

'She's very perceptive,' Jolinda murmured.

'. . . and she said, "Say, there's an American lady living at the big house on the hill. The Bayley place," she said. "Why don't you look her up?" So . . . here I am.'

Jolinda started to push the chair again; Little Mark had woken up. Rufus padded beside her, issuing vague rumbles of discontent with the situation. 'But I'm not at the house,' she reminded the sergeant, who had fallen in on her other side, safely separated from the dog by the pushchair.

'I called there first, and they said you were out walking the baby. Mrs Bayley, they said. That you?'

'That's me.'

'And the child?'

'His name is Mark Bayley, and yes, he's my son.'

'Son of a gun. So, is there a Pa Bayley?'

'My husband's name is Wing-Commander John Bayley, Sergeant. Now how about telling me your name?'

'Wing-Commander! Hell! That's pretty senior, ain't it?'

'Yes it is. But as he isn't here right now, he can't bite you either. Your name?'

'Mike Lonergan. I'm just a sergeant in the infantry.'

'I can see you're a sergeant. Well . . .' She gestured at the house that they had now reached. 'Home.'

'Oh. Ah. Right. Well, I'd better be going.'

Jolinda regarded him for several seconds. 'You say you're on a furlough. Most GIs on a furlough head for the bright lights of London.'

'Yeah. Well, I'm not big on bright lights.'

'So you came down here instead? What on earth for?'

'Well, you see, my folks came from round here. My ancestors, right? So I thought I'd have a look see at what the place was like.'

'What place, exactly?'

'Place called Arundel.'

'Arundel,' Jolinda repeated thoughtfully. She was tempted to say that everyone knows of Arundel, but she didn't want to snub him. And while she personally only associated Arundel with the Dukes of Norfolk and the large Howard family, she knew there was a village there, and not everyone in it could be an aristocrat. So she contented herself with commenting, 'You're a bit far east.'

'Is that a fact? Shucks. Well, I'd better be on my way. But I tell you what, Mrs Bayley: I sure am glad I got lost and wound up here. Or I wouldn't have met you.'

He was laying it on with a trowel. But he looked so forlorn. And she was in the mood for company; her stepmother-in-law Helen was out visiting friends and would not be back until six at the earliest. Not that Helen Bayley was ever stimulating company, and for all her careful kindness Jolinda knew she still, after two years of marriage, did not entirely approve of her outspoken and occasionally abrasive step-daughter-in-law. And it was so very long since she had heard an American accent in the flesh. 'Tell you what,' she said. 'As you've come all this way to no purpose, let me at least give you a cup of tea. There's a late train.'

'Say, that'd be great. Ah . . . did you say tea?'

'It's an old English custom. Off you go, Rufe. You can bite him on the way out.'

Rufus licked her hand, gave Lonergan an unfriendly look, and went off to his kennel, which was situated under his favourite tree.

'Some dog.' Lonergan watched her open the front door. 'Say, wasn't that locked?'

'No. Should it be?'

'Well, out here . . . it's kind of lonely, ain't it? And this looks like some house.'

'It is some house. And it belongs to my father-in-law, who's an important man around here. As everyone knows.'

'Wow! Say, let me do that.'

Jolinda was stooping to lift the pushchair up the short flight of steps, and he took it from her and lifted it himself. Baby Mark stared at him.

'Thank you. Oh, Clements, Sergeant Lonergan and I would like some tea.'

The butler, foursquare and red-faced, with a huge head surmounted by greying dark hair, and who apparently had been in the Bayley service since before time began – certainly

since long before she had appeared on the scene – gave
Lonergan an inquisitive look, but also a brief incline of the
head. 'Of course, Miss Jolinda. Ah . . . ?'

'We'll take it in the study.'

Clements looked more disapproving yet. The study – it was
actually a small library – was the Bayley family holy of holies.
'Of course, Miss Jolinda.'

'Thank you. Penny, I think Baby needs changing and I
know he's ready for his tea.'

The young woman descending the stairs, wearing a nurse's
cap and uniform, also looked somewhat taken aback at the
soldier standing beside her mistress, but bobbed in a brief
curtsey. 'Come along, Markey.' She scooped the boy from the
pushchair and returned up the stairs.

'It's through here.' Jolinda gestured at the drawing-room
doorway.

Lonergan had been gaping, first of all at Clements, then at
the panelled walls of the hall with the several portraits, the
stairs, and then at the nurse. 'This is something,' he said again.
'That girl . . .'

'She's Mark's nanny. I wish she wouldn't call him Markey,
but she's very good with him, and he's very fond of her, so
there it is.'

She led him across the room in the direction of the library,
and he stopped again to look around him. 'I ain't never been
in a room like this, ma'am. Is that what I should call you –
ma'am?'

'Actually, it is.'

'I knew it. You're a duchess or something.'

'No. But I am a commissioned officer in the Women's
Auxiliary Air Force. My correct title is Section Officer Bayley.'

'Holy sh— I beg your pardon, ma'am.'

'Feel free.'

He stood before the fireplace, in which there was a roaring
blaze, and looked up at the full-length portrait of a yellow-
haired woman above it. 'Wowee! That your mom? She is just
beautiful.'

'Some people thought she was the most beautiful woman
of her time. Her name was the Countess Karolina von
Bitterman.'

'Did you say, Countess von . . . your *mother*?'

'She would have been my mother-in-law, had she lived. I did meet her, a long time ago, when I was a little girl, and when I regarded my husband as a noisy little brat. But then we drifted apart. She was German, you see.'

'What? You mean your husband is a Kraut?'

'My husband is one of Britain's leading fighter aces,' Jolinda said severely. 'It is a complicated story. In here.'

Clements had brought in the tray of tea with, needless to say, a plate of sandwiches, and she followed him into the library, Lonergan at her heels. Clements gave his usual brief bow and withdrew.

'I don't think that guy likes me,' the sergeant said, 'any more than the dog.'

'They are conservative Englishmen,' Jolinda explained, and poured tea. 'In fact there is nothing more conservative on the face of the planet. They regard all strangers with hostility, until said stranger has proved his or her worth. Lemon or sugar?'

'Whatever you say, ma'am. How long did it take you to be assimilated then?'

'I had a built-in cachet. I told you, it's a complicated story.' Jolinda added two lumps of sugar, a splash of milk, and held out the plate. 'Have a sandwich.'

Lonergan regarded the small pieces of bread suspiciously. 'I'd sure love to hear it.'

'I'll be brief. My father is Air-Vice-Marshal Hargreaves, Royal Air Force.'

'Jesus! A countess! A general! I'm getting a little out of my depth here, ma'am.'

You were out of your depth from the moment you first addressed me, Jolinda thought. But she was enjoying herself. 'Then you must learn to swim. My father and my father-in-law, Mark Bayley, were both fighter pilots in the Great War. Both became quite famous. But while Dad made a career out of the RAF, Mark Bayley was shot down in 1918 and so badly wounded that he could never fly again, at least in combat. But it wasn't all bad. While in hospital in Germany he met the Countess von Bitterman, and they fell in love. As she inherited a fortune, he never had a care after that.'

'And she's the mother of your husband.'

'No. I told you it was complicated. My husband is Mark's son by a previous liaison.'

'You mean he was . . . well . . .'

'He is technically a bastard, yes.'

'I didn't mean . . .'

'So don't worry about it.'

'I guess it's a good thing this Bayley character and the countess never had kids of their own. That sure would have complicated matters.'

Jolinda poured more tea; Lonergan had absent-mindedly finished his. 'Mark and Karolina did have a son. He's the Luftwaffe's principal fighter ace.'

Lonergan put down his cup and stared at her.

'Like I said, it's complicated.' She looked at her watch. 'Here have I been boring the pants off you, and time has been rushing by. It's a half-hour walk to the station.'

'I sure haven't been bored, ma'am. But I can see I've been taking up your time. Tell you what, though, I'd sure like to see you again.'

Jolinda looked into his eyes. 'Why?'

'Ah . . . you're a very pretty, lovely lady. Shucks, I know I'm not in your class, ma'am, but I sure have enjoyed talking with you. Kind of makes me feel less homesick.'

'What part of the States are you from?'

'I'm from Connecticut. New Canaan. I don't suppose you know it, being a southern lady and all.'

'I'm not a southern lady, Sergeant. I was born in this country, and I lived most of my life on the West Coast.'

'Is that a fact? I've been to Los Angeles. Did one of those bus tours through Hollywood.'

'I lived in San Francisco. But, you'll never believe this: I was stationed just outside New Canaan for, oh, six months. Back in 1938. When I was a rookie.'

Lonergan stared at her for several seconds. 'A rookie what?' he asked at last.

'I was in the Air Corps over there, before coming back here. America wasn't in the war then, you see. And I wanted to do my bit.'

'You sure have had an interesting life.'

'So, we could have met each other four years ago. I wasn't an officer back then.'

'Yeah. That would have been fun. But we did meet each other. I'm sure of it.'

'Say again?'

'I knew there was something familiar about your face. And your name. Hargreaves! Yeah. That rang a bell the moment you said it. I was in New Canaan in '38.'

'Are you serious?'

'Cross my heart and hope to die. Of course, we didn't mix. You were a trainee officer, right, and I was simply a GI Joe. But I could hardly forget a looker like you. You know something, ma'am? We were at a dance together once. I mean, we were at the same dance, not that you were with me. But the guys I was with could tell I was gone on you, and they said, "Go on, Mikey, be a devil. Ask her to dance with you. She can only say no."'

'I remember those dances,' Jolinda said, a whole rush of memories coming back. 'But I don't remember ever being asked to dance by an enlisted man.'

'That's because I never asked you. I actually stood up, and then I guess I lost my nerve, and sat down again. And here I am, running into you again four years later. Ain't that fate or something?'

'Yes,' Jolinda said thoughtfully.

'Say, ma'am, may I ask you something?'

'Why not.'

'If I had asked you to dance that evening, would you have said yes?'

Jolinda regarded him for a few seconds. 'You know, I might have done. I was a little wild when I was a girl.' *And how much would I like to be a little wild from time to time now that I'm a woman*, she thought.

'Then I sure was a sap to pass it up. Well, ma'am. This has been a real pleasure. I can't remember anything better than meeting you again after all these years. But like you said, I'd better move if I'm gonna catch that train.' He stood up. 'This sure has been a treat, ma'am. And that tea and all.'

Jolinda stood. 'I enjoyed it too.' She held out her hand, and he gave her fingers a gentle squeeze. 'Do you know,' she said, 'it's damn near three years since I heard an American voice.' Except over the phone, she reflected, and conversations with Mom were always inclined to be fraught.

'Well, like I was saying, I don't suppose, if I found myself in this neck of the woods again sometime, you'd want me to call again?'

'I think that would be rather nice. But don't forget I'm on duty a lot of the time. You just struck it lucky today. On the other hand, if you struck it really lucky next time, my husband might be home. I'm sure he'd enjoy meeting you.'

'Sounds great.' He had retained her hand, and now he gave it another squeeze. 'You reckon that hound of yours will let me out?'

'I'll come out with you.'

Jolinda stood with her hand on Rufus's collar to watch Lonergan disappear down the drive. What on earth was she doing, inviting him back again? But she *had* enjoyed this afternoon.

That needed analysis. She gave Rufus a last stroke and returned to the study, where Clements was clearing away the tea things. 'Seemed a nice young gentleman, miss. Old friend, is he?'

'Apparently.'

Clements did not comment, but his silence was more meaningful than anything he might have said.

'I don't actually remember him,' Jolinda confessed. 'But it was nice to talk about, well, old things.'

'Of course, miss.' Clements removed the tray, and Jolinda sat down and gazed into the fire. They hadn't actually talked about any old things, apart from that one evening she couldn't really remember. They had only really talked about the Bayley family background. And they came from as far apart as it was possible to be, but perhaps that was why she had so enjoyed his company . . . apart from his obvious, and apparently long-standing, yen for her.

Her background was one of such confusion. She had thought that returning to live with her father in England, not to mention marrying her childhood friend, would have sorted out all the uncertainties that had bedevilled her for the past seventeen years.

She had been only eight when her mother had finally become fed up with the protocol and lifestyle of being a service wife and done a runner back to her home in California, taking her daughter with her. It had been totally unexpected and utterly confusing to a little girl, happening as it did without warning. Mom had met the dashing young RFC pilot Cecil Hargreaves while in London in 1917, and they had married a few months later. By then *she* had been on the way, but the fact that she was just as illegitimate, at least on conception, as Johnnie had never been mentioned, probably because, unlike Mark Bayley, Cecil Hargreaves had married his so-productive one-night stand. All she could remember was a world of uniforms, parades and, of course, visits to Hillside, where she had been sent off to play with the two Bayley boys, a reluctant chore as they were both younger than her and not in the least interesting. Mom had always seemed perfectly content with her marriage, until the day she had announced she was leaving.

Jolinda – the name had been chosen by Mom for some unfathomable reason, but was perhaps an indication of her basic antagonism to stuffy English mores – had never discovered what had been the final straw for her mother. Logic suggested that there should be another man involved; Deborah Hargreaves had been, and indeed still was, a very handsome woman. But there had never been any solid evidence of an adulterous affair. More reasonably, when *her* mother had died, Mom had suddenly found herself a wealthy woman in her own right and had determined that she was through with kowtowing to the pompous wives of air-commodores and the like. Clearly she had never considered the possibility that her husband might one day be an air-commodore himself.

So Jolinda had found herself in the stultifying environment of long bridge parties and banal conversation on the west coast of the United States. As she grew into a teenager that gradually turned into total neglect, so that she had been permitted to do her own thing. She had in fact done very well, although going to college had been simply a matter of following the example set by the children of Mom's friends. But doing her own thing, and keeping her own counsel, had by then become a way of life. Confiding anything to Mom had never been an option, because Mom lived from one hysterical outburst to another.

So losing her virginity had been an entirely personal matter. There had been no question of marriage: Al had been from as far the wrong side of the tracks as Sergeant Lonergan. She had just been fortunate not to get pregnant. But the affair had undoubtedly influenced her decision, on leaving college, to join the Women's Army Air Corps. Mom had had one of her outsized explosions, but being Mom, as she had been unable to get her daughter back out until the period of her enlistment had been completed, had pulled strings and secured a commission for her wayward child.

Then the European War had come along. Like most young Americans, Jolinda had known very little about European politics, and had held even less interest in them. But she had suddenly woken up to the realization that her father, whom she loved dearly, was apparently fighting for his life. Without hesitation she had resigned her commission and crossed the Atlantic. That maternal explosion had probably been heard in Moscow. But Dad had welcomed her with open arms, got her enlisted in the WAAF and, like Mom before him, obtained a commission for her, with more justification, as she already held one.

That Dad had also virtually thrust her into the arms of his best friend's son, a young man he had apparently always dreamed of having as a son-in-law, had seemed a bit much at first, and she had resisted vigorously. But being stationed at the same airfield as Johnnie, she had gradually come to realize John Bayley's worth, as well as to respect his standing as a fighter pilot. And she had never regretted her decision to marry him. Johnnie was great fun, and could be a most passionate lover. That he had also been, and was, a most private person, had been disappointing, at a time of her life when she had wanted to stop being over-private, and share everything, at least with her husband. But she had understood not only that he was still suffering from confusion over his tangled background, and his equivocal feelings about his half-brother, who he knew had a better claim to the Bayley – and von Bitterman – millions than himself, but whom he was now committed to killing on sight. And of course there was the simple fact that he was equally committed, almost every day, to risking his own life in battle.

All of these sombre shadows lying across his personality would pass with time, she had never doubted, and certainly would when the war finally ended. But that was clearly not going to happen for the foreseeable future, no matter what might be developing in North Africa. And then there was that four-month separation while he had been an Evader, a shadow across both of their personalities. Suddenly she had found herself recalling those carefree days in various army camps in the States. And now, just as suddenly, a half–remembered figure had appeared from those days. But she might never see him again. Did she want to see him again? That was dangerous ground. They were several light years apart, in every way. But he had been a breath of fresh air.

It was well before dawn when the flight of de Havilland Mosquitoes touched down and rolled to a halt, to be immediately surrounded by teams of mechanics. With their twin engines and their two-seater cockpit, they did not look like the fastest aircraft ever built. Their secrets, their all-wood construction and their revolutionary exhaust system that gave them speeds of well over four hundred miles an hour, were not readily obvious. But their twin thirty-millimetre cannon, and the accompanying pair of machine-guns, mounted behind and above their radar aerial, and their rack capable of carrying a thousand-pound bomb, left no doubt as to their hitting power.

Originally designed as unarmed reconnaissance machines – reckoned, correctly, to be too fast for interception even by a Messerschmitt – their potential, accentuated by their enormous two-thousand-mile range, had quickly led to their development as a strike aircraft, a joy to fly and a terror to the enemy.

Wing-Commander John Bayley swung down from the cockpit, followed by his navigator, Flight-Sergeant Chris Langley, and they strode to Dispersal with the other crews.

They moved with the confidence of successful men, who knew they had been flying the best fighter-bomber in existence, and who had the aura of continued success. This was especially the case with John Bayley, who now had more confirmed kills – forty-five – than any other RAF pilot. He had not had a career of unfailing success. He had been shot down four times, once by his own brother, had been badly wounded and spent some time in hospital, but continued survival had brought with it increasing certainty that he would survive to the end.

And he had so much to survive for. He held the rank of

Wing-Commander with a huge future in front of him. When his father died, he would be a very wealthy man. He was married to a virile and attractive woman, and he had a son to carry on the name and the family. And he was still only twenty-four years old. Some thought that was old for a fighter pilot, in these days of ever-increasing speed and complicated technology, but few would deny that he was close to being a legend in his own lifetime.

As for the shadows that sometimes threatened to cloud the real happiness of his existence, he felt he was becoming adept at keeping those hidden. They could not, in any event, be adequately shared, least of all with Jolinda, who lived her life on a very even and uncomplicated level, at least, he felt, since she had married him.

'Almost no activity,' Wing-Commander Hoosen was reporting at the desk, 'They just let us get on with it. What's the news from the desert?'

'They seem to have Rommel reeling,' reported Squadron-Leader Portman, on despatcher duty. 'Mind you, they thought they'd done that before, and he's always bounced back.'

Group Captain Hastings appeared in the doorway of the inner office. 'Do I gather all went well?'

'Piece of cake,' Squadron-Leader Evans said.

Hastings looked at John. He knew he was likely to get the most accurate report from his most experienced pilot.

'Jerry does seem to have his mind on other things,' John agreed.

'Well, that can't be bad. You have forty-eight hours. See you on Thursday afternoon. Will you step in here a moment, Johnnie?'

John raised his eyebrows, but followed the Group Captain into the inner office.

'Interesting piece of news just came in via Switzerland,' Hastings said.

John waited. It could only be news of Max. Perhaps he'd bought it at last.

'The Luftwaffe Tactical Air Fleet in southern Russia – that's the fighter wing, of course – has just received a new commanding officer: General Maximilian Bayley.'

John stared at him. 'That has to be a mistake.'

'Why?'

'Well, for one thing, Max was christened Max, never Maximilian.'

Hastings nodded. 'That could be a mistake, yes. Some editor adding his own take. But that doesn't prove that this chap isn't Max.'

'For God's sake, sir. A general? Max is a year younger than I am.'

'Hmm. Well, it seems Jerry believes in promoting by talent rather than seniority. You going to tell your dad?'

'Of course. He'll be interested.'

'Your brother seems to be quite a fellow. According to the report, he has over a hundred kills.'

'Mostly obsolete Russians.'

Hastings studied him. 'You jealous?'

'No, sir. Just irritated. I've been trying to bring him down since this show started. And now he's gone off back to Russia, where I can't get at him.'

Which, in view of the obvious depths of antagonism between you, is probably no bad thing, Hastings thought. But he said, 'Well, no doubt one day he'll come back. Go home and forget about it for a couple of days. We have something big coming up.'

'Sir?'

'Top secret. How does Berlin sound to you?'

'I thought that was strictly heavy stuff. I mean, we can't carry any worthwhile load.'

'That's true. But the heavies always go in at night. And they miss far more than they hit, even with these new bomb sights. The evidence that we are getting from our agents is that the German attitude is, ho-hum, here they come again, what a bore.'

John was frowning. 'You mean they're going in by day, with us as escorts? Right across Germany, in daylight? That is going to be expensive, even with us around.

'No one can argue with that. Not even Harris is prepared to risk his Halifaxes on such a jaunt. No, you won't be flying escort. You'll be on your own. A squadron of six planes. Our six best pilots.'

John gave a low whistle. 'That'll be a do. But what's the point? So, maybe we can knock out a couple of trains or something. That's not going to win the war.'

'The point, Johnnie, is propaganda. Morale. The Russians are screaming for us to do something, anything, here in the west to take the pressure off them. Well, you know we can't do anything worthwhile right now. Nor will we be able to until the Yanks move into high gear, and that can't be before next year at the earliest. So we've tried these thousand-bomber raids. They seem to have done a lot of damage, but morale is still high, and the damage has been confined to the west of the country. The east is inviolate, because of the range and, as you say, the certainty of heavy casualties. But you chaps are so fast *you* are virtually inviolate, and for you Berlin's seven hundred miles is a matter of there and back for lunch. And the sight of you flying right across Germany in broad daylight, shooting up Berlin, and coming home again, is going to shake up the Nazis no end. They'll have to wonder when we'll start doing it for real, a thousand bombers, in daylight. The theory is that they'll have to pull planes back from Russia to defend the home front. You on?'

'Of course I'm on,' John said. 'When?'

'It won't be before the New Year. Just remember, until then, it's top secret.'

'Lift, Chris?' John asked as they walked outside into the crisp pre-dawn air.

'That would be very kind of you, sir. But I'll be taking you out of your way.'

'I can spare an hour. My wife doesn't take too kindly to being woken up at dawn when she's not on duty. Anyway, it's only a slight detour.'

He mounted the Harley-Davidson, his proudest possession after his wife and son, and Langley settled himself on the pillion, wrapping his scarf round his face, as John was doing, to give as much protection as possible against the near-freezing air. 'This is some machine. May I ask how long you've had her, sir?'

'Four years. She was a present from my dad when I passed out from Cranwell. Seems like another world. Do you know the first combat machine I ever flew?'

'Ah . . . Bristol Gladiator?'

'Not quite. Boulton-Paul Defiant.'

'I remember them, sir. They were two-seaters, just like the Mosquito.'

'There were a few differences,' John said thoughtfully. 'Such
as speed, firepower, and general capability. The first time I
ever flew one in combat I encountered a 109. That was the
old E model. I think I lasted precisely one minute, which was
the length of time it took him to get on my tail and loose a
burst.'

'But you survived.'

'My gunner didn't.' Max, he thought, a general, at twenty-
three, with a hundred-plus kills. But then he thought, Berlin,
in broad daylight! That might indeed bring the bugger back
from Russia. John opened the throttle and the noise precluded
further conversation.

'The third on the left, sir,' Langley said, and John pulled into
the side of the street before the row of darkened terraced
houses.

'Will your wife be awake?'

Langley dismounted. 'I'm not married. I live with my
mother. She's a widow.'

John realized how remiss he had been in not finding out
more about his crew at an earlier stage; they had now been
flying together for several months. But suddenly he wished
he hadn't found out now. If Langley was an only son, the only
support of a lonely mother . . . were the risks they took on
every sortie worth it?

But then, what of the risks he took? He pondered on this
as he waved goodbye and roared out of the town. Of course
Jolinda would never be alone. Dad and Helen and her father
would always be there, and she had Baby Mark. But he could
not deny how upset she had been when he had been reported
missing, believed killed – and how emotional they both had
been when he finally returned to a joyful reunion.

But it *hadn't* been that joyful, there was the rub. Too much
had happened to disrupt the tremendous intimacy of their
first year of marriage. He knew what it was, from his point
of view at least: he could not get that magnificent woman,
Liane de Gruchy, out of his mind. The Frenchwoman had
risked all, had shared all, from the chance of capture, and
torture and death, to that last tumultuous night when she had
bade him farewell in her own inimitable manner. He knew
now, as he had known then, that to her he was a job of work,

that having seen him to safety she had immediately retraced her steps to rejoin her resistance group, and probably soon to escort another and then another downed airman to the Spanish border, sharing with each of them everything she had shared with him. It was not possible to be jealous of a woman like Liane de Gruchy, certainly when one had a lovely, loving wife waiting at home. But equally, it was not possible – for him, at least – to forget her.

Jolinda knew nothing of Liane, nor could she; he would not have dared tell her, however unforgettable and morally reprehensible their affair had been. The way he saw it, he had been engaged in saving his life, and there was no possibility of his ever encountering Liane again. He had also been forbidden by MI9, the branch of the Secret Service that dealt with returning Escapers and Evaders, to discuss any aspect of his time in France – of the means used to get him out, the people who had helped him – with anyone, even his own comrades. It had been impressed upon him that one careless word could endanger a member of the Escape Route team, and once one was taken, to be subjected to unthinkable tortures in order to extract more names, could bring the whole structure crashing down. The thought of Liane de Gruchy tied naked to a triangle waiting to be flogged, or strapped to a table to have her toenails pulled out or electrodes thrust into her genitals could, and often did, keep him awake at night.

Jolinda could not know of those thoughts or the events that had led up to them. But her instincts had told her that her husband had undergone a character-changing experience, and if she accepted that he could not share it with her, at least until after the war, she would not have been human had she not felt that a wedge had been driven between them. And so she had changed too, and he did not know how to change her back. He had thought several times that perhaps Dad was the answer. Dad had experienced so much, suffered so much, triumphed over so much, and Dad, he knew, was as fond of Jolinda as if she had been his own daughter. But Dad was married, to Helen. Had Stepmother Karolina lived, it would have been so simple. Karolina had never been shocked, never criticized, never doubted. She had believed that every human being had to make the best of what they had been decreed by Fate, without regret or recrimination, and she had been willing to help anyone who drifted into her orbit to do that, without hesitation. Helen had a complete lack of ability to understand the mental or physical make-up of anyone who was not strictly orthodox, according to her interpretation of the word. Her world was governed by 'But is it *right*?' or 'But that's *terrible*,' or, most important of all, 'What will the neighbours say?'

She seemed to keep Dad happy enough, although it was difficult to imagine a man who had spent fifteen years sharing the bed of the most beautiful and passionate woman of her time finding any great pleasure in riding a farm horse such as Helen. But perhaps Dad had simply settled for comfort after losing Karolina. John was certain only that he could not contemplate the idea of Helen knowing anything about his problem.

'Well,' Mark Bayley observed, 'he is travelling very fast. Clements, I think we'll have the Bollinger, and drink to Max.'

'Right away, Mr Mark.'

'You don't mean we're going to celebrate . . .' Helen's voice was strained with outrage.

'The success of my son,' Mark said quietly, but in that tone which left no room for argument or disagreement.

Six feet tall, even if twenty-four years of trailing a crippled leg had left him a little bowed, and with the shock of white hair above the craggy features he had bequeathed to his eldest son, Mark Bayley came across to most people as a somewhat grim figure. He certainly lived his life according to his own ideas and decisions, as he had been encouraged to do by his first wife. Helen, of medium height and inclined to be dumpy, with a pleasantly plain face, worshipped him and was terrified of him in equal measure. So now she offered an explanation for her remark. 'I meant, at eleven o'clock in the morning.'

'Best time to drink champagne,' Mark said. 'What do you think, Johnnie?'

'I think he deserves it,' John said. 'Don't you, Joly?'

'A general at twenty-three. That's going it a bit.'

'Well, that fellow Molders, who was their leading ace after Marseille, and went in last year, was a general, and he was only thirty. I don't know how long he had the rank.'

Helen, who hated phrases like 'going in' uttered so casually, shuddered, and decided to change the subject. 'Well,' she said, 'we've had an exciting day here as well.'

'Have you?' Mark and John spoke together. Mark, having spent the night in London after an aeronautical conference, had only arrived a few minutes before John.

'She means yesterday,' Jolinda said.

'I was returning from visiting Marjorie Cresswell,' Helen said importantly. 'Yesterday afternoon. I was driving the trap. And as I came down the lane to the house, you'll never guess who I saw.'

'The invisible man,' John suggested wickedly, and winked at Jolinda, who was pulling a face.

'It was an American serviceman. A sergeant, I think.'

'There are a few of them about,' Mark observed, accepting a glass of champagne from Clements. 'Not many down here, though,' he added thoughtfully.

'He was walking along the lane,' Helen said.

'And he leapt on to the trap and assaulted you,' John suggested. 'And you hit him with your handbag and killed him, and he is lying dead in a ditch, and you want us to go and get rid of the body. Now that *is* a story. I'll just finish my drink, then get a shovel.'

'Really, John, that is not the least bit funny,' Helen snapped, and looked at her husband. 'He was coming from the house. Don't you want to know what he was doing here?'

Jolinda sighed. 'He was having tea with me.'

Both men turned their heads to look at her, and Mark said, 'I think we should drink that toast. To Max, if not necessarily to the Luftwaffe.'

'To Max,' they agreed, raising their glasses.

'Now, Joly,' Mark said. 'What guilty secret are you about to reveal?'

'It really was quite remarkable,' Jolinda said. 'I was walking Baby and Rufus, and this guy suddenly turned up. Seems he was down here trying to find some relatives – they actually live over at Arundel – and apparently he'd been told in the pub that there was an American lady living in the big house, so he came along to pay his respects.'

'That sounds very civilized,' John said. 'And as you brought him back here for tea, *he* must have been quite civilized.'

'I brought him back here for tea,' Jolinda said, 'because we discovered the most amazing coincidence. It turned out that I had known this guy in the States. When I was serving in the WAAC, he was in the same camp.' Which was not true, she reflected: she had brought him back here *before* he had remembered meeting her in New Canaan. But they could never know that, and it was the safest way to play it.

Helen uttered one of her monumental sniffs.

'You mean he was an old boyfriend?' John asked. He had never resented the fact that Jolinda had not been a virgin when they had married, or the knowledge that she had lived a fairly free and easy life while an American soldier, but he wasn't sure he wanted old bed-mates turning up.

'Of course he wasn't. In fact, to be honest, I didn't remember him at all. But then, there were a lot of guys about.' She gave Mark an apologetic glance, but he merely winked at her.

'But he remembered you,' John said.

'Well, yes, he did. Or so he said.'

'You do realize that's the oldest ploy in the world,' John pointed out. 'Meeting a pretty girl and pretending to have met her before. After four years?'

'I don't think that's necessarily untrue,' Mark argued. 'If you'd met Joly four years ago, wouldn't you still remember her?'

'I would be very careful how you answer that,' Jolinda recommended. 'But this guy was genuine. He knew my name.'

'He'd have got that in the pub,' John said.

'My maiden name.'

'That too. Everyone around here knows you're Air-Vice-Marshal Hargreaves's daughter.'

'No one around here except us knows that I once served in the WAAC. Anyway, like I said, he was merely paying a courtesy call on a fellow national. But when we got talking, he remembered me.'

'If I may use an American expression,' John said, 'that is bullshit.'

'John!' Helen remonstrated.

'What was this fellow's name?' Mark asked.

'Mike Lonergan.'

'Mike Lonergan,' Mark repeated, clearly committing the name to memory. 'Helen, my dear, I think we should have lunch. I suspect that Johnnie would like to get to bed.'

* * *

'Good-looking fellow, was he?' John asked as he undressed after the meal.

'I wouldn't say that. He was . . . pleasant looking. Don't tell me you're jealous.'

Naked, John lay on the bed. 'I am jealous of any man who spends time in your company when I can't.'

'Why, John Bayley, I never thought to hear you say that.' She stood beside him, fingers playing with the buttons on her dress. 'Are you really interested only in sleep?'

He put his arms round her thighs and brought her down on top of him, sliding his hands under her dress to find her knickers. 'Suddenly not. At least for a while.'

She raised her body to allow him to slide the silk down her thighs. 'I must find some more guys to come calling, if they are all going to have this effect on you.'

'Ah, Kesten. Come in. Sit down.'

Pieter Kesten closed the door of the office, shutting out the garish lights of the seedy nightclub at his back, pulled up a chair and sat down. This evening he was in civilian clothes.

'Well?' said the man behind the desk. 'Tell me that all is going well.'

'It is going as well as can be expected, Herr Wolfert,' Kesten said.

'What do you mean by that?'

'I mean that the information you have given me, while very accurate as regards her American background, was not so accurate with regard to her present situation. The lady is very obviously happily married. She is also surrounded by the trappings of wealth, which means mainly, in the context of our operation, faithful and protective servants. Not to mention her dog. She also has a father-in-law who is not only big in the aircraft industry but is important in the vicinity where she lives.'

'Well, we knew all that,' Wolfert pointed out. 'What are you trying to say? That you cannot carry out the assignment?'

'No, sir. I believe I have made some progress, and that I can carry out the assignment. But I am warning you that it may take some time. It cannot be rushed. If the lady were to take either alarm or umbrage at anything I might say or do, we could lose everything. In any event, I am not convinced that she knows anything about her husband's aircraft.'

Wolfert leaned across his desk. 'Kesten, we do not have *some* time. The Luftwaffe needs to know the secret of these planes as quickly as possible. Certainly before next spring. If you have to take chances with this woman, do so. You may well be pleasantly surprised. There is no woman who is *entirely* happily married. However, if you cannot seduce her, we shall have to employ direct methods.'

Kesten swallowed. 'I would not like to have to do that, sir. She is a very . . . well, attractive, vibrant personality. I would not like to harm her.'

Wolfert sighed. 'Kesten, it is your business to destroy her. Whether or not you do it by screwing her brains out, with her consent, and then blackmailing her to do what you require, or by simply kidnapping her to force her husband to do what you require, either way she is going to be destroyed. I agree that the first option would be preferable. But it has to be one or the other. I am sure you do not wish to have to return to Berlin and admit to Admiral Canaris that you could not carry out your mission because you developed a soft spot for your target. Go outside and pick one of the girls. Tell her it is on the house and that she is to spend the night with you. And remind yourself that there is more than one attractive woman in the world. Then get back to work. Heil Hitler!'

The East

'Ah, General Bayley. Welcome to Kiev.' General Lutyens was clearly taken aback by the youth of his new fleet commander, even if they had met before, two years previously. 'I hear you have been doing great things.'

'That depends on your interpretation of the word, Herr General.' Max was not merely being polite. His trouble when dealing with other officers was that he never knew just how much they knew of him – the questionable, that he had an English father; the creditable, that he should have more than a hundred kills; or the discreditable, that he had managed to fall foul of both the Gestapo and the SS. But he had long deduced that whatever his new superior actually knew of him, the man had not the slightest sense of humour.

'The impression I have been given, General Bayley,' Lutyens said, 'is that you are our best fighting airman, and that is what I, and the Reich, require at this moment. Tolder could see nothing but difficulties, impossibilities. I am told that you do not accept those words, in relation to your duties. Your squadrons are assembling now. I understand that you have flown with some of them before.'

'Yes, sir.'

'Excellent. So you will know of what they are capable, and more important, they will know what you expect of them. You are satisfied with your quarters?'

'I have not yet actually been to my quarters, sir. I came here direct from the airfield.'

'You are zealous. I like that. I am sure you will find your quarters comfortable. They are situated in a very good hotel, and you will, ah . . . lack for nothing. But you are here to fly, and as you are here now I will acquaint you with our situation.'

He walked to the large table against the far wall of the office. 'You will see that I have marked the perimeter of the Stalingrad position here. It is, of course, constantly changing.'

Max studied the map stretched across the wood. 'It looks formidable.'

'Yes. Unfortunately, it is not as formidable as it looks. At the present time we do hold these positions on the Volga, north and south of the city. But we do not yet have complete control of the city itself. I know it looks like it on the map, but it would be quite impossible to delineate with any accuracy where there are Russian positions. They seem to be everywhere. They are in shattered buildings, lurking in the cellars, and they infest the sewage system. They are like vermin. They *are* vermin.'

'Well, I can see that it may take time,' Max suggested, 'but surely they will be eliminated, with time.'

'Perhaps. The trouble is that we do not yet adequately control the river crossing. Again, we may appear to do so. We have heavy guns trained on it, and it is bombed every night. But yet every night they manage to take out most of their wounded, and to get replacements across. This means that every morning there are fresh troops for our people to overcome. It is a serious problem. But not, of course, as serious as the problem to the west of the city. Which is why you are here. You'll see the Gumrak air strip is marked.'

Max peered at the map. 'And those marks?'

'Are the latest known positions of the Russian forces.'

'You mean the northern and southern fronts have made contact.'

'We knew that was inevitable. Everything depends on how soon Manstein can bring his army back. And on the ability of the Sixth Army to maintain itself until he does. Which is where we come in.'

Max continued to look at the map. 'Gumrak is the only air strip?'

'It is the only one remaining in our hands, yes.'

'But if those estimates of the current Russian positions are accurate . . .'

'Absolutely. It could soon be lost as well.'

'In which case . . .'

'The supplies will have to be dropped.'

Max gave a low whistle. 'We are going to *drop* eight hundred tons of food and munitions every day?'

Lutyens gave a sour smile. 'General, on this front we have to deal in reality, not the rubbish they put out in Berlin for public consumption. Eight hundred tons a day means thirty-three tons an hour, supposing we had twenty-four hours of daylight, and there were no interruptions. However, we currently have about ten hours of daylight, and that is very soon going to drop to eight or less. We are of course flying by night as well, but the losses are frightful. There is also the small matter of Russian interference. They are putting up more and more planes, mainly bombers but they are now increasing their fighter strength as well. They sense the opportunity for a very big victory. That is why I sent for reinforcements.'

'Yes, sir. May I ask exactly how much we have actually been able to deliver so far?'

'A week ago we delivered five hundred tons in one day. That is our best so far.'

'But . . .'

'I know, General. Stalingrad is short of its requirements by more than three hundred tons a day. They have of course some reserves of ammunition with them, but we are told the winter will last until next March at the earliest. We must do the best we can.'

Max had continued to study the map. Now he used a pair of dividers to measure distances. 'It is a thousand kilometres from Kiev to Stalingrad.'

'Give or take a hundred or so, yes.'

'That is the maximum range for my planes. Will we be able to fuel on the ground?'

'It might be possible, as long as they hold the air strip. But I do not think they will have any to spare. We are flying some in, but not really enough, and should the Fuehrer authorize a break-out, they will need every drop they have for their tanks. You will move your squadrons up to Kharkov. That will halve the distance, so you should be able to get to Stalingrad and back without difficulty, and even have the time to attack the enemy forces on the ground.'

'And there is no risk of Kharkov being overrun?'

'None at all. I would like your people to be in place and operational by the end of this week.'

'They will be, Herr General. I will leave tomorrow.'

'You realize that not all of your squadrons have yet arrived?'

'I will take what I have. The rest will follow as they come in.'

'Excellent. I was told I was being given a man of energy and decision. I congratulate you, General. Heil Hitler!'

Heinrich, Max's servant, who had been with him since the war had begun, habitually wore a lugubrious expression, but today it was more lugubrious than usual. He stood in the hallway outside the suite, waiting for his master.

Max was feeling pretty lugubrious himself. For some time he had had a growing impression that the war was being sadly mishandled, even if he knew that to criticize the high command – which was now essentially Hitler and his personal staff – was a dangerous course, not to mention a futile one. But to consign an entire army to a desperate enterprise, and then commit God alone knew how many other armies and units in an effort to keep it alive . . . And as for recalling Manstein, he did not believe that cutting the Volga could possibly be a decisive coup, certainly at such a place, where it was about to spread into its delta above the Caspian Sea. Securing the Caucasus oil definitely would give them an advantage, helping both the Wehrmacht and the Luftwaffe, while at the same time limiting the resources of the Red Army and Air Force.

He found Kiev, even after an acquaintance of no more than a few hours, a most depressing place. He was no stranger to being on the receiving end of bombardments and air raids, although what he had recently experienced in Berlin, had not devastated the city. But this place . . .

When he had served in Russia during the early summer of the previous year, the advance had been so rapid and so overwhelming, the speed with which the Russian armies and cities had surrendered so decisive, that the necessity for mass destruction had never arisen. Kiev had apparently been one of the few places where the Reds, although surrounded without hope of succour, had held out for some weeks before surrendering. In those weeks the German artillery had systematically pounded this most ancient of Russian capital cities into rubble. Nothing appeared to have been done in the direction of any rebuilding, save where it was considered necessary by the conquerors. It reminded him too much of Warsaw, which he had visited in the company of Hildegarde in the spring of 1941.

As did the surviving people of Kiev remind him of the Poles, but with one terrible difference: the Poles had been sullenly hostile, but their war had been over. Russia was still at war. If her people, like the Poles, hastily stepped off the pavements into the gutters at the approach of a German uniform, and shuffled away down side streets as rapidly as possible, they could not escape the daily reminder of their fate. In the central square the bodies of those who had not accepted surrender with good grace dangled in the wind, and while it was already cold enough to prevent rapid decomposition, Max's practised eye convinced him that several of the victims had only recently been executed – more than a year after the city's capture. And three of them were women.

But he forced a smile. 'Is it a dump?'

The hotel did not look like a dump. Its tarnished appointments suggested that it had once been the height of elegance. And as it had been taken over by the Wehrmacht for the use of its officers, a modicum of its past glory had been restored, while the staff were nauseatingly obsequious. And Heinrich replied, 'The apartment is very comfortable, Herr General.'

'Well, don't get too comfortable: we leave again tomorrow. But I'm sure they'll find us somewhere equally comfortable in Kharkov.' He opened the door.

'Ahem,' Heinrich coughed.

Max turned his head.

'There is an occupant, sir.'

'What? I am not sharing with anyone.'

'I tried to tell the young lady this, sir. But . . .'

'Young lady?' Max threw the door open and entered the sitting room, which did indeed look very comfortable, and was made more so by the woman who had been seated in a chair by the window, but who stood at his entrance. She was certainly young; Max doubted she could be even twenty. She was also pretty in a gamine way, with short black hair. She was far too thin, but her dress and high-heeled shoes looked clean and even new.

She licked her lips, perhaps at the sight of his expression. Then she said, in German, 'General Bayley?'

'I am General Bayley. And you?'

'I am Rena Gorbalov.'

'My pleasure. Now tell me why you are here.'

Rena Gorbalov moved her hands to and fro. 'I belong here, sir.'

Max took off his cap and belts, handed them to the waiting Heinrich. 'You mean you're a member of the hotel staff.'

Rena made a moue. 'I am not a chambermaid.'

'I think I had worked that out.' Max sat down, crossed his legs. 'But, Fraulein, I really am very tired. Now tell me exactly why you are here, and then you can leave.'

Rena went to the sideboard. 'Would you like schnapps?'

'I think I would, yes.'

She filled a small glass with the clear liquid, and brought it to him, standing immediately in front of him. She had a pleasant scent. Max drained the glass, and she took it away to refill it, brought it back. 'I belong to the room,' she explained. 'For your comfort, sir.'

Max looked her up and down, with more interest this time. '*My* comfort?'

'The comfort of the gentleman who occupies this apartment, sir.'

'I see. You are in lieu of a bottle of champagne from the management, is that it?'

'I am not employed by the management, sir. This hotel is operated by the SS.'

'Light comes bursting through the clouds,' Max said. 'Sit down.'

Rena sat beside him, very straight, knees pressed together. Max handed her the glass. She hesitated a moment, then took a quick sip. 'Heinrich,' Max said. 'I wonder if you could rustle up some lunch.'

'Of course, sir. For . . . ah . . .'

'Three. You want some as well, don't you?'

'Thank you, sir.' Heinrich closed the door behind him.

Rena was still gazing at him.

'I am assuming that you would like some lunch as well,' Max said.

'Thank you, sir.'

'You look as if you could do with a square meal. When did you last eat?'

Another lick of the lips. 'Yesterday, sir.'

'Yesterday sounds like a long time ago. Be explicit.'

'The gentleman who was here left at lunch time, sir.'

'And you only eat when there is a gentleman here? Christ Almighty!'

'The apartment is in use almost every day, sir.'

'Almost? Isn't the hotel responsible for feeding you?'

'The hotel staff do not like me, sir. Us.'

'Because you work for the SS. You volunteered for this work?'

'No, sir. We were conscripted.'

'I see. You are what I believe the Japanese refer to as "comfort girls". And the SS taught you to speak German? You do so very well.'

'No, sir. One of the criteria required was that we speak German. The language is widely used in the Ukraine.'

'I see. So they rounded you up . . .'

'They came to our school, sir. They lined up all the senior girls, and they selected which of us they wished to . . . use.'

'On the basis of whether or not you spoke good German?'

'Well, no, sir. There were other requirements.'

'I imagine there were.' Max studied her. It was very obvious, from her choice of words, her clothes, and her general demeanour, that she came from a good background. 'What does your father do?'

'My father is a lawyer, sir.'

'And he did not object to your being requisitioned for the service of German officers?'

'Yes, sir. He did. So I have been told.'

'But he wasn't very successful.'

'He went to the SS headquarters, and they beat him up, and threw him on to the street. So I have been told.'

'How is he now?'

'I do not know, sir. I have not seen any of my family for over a year. Since I was recruited.'

Perhaps four hundred days, Max thought. *Every one of which you have had to service a German officer, or starve.* There was a fascinating story here. But it was not one into which he dared delve, however much he might be tempted. He was relieved when the door opened and a waiter wheeled in a trolley laden with food and drink, followed by Heinrich. 'Oh, good man. Fraulein.'

She glanced at him, her lips working, perhaps because of the sudden flow of saliva.

'Eat,' he commanded. 'And you, Heinrich.'

The waiter gave them all a scandalized look, and then withdrew, closing the door. Max pulled up chairs and they sat around the trolley, making, he supposed, a considerable contrast. Heinrich ate sparingly. Max himself was hungry, but was more interested in the bottle of wine, in view of everything he had heard that morning, from both sides of the fence. Rena was clearly very hungry indeed, and although she tried to practise manners, found it difficult not to cram her mouth with food. Eventually he felt he had to stop her. 'If you eat any more at that rate you will make yourself ill,' he pointed out. 'Do not worry, there will be another full meal tonight, and we will leave you food tomorrow.'

She gazed at him with enormous, tear-filled eyes, and again he was relieved when there was a smart rap on the door. Heinrich hastily stood up, but Max called, 'It is open.'

The door swung open to reveal a handsome, very smartly dressed Luftwaffe officer. 'Heil Hitler!'

Max leapt to his feet and hurried across the room. 'Gunther!'

Gunther Langholm shook hands and then embraced his oldest friend, at the same time looking past him at Rena, who was also on her feet. 'I am not intruding?'

Max released him and turned. 'This is Rena. Rena, say hello to Colonel Langholm.'

Rena advanced to shake hands and give a brief curtsey.

'Now off you go, Rena,' Max said.

'Sir?' Her lips quivered.

'Go into the bedroom and lie down. I will see you later.'

'Yes, sir.' Another curtsey, and she hurried off.

Gunther was shaking hands with Heinrich.

'Have you eaten?' Max asked.

'I have.'

'Then you can take this trolley out, Heinrich. But leave the wine. You'll have a glass, Gunther? It appears to be Russian, and is not very good, but it is reasonably alcoholic.'

'I would enjoy that. But . . .' From the side pocket of his tunic he took a half bottle. 'French.'

'Cognac?'

'The best.'

'But we'll drink the wine first. I feel like getting drunk. It may be our last opportunity for a long time.'

'Why not?' Gunther sank into a chair, tasted the wine, made a face, and then drank some more. 'I see you are being taken care of.'

'She comes with the room.' Max also sat down, while Heinrich wheeled the trolley out and closed the door. 'Sad little thing. I have no idea what to do with her.'

'I am sure you'll think of something. But I agree, it is sad.'

'At least she seems reconciled to her situation.'

'That is because she does not know what her situation is.'

'Oh, I know she must get knocked about from time to time,' Max agreed. 'But that can happen in even the best of homes.' He was thinking of Erika.

'It is not what happens to her here that is important,' Gunther said sombrely. 'But if the Reds ever regain Kiev . . . there was a town, maybe even a city – I can't remember its name – that we occupied towards the end of last summer. There the SS rounded up all the pretty girls and made them service our officers. Then the Reds counter-attacked in the winter and we were driven out. We regained our position, and the town, this last spring. And we found those girls, stripped naked and crucified to the doors of the houses, by nails, not ropes.'

Max stared at him with his mouth open.

'It is not a pretty story,' Gunther agreed. 'But as it is extremely unlikely that the Reds will ever recapture Kiev, your popsy should be all right. It is so good to see you again, and looking so well.'

'And the same to you,' Max said, although he reckoned he was not being truthful. Gunther's face was haggard, and for all the immaculate perfection of his uniform his body language was that of an unhappy man. Perhaps he had seen too much horror. And *he* had to get rid of the image that was suddenly clogging his brain, of that poor little waif in his bed being dragged naked through the streets to be nailed to a door! 'And the Wing? The old crowd?'

'They are all here. Those of them that are left.'

'Ah. Horst?'

'Dead. Shot down by anti-aircraft fire over Moscow.'

'Then you don't *know* he is dead.'

'He may as well be. The Ivans do not treat their prisoners very well.'

Obviously they have learned from us, Max thought, remembering the summer of 1941 and the long lines of Russian soldiers, starving and shambling, being driven by whips and dogs towards the camps where they would be encouraged to die. But he decided not to say it. Although the best of men, Gunther was a dedicated Nazi.

'And Hildegarde?' Gunther asked.

'I was with her a week ago, and she is in the pink. If somewhat frustrated. She is in Munich.'

'You mean she was posted there, despite being your wife?'

'I posted her there. She is on maternity leave, and I felt she would be safer well away from any fighting.'

'Maternity leave? But that is splendid news.'

'I think so.'

'And you are a general, with a hundred kills . . .'

'A hundred and fifteen,' Max said quietly.

'There is a target.'

'And you?'

'Oh, eighty-three. I have a way to go. A hundred and fifteen! You know, when you were, well . . .'

'Virtually cashiered?'

'That's what we all thought.'

'But Milch sorted it out, gave me another chance. As for the hundred and fifteen – the Yanks do not seem to realize they are in a shooting war. They come over in droves, in broad daylight. Their bombers bristle with gun turrets, but they are so slow. Sometimes they have Spitfire protection, but that is limited by range, and when they are on their own they are sitting ducks.'

'And you have the new 210s.'

'Yes,' Max said thoughtfully. 'Sometimes I long for the old Gustav.'

'But aren't these the best fighter-bombers we have? And at last they're giving them to us. I saw them on the field when I came in.'

'Yes. You know why we are here?'

'The main campaign is being fought down here. Although . . .' Gunther finished the wine and poured two glasses of cognac. 'I would have supposed that campaigning is just about over for the year. Going on last winter, it will soon be impossible to fly.'

'This campaign is going to go on all winter,' Max said.

Gunther, sipping cognac, slowly put down his glass and listened as Max outlined the situation. Then he said, 'It seems to me that we may have got ourselves into a bit of a pickle.'

'That's a fairly accurate assessment. But we have our orders, and we will carry them out. Our first business is to establish our base at Kharkov. We take off at first light tomorrow.'

'Yes, sir.'

'Then we fly daily sorties, and we keep the skies over Stalingrad clear.'

'But we also shoot up the enemy whenever possible,' Gunther said eagerly. 'It will be like old times, in France – or even here in Russia, last summer.'

'Yes,' Max agreed. *Just like old times*, he thought. 'You are hogging the brandy,' he complained.

'You are welcome to spend the night here,' Max suggested, when the cognac was finished. It was still only four o'clock in the afternoon, but it was already getting dark, and as tomorrow promised to be a very long day he intended to go to bed early, with perhaps a meal later on. And with Gunther here he might be able to resist the temptation in the next room – a temptation that had suddenly taken on a completely new dimension, thanks to what his friend had told him, as well as the wine.

'You mean three in a bed?' Gunther shook his head. 'I am an old stick-in-the-mud when it comes to the treatment of women. Anyway, there may be someone like her waiting in my quarters. I will go and find out.' He stood up, swaying slightly, and made his way to the door. 'I will see you in the morning, Herr General. Heil Hitler!'

The door closed behind him, and Max remained staring at it for some minutes. Thinking about the future was a mistake, in this present situation. If he came through, there would be Hildegarde – and a son, or a daughter; it did not really matter which – and some peace, and maybe even happiness. Until then, it was a business of survival, from one minute to the next, and seeking whatever comfort was available.

He moved, as unsteadily as Gunther, to the bedroom door,

and opened it. Rena was beneath the covers, her clothes on
the chair beside the bed. Now she hastily scrambled out of
bed to stand to attention. In his present mood and with the
slight chill in the room he could not suppose there was a more
evocative sight in the world, especially as he could not stop
himself from imagining nails being driven into the pale flesh
by a mob of jeering men. 'Oh, get back into bed,' he
commanded. 'You'll freeze.'

She slid back beneath the covers.

'Did you hear anything that was said in the other room?'

'No, sir. I did not listen.'

He was sure she was telling the truth; if she had overheard
he did not think she could be so unchanged from her earlier
demeanour. 'Are you still hungry?'

'I . . . whenever it is time, sir.'

'Well, it will be time later. But I wish to come to bed for
an hour or so.'

The body beneath the covers gave a wriggle, whether of
apprehension or anticipation he could not be sure. She watched
him with wide eyes as he undressed. 'Are you going to beat
me, sir?'

'Eh?'

She did her habitual lick of the lips. 'Well, sir, some men
find it stimulating.'

'You mean they find it necessary in order to get it up. Would
you believe that I have never beaten a woman in my life . . .
Except . . .' He remembered that Heidi Stumpff had liked to
be spanked. But that had been to get *her* going, not him.
'Except when they wanted it for pleasure.' He got in beside
her. 'You'll get the full treatment when I've had a nap. Can
you wait?'

She snuggled against him. 'Must you leave tomorrow?'

'Yes, I must.'

'But you will come back?'

'Now that I really cannot say. Keep your fingers crossed.'

For us both, he thought.

Heinrich tapped on the door. 'Four o'clock, Herr General.'

'Shit!' Max muttered. He had never felt less like leaving a
warm bed. There had been another bottle of wine with his
supper, and he had sent down for some more cognac; it was

the first time in a very long time that he had deliberately set out to get drunk.

It had nothing to do with any feelings that he might be going to his death. Rather it was a growing awareness that this great but so misguided nation to which he had tied himself was now facing catastrophe, plunging madly onwards like a runaway train, certain only that somewhere the track had to end in disaster.

The girl moved against him and brought him back to reality. He *had* been drunk the previous afternoon. But she had been the most satisfying companion he could recall. Perhaps more satisfying even than Hilde. Now there was a sad admission of his own inconstancy. But where Hilde proceeded through life with a calm certainty, in herself and her surroundings and her place in the future, this girl had offered only a desire to please, which made him the more anxious to please her. As if she had no future at all, she seemed prepared to live only in the present. He began to wonder how he could ever have been so naïve as to desire anything else.

He switched on the light and kissed her forehead. 'Time to go.'

He swung his legs out of the bed, and she caught his hand. 'Take me with you.'

'To Kharkov? That is where I am going, you know.'

'I heard you say that, before.'

'And you wish to go there? It is not in the Ukraine, you know. It is five hundred kilometres east of here. Five hundred kilometres nearer the Russian army.'

'But you are going there.'

'It is to be our base, yes.'

'Your army holds it.'

'And we are going to go on holding it.' *According to Lutyens,* he reflected.

'Please take me with you, sir.'

'Why? Why do you want to go with me?'

'Because . . . because you have been kind to me, sir.'

'Has no on else been kind to you?'

'I did not know there were any kind Germans, until last night.'

You poor, forlorn little girl. 'But you will know no one in Kharkov.'

'I would like that.' She gave a little shiver. 'I know too many people here. And they know me.'

'I understand. But you work for the SS.'

'You are a general, sir.'

He gazed at her. *Out of the mouths of babes and sucklings,* he thought. *I am indeed a general.* That realization had not truly sunk in before. And putting a twist in the SS tail was what he wanted to do more than anything else.

'What is the name of the SS commander in Kiev?'

'Colonel Fehrlein, sir.'

'Very good. Get yourself ready to leave.'

He got out of bed, shaved and dressed, sat at the desk and began to write on a sheet of the hotel notepaper.

> *Dear Fehrlein,*
> *I have found Fraulein Gorbalov such pleasant company that I am taking her with me to Kharkov. It follows that you will require a replacement for this room.*
> *With every good wish,*
> *Bayley, General, Luftwaffe.*

He folded the note into an envelope and wrote Fehrlein's name on it. Heinrich was serving breakfast, and Rena was already seated at the table, clearly in a very excited state.

Max gave Heinrich the letter. 'Please take that down to the desk and tell them that it is to be delivered to Colonel Fehrlein's office this morning.'

'Of course, sir.' Heinrich looked at Rena, and the small suitcase beside her. 'The young lady . . .'

'Is coming with us, Heinrich.'

'Of course, sir.'

Heinrich left the room.

'You have made me so very happy,' Rena said.

'Let's hope it stays that way,' Max replied.

The future would have to take care of itself.

From twenty thousand feet on a surprisingly clear early winter's day it seemed that all of Russia was displayed beneath the German fighters as they flew east in formation. Kharkov was nearly five hundred kilometres behind them now, and they could see the great serpent of the longest river in Europe winding its way through the bluffs to either side. Directly in front of them, a huge pall of smoke indicated the city of Stalingrad.

Below them there was snow on the ground, although Max did not imagine there was any lying on the shattered houses of Stalingrad, or the decomposing bodies contained within. And amidst the snow were their targets. The railway line had carved its way across the countryside all the way from Kharkov, through innumerable towns and villages. In the beginning it had been busy enough, but now it was virtually empty; it had been cut by the Russians. To either side of it, heading west, could be made out streams of men, and some vehicles: the broken Romanians.

Beyond them the Russian concentrations could be seen, and beyond those, the positions still held by the Sixth Army. At first glance these appeared a comforting distance west of the city, and well west of the airfield, which was now coming into view, and above which the bombers that had been converted into transports were circling as they waited their turn to get down, and circling again as they rose for the flight out. These planes were stripped-out bombers such as Heinkels, Dorniers and Junkers 88s, but also a number of civilian aircraft – everything that could fly and could be spared from other duties had been pressed into service. Disturbingly, there were quite a few wrecked machines to be seen on either side of the strip.

And now Max could see the main reason for the casualties: the host of Russian fighters rising from the other side of the river. They of course had a far shorter distance to fly to and from their base, and therefore much more time to attack the transports, whereas his machines had at most half an hour before they had to start their return journey, hopefully soon to be replaced by the next wave.

That precious half hour clearly had to be put to good use, but by now their tactics had been well formulated and rehearsed in combat. He now spoke into his oxygen mask. 'Your turn today, Gunther. B Wing ground attack. A Wing will follow me.'

Even after Gunther had detached to go hurtling down to launch his rockets at the Russian troops, Max still had six squadrons to lead into battle, and although none of these was at full strength he yet commanded over fifty planes. Even a year ago these should have been more than enough to destroy the hundred-plus Russians over the city. Now though, while he never doubted the superiority of the machine he was flying, he had become too aware of the inferior quality of most of his pilots. Only eighteen months ago he had commanded a wing composed of youthful veterans. Many had fought in the Battle of Britain. All had been trained to perfection over at least a year. And all had followed their famous young commander without question or hesitation. Now most of those men were dead, or too badly wounded to fly. These pilots were certainly young, and he could not criticize them for any lack of enthusiasm, any unwillingness to follow him wherever he led, but they lacked experience of flying, much less combat. Half of them had been sent to Russia straight out of flying school. He supposed he should be grateful that they were not about to engage Spitfires, or worse, Mosquitoes, flown by veteran RAF pilots. Even so, he was losing men and machines at an unacceptable rate. For what, he wondered? It was an attempt to keep alive a dying army merely to satisfy an egotistic lunatic.

'Remember,' he said. 'Mutual support.'

There was no time to remind his fledglings of the various essential rules of combat. He had lectured them often enough on the ground. But the implementation of those rules, under combat conditions, was another matter. The most important rule of all was do not fire until you are close enough to be sure of a hit. That meant waiting until your gun sight was entirely filled by the enemy aircraft; the art of deflection fire – the ability to calculate an opponent's speed and the exact direction of one's aim to intercept the plane – could only be learned by experience.

Soon he was surrounded by streams of tracers. The Russians had ceased strafing the buildings beneath them, for the moment, and were rising to meet the German onslaught, but were still a kilometre away. And most of the Messerschmitts were blazing away, wasting precious bullets. They only had a maximum of 2500 rounds per gun – which would give perhaps twenty-five seconds' sustained firing – and twenty rockets each.

He sighed, and closed in on the enemy. They were splitting

up, moving to each side; they knew they had superior numbers and were thinking of encirclement. Max moved his stick and sent his machine round in a tight turn. The fighter in front of him twisted and then dived. Max went down with him, closing his cooling vents to give him additional speed, a risky manoeuvre as the engine would only function without air for a few moments before seizing. But those few moments were all he wanted. His sight was filled, and he squeezed the triggers, firing one of his rockets almost at point-blank range. The rocket struck and exploded, as did the Russian plane, filling the sky with burning fragments. Max opened his vents and pulled back the stick to climb steeply away from the flying debris; he reckoned the pilot must have died instantly.

Then he was back in the battle, trying to mother his flock, shouting both warnings and instructions while seeking targets for himself. The action was brief. Even if vastly superior in numbers, the Russians broke off the engagement after only ten minutes and hurried to the east. 'No pursuit,' Max snapped as one or two of the Germans started in the same direction. 'You haven't the fuel. Home!'

He made sure they had all obeyed before following, circling over the fires below, and counting. He reckoned a good fifteen of the Russians had gone down. But so had six Messerschmitts.

Max read the letter with a pounding heart. Gunther, seated across the table in the Kharkov mess, watched him with a frown, trying to decipher his expression. 'How bad?'

'Not bad,' Max said. 'Not bad at all. Fritz!' he shouted. 'Champagne! Champagne for everyone. It's a boy!'

The pilots crowded round to shake his hand.

'And Hilde?' Gunther asked.

'On top of the world.' Then Max's smile faded. 'She wants to know when I'm coming home.'

'Well,' Gunther said. 'Now the Ivans have taken the airstrip . . .'

'You understand,' Max said, 'that if Stalingrad falls – or perhaps I should say when – it will be the greatest defeat ever suffered by any army in history?'

'Didn't the British surrender more than eighty thousand at Singapore?' Gunther asked. 'And what about Cannae? That cost the Romans at least eighty thousand.'

'Agreed. But Paulus has a quarter of a million.'

'Well . . . he's not done yet.'

'It still looks as if, barring a miracle, an army of two hundred and fifty thousand men is going to be swallowed up.'

Gunther drank some champagne.

'I am too serious,' Max agreed. 'Was that not your ninetieth kill this afternoon?'

'Ah . . . yes, I think it was.'

'Are you trying to say you haven't been keeping count? Fritz, another bottle. We have two causes to celebrate.'

'What will you call the boy, Herr General?' one of the pilots asked.

Max opened the letter again. 'My wife wishes to call him Max.'

'That is as it should be,' Gunther declared. 'We will drink a toast to Max.'

'And then I am going to bed,' Max announced.

His officers exchanged glances; they all knew exactly what was waiting in his bed, but none of them was prepared to criticize the morals of someone who was not only their commanding officer but also a hero to every man in the fleet.

Max closed the door behind him, and Rena rose from the chair in which she had been seated, looking out of the window at the snow. 'I heard the cheering,' she said. 'Is it good news?'

'My wife has given birth. I have a son.'

'Then I congratulate you.'

She made no move, but waited for him to come to her, which he did. He put his arms round her. 'She is my wife.'

'And you love her.'

'Yes, I do.'

'I envy her. Do you wish sex?'

She made to turn away, and he caught her arms. 'She is my wife,' he repeated. 'But you are my responsibility. I have made you so. I shall not abandon you.'

'You will take me to Germany when you return?'

'Yes. You will have to go as my servant. You understand this?'

'I am happy to be your servant, sir.'

'Well, then . . . Oh, damnation,' he muttered as he heard a tap on the door. 'What is it?' he shouted.

'It is Fritz, Herr General. I am sorry to trouble you, but there is a telephone call for you. From Kiev. General Lutyens.'

'Thank God for that. I'll be back in a moment,' Max told Rena, and hurried down the stairs to pick up the receiver. 'Herr General! Good evening. When will my replacements be arriving? I'm getting a little short of pilots.'

'There are no replacements, Max.'

'Herr General?'

'You have done all you can, and you have suffered unacceptable casualties. Your command is now dissolved, and your wings are to return here for re-assignment.'

'You mean I have failed in my mission.'

'No, Max. *You* have not failed. But Field-Marshal Manstein has informed us that it is now impossible for him to relieve Stalingrad, and equally it is now impossible, given the numbers of enemy troops surrounding the city, for the Sixth Army to break out, even were they to be given permission to do so, which they have not.'

'So they are just to be written off? Two hundred and fifty thousand men?'

'I doubt there are quite that number left. The point is that it makes no military sense to continue pouring our resources into a lost battle. So you will bring your men and your machines out, and await re-assignment to more important duties. There will be leave. Is it true that you have just become a father?'

'Yes, Herr General,' Max said slowly. 'It is true.'

'And you wife is well?'

'Yes, Herr General. My wife is well.'

'I congratulate you, and her. You will be with her for Christmas. I expect you here by the end of the week.'

'And my ground staff, sir?'

'They can follow by truck.'

'I do not have sufficient vehicles, sir.'

'General Bayley, your planes and your pilots are what matter. Bring them out, and allocate the more important of your ground personnel to what transport you have.'

'If we could requisition the railway . . .'

'The railway is required by the Wehrmacht for the movement of troops and supplies. I understand your difficulty, but we are fighting a war. Bring out who you can, whoever you regard as most important. When you are in Kiev, come to see me, and we will see what we can do about the rest of your people. Heil Hitler!'

'Heil Hitler!' Max repeated, and replaced the phone. *The greatest disaster in military history*, he thought. So we shrug, and walk away. Better luck next time. But would Paulus's men have a next time? Would any of them?

Most of his pilots were still drinking, boisterously. But the noise ceased as their CO appeared in the doorway. 'Orders from Kiev,' he said. 'We are pulling out, at dawn tomorrow morning.'

'Pulling out? To go where?' Gunther demanded.

'I have not the slightest idea. But I suspect that we are going to be split up and assigned to other duties.' He held up his hand to silence the immediate deluge of questions. 'We have been given an order, and we will carry it out. I shall be sorry to lose any of you, but I will see each of you in Kiev, when we have received our new orders.'

'Does this mean that Stalingrad has fallen?' Gunther asked.

'It means that our part in the campaign is over,' Max said carefully. 'I should get some sleep, if I were you. Major Lippner, a word.'

The adjutant hurried over.

'We – that is, the aircrew – are expected in Kiev tomorrow,' Max told him. 'I am leaving you in command of the ground personnel. These are to be evacuated as rapidly as possible, by truck.'

'Herr General, we do not—'

'I know, Lippner. I wish you to make up a list of the more important personnel and give them priority. When I get to Kiev, I will arrange for additional transport to be sent to you.'

Lippner gazed at him.

He knows I am promising the impossible, Max thought. 'I know it is a shitty assignment, Lippner. But I know you will carry it out.'

'Yes, sir. I assume it is my duty to remain until the last man has been evacuated?'

'I'm afraid it is.'

'Very good, sir. And, ah . . .'

'The Fraulein is my servant, Major. As is Heinrich. I would like them given as much priority as is possible.'

PART TWO
THUNDERBOLTS

'Be ready, gods, with all your thunderbolts;
Dash him to pieces!'
>> *Julius Caesar*
>> William Shakespeare

Casualty

'Well, gentlemen?' Group Captain Spencer surveyed the five officers standing before him; he intended to lead the raid himself. 'You have all been very good in not asking questions, but I feel some sort of explanation is due. You know we are going to strafe Berlin, but I am sure you are asking yourselves just what we hope to achieve with only six aircraft. The answer is very little, in physical terms. The objective is to show the Nazis that it can be done – and will be done, in the not too distant future, but with a vastly increased force. This certainty will also greatly encourage the Russians, and it is the best thing we can offer them at this time when they continue screaming for a second front in Europe. As for the choice of today for the exercise, I suppose you could call it a bit of mischievousness on the part of our superiors. It has been learned that today both Messrs Goering and Goebbels are making important speeches in Berlin, extolling the greatness of Nazi Germany and proclaiming the certainty of ultimate victory. I suppose this is intended to offset the fact that they are committed to another winter in Russia, with people no doubt remembering that last winter did not go entirely according to plan. From our limited point of view, it's an opportunity to show people what we really can do. So, synchronize.' They checked their watches. 'Oh-six-twenty-five. We are going in two flights. I will lead A Flight. We take off at oh-six-forty-five. Wing-Commander Hoosen will lead B Flight, and will take off at oh-seven-fifteen. Twenty-five thousand feet, and four hundred and twenty mph. Keep your eye open for ice on your wings, and use your de-icers; it doesn't matter if you get home with flat batteries, as long as you get home. A Flight should be over Berlin at oh-eight-thirty, and commence its return journey at oh-nine-hundred. B Flight will maintain its half-hour interval. We should be back here by eleven hundred. Questions?'

No one spoke, no one moved.

Spencer nodded. 'Good luck and good hunting.'

They filed from the office out into the gloom of the winter morning; the sun had not yet risen, and even its prospect was hidden behind a bank of cloud on the eastern horizon. 'You'll take the right, Johnnie,' Hoosen said. 'You on the left, Taffy.'

'Wilco,' Squadron-Leader Evans acknowledged.

'And as the man said, good hunting. Just remember, we stick together unless there is real trouble, I won't be communicating again until we are over the target, and that goes for you too.'

The pilots nodded, and soon reached their planes. John remembered how sceptical he had been when first shown the prototype model, and invited to fly it, and how instantly he had fallen in love with such deadly perfection. Now he asked, 'All set?'

Langley nodded. 'She's ready, sir.'

He waited. As with all the air crews, he had asked no questions about this sudden alteration to their usual arrangements, from night to day flying. But there could be no doubt that he was curious. And when they were both seated, he could not resist remarking, 'At least we'll be able to see where we're going, for a change.'

The engines were ticking over, and John was checking his instruments. He watched A Flight soar into the sky. 'Don't you like daylight, Sergeant?'

'It'll make a change. I seem to have been issued with new charts.' He sifted through the several sheets of stiff paper. 'These rather look like . . .'

'The eastern half of Germany, yes. Berlin, to be precise.'

Langley did not immediately reply, and John glanced at him; he was still sorting out the charts. 'Will it be as a crow, sir?'

'Hopefully, yes. At least on the way out. Coming back may not be quite so easy.'

'Well, then, we're looking at virtually due east. Straight at the sun, if it ever shows up, until we close the target.'

'No reservations?'

'I always reckoned these machines were made for something like this. But only six? Do we have a specific target?'

'Believe it or not, it's a propaganda exercise. We fly to Berlin in broad daylight – something that has never been tried before – we shoot up everything we can find, railway stations, public buildings and so on, and we come home again. The idea is to put the wind up Jerry, let him know that we can do it, make him worry that the next time we may do it with a thousand planes. Strategically, we are trying to make him look over his shoulder from the Russian front, maybe take a little pressure off Uncle Joe's lot.'

'Yes, sir. Do we have a thousand aircraft capable of flying to Berlin and back?'

'No, we don't. But Jerry doesn't know that. There's the signal. Let's go.'

They climbed into the overcast sky, and at no more than six thousand feet the ground was lost. At thirteen thousand they emerged into brilliant daylight, with nothing to look at but the sky and the glowing orb of the sun emerging in front of them. That provided a rough course but for the first three hundred miles they could follow the radio beacons that thrust into Western Europe; Langley had simply to keep listening for the nuls and request only the smallest alterations of course whenever they wandered slightly to left and right and picked up the Morse signals. Reassuringly the other two aircraft were always in position, Hoosen out in front and Evans to the left.

At twenty-five thousand feet traces of frost began to appear on the wings. 'Keep those clear,' John said.

'All the way, sir?'

'If necessary, yes. But the sun should help, when it gets high enough.'

Langley clicked the de-icers into action.

Ice apart, John knew that the first obstacle – at least to conventional aircraft – would be the Kammhuber Line. The Germans, over the previous year, had developed an in-depth series of defences to cover France and the Low Countries. The entire area was divided into boxes, each box being defended by a separate fighter group, and the whole connected by a central radar control. Thus when a flight of Allied bombers was reported over the Channel, its speed and direction were plotted, and sent out to the various boxes. For instance, Box A might receive a message that a flight of seventy-plus bombers was approaching him, distance a hundred kilometres, speed three hundred and twenty kph. The group commander would calculate the best interception point, and put up his entire command to meet the enemy. He could do this with perfect confidence, certain that Box B, behind him, would have received the same information, updated as regards distance, and would therefore be ready to take over the interception the moment the enemy entered his air space, while Group A could return to its base, land, refuel and re-arm, and be ready for any secondary incursion – or, more to the point, to take to the air again – when it was warned that the raiders were on their way back.

The system had worked very well against conventional aircraft, certainly when the bombers had outstripped the range of their escorting fighters. But it had proved all but useless against such things as the Mosquitoes, and, it was rumoured, the newly developed American P-38 Lightnings. These had not been seen in Europe as yet, but John did not doubt that they soon would be, as the USAAF bombers were presently suffering unacceptable casualties.

But those were matters for the high command. His job was immediate. 'Anything?' he asked.

Langley, who also spoke German, had been fiddling with various wavelengths. 'They know we're here. But they can't decide where we're going.'

'I imagine they'll work it out.' John looked at his watch; they had been flying for an hour. 'Still in contact?'

'No, sir.' Langley looked across at Hoosen. 'But the boss seems happy enough.'

The flight-commander came on the air fifteen minutes later. 'Time to have a look.'

The cloud was now starting to break up, and at ten thousand feet they could see the ground. The sun was also making good progress, and Langley switched off the de-icers. 'Nice day,' Hoosen remarked. 'And that looks like the Hanover–Berlin autobahn. Well done, navigators.'

'Bandits,' Evans commented.

'Those are FWs,' Hoosen said. 'Ignore them.'

The Focke-Wolfes were climbing rapidly, but long before

they could reach the British squadron the Mosquitoes were
past them.

'There!' Langley said.

Several columns of smoke were rising into the morning air.

'And there!' John said, as he saw the three other aircraft
streaking back towards them.

'All the best,' Spencer said. 'See you at home.'

Now the city itself was clearly visible. 'I reckon we'll go
straight up the Unter den Linden,' Hoosen said, 'and see what
we can do about the Brandenburg Gate. Going down.'

He dived, and the other two aircraft followed. Now the sky
was a mass of black puffballs as the anti-aircraft guns opened
up. John supposed they had been practising on A Flight only
a few minutes earlier, but they still hadn't got the deflection
angle right.

'More bandits,' Langley remarked.

'210s,' Hoosen replied. 'We'll have to take a couple out.'

He was already flying low, close to the rooftops, and now
he loosed his rockets before climbing steeply to confront the
swarming fighters. John, following, had a peculiar sensation
as he looked down on a scene he remembered from his childhood, when he had come here with his father and stepmother
Karolina. They had stayed at a hotel called the Albert, which
was apparently always used by the Bitterman family when
visiting the city. It should be just beneath him . . . He frowned.
The street where the Albert had stood was a wreck, the hotel
itself just a pile of rubble. Another link with the past gone
for ever.

'There's a target,' Langley said.

John blinked, regained his concentration, saw the railway
line and the station, lined it up, and squeezed the trigger. The
rockets ploughed into the station, and it seemed to explode,
carrying a train with it. He hoped there hadn't been too many
civilians on board. Then he pulled the stick back to climb
away from the smoke.

'Fucking hell!' Langley shouted.

John turned his head sharply: his navigator was not given
to expletives. Above them, Hoosen's machine was spiralling
down, followed by a trail of smoke.

* * *

It had been an incredibly mild January, at least in the south of England, although it was cold enough to make riding a bicycle in a skirt an extremely chilly business. But, not having the use of a car, it was still the quickest way to get to and from the station, and hard peddling at least kept the circulation going.

The annoying thing was that there were two cars in the garage at Hillside, not to mention the Rolls that was used by Mark Senior. But there was no petrol to spare. Anyway, Jolinda reflected, it wasn't raining – in fact the sky was quite blue – and there was no wind, while the lane along which she rode was as attractive as ever, even if the trees had shed their leaves and now stood gaunt and bare.

As there was no traffic to worry about – this lane was invariably devoid even of pedestrians – Jolinda lost herself in a daydream of the warm fire, and the even warmer baby, waiting for her at home, and was taken entirely by surprise when a man suddenly stepped out of the hedge in front of her. Quickly she braked, putting her foot down as the bike fell over. 'That was a damned silly thing to do,' she snapped. 'I could have ridden straight into you.' Then she frowned as she recognized his uniform. 'Mike?'

He saluted. 'At your service, ma'am. Say, you sure look cute in that uniform.'

'You can't see my uniform,' she pointed out; she was wearing a greatcoat. 'What are you doing here, anyway?'

'Well, ma'am, you told me I could call, next time I could get down to this neck of the woods.'

'Yes, I did,' she agreed. 'But I expected you to come to the house.'

'Well, I reckoned I'd be safer if I could come across you when you didn't have that man-eating monster around.'

'I don't think Rufus has ever actually eaten anybody. Although I'm sure he's considered it from time to time. Well, you're welcome to visit, and I'll make sure he doesn't bite you. But it's two miles to the house, and there's only one bicycle, so . . . How did you get out here, anyway? It's a long walk from the village and the station.'

'Not a problem. I have transport.'

'You have?'

'Over there.' He pointed, and now she saw, beyond the hedge and the fringe of trees, the roof of a van.

'That's yours?'

'Let's say I have the use of it. And there's lots of room. We can put your bike in the back.'

'Well . . .' She slid off the seat and he was soon grasping the handlebars to push the bike towards the van. 'How'd you get the coupons?'

'Aw, you can get anything you want if you want it badly enough. Certainly in London.'

She walked beside him, and he parted the hedge so that she could get through. 'You mean you've been using the black market. That's not really right, you know.'

'What the hell. A guy's gotta do what a guy's gotta do. Right?'

She considered for a moment. 'And you had to come down and see me?'

'That's why I'm here.'

They had reached the van, and he opened the rear doors and put the bike inside, then closed the doors again. Then he opened the passenger door, and Jolinda got in, taking off her side cap as it brushed the roof. Lonergan walked round the front and got in the other side.

'Wait just one moment,' she said. 'You say you came down here to see me. But as I wasn't home you came out here. Right?'

'First time.'

'How did you know I'd be here at this hour?'

'I'm a patient guy.'

'You've been sitting in this van, waiting . . . for how long?'

'A couple of days.'

'What?'

'Well, I knock it off every night. I mean, you're not on duty at night, right? I've a room in the village.'

'And you prefer to wait for me out here in the cold rather than come straight to the house? You are an absolute nut. Come on, take me home.'

'You wouldn't describe me as a man in love?'

Jolinda gazed at him, open-mouthed.

'Shucks, ma'am, the first time I saw you, I just knew you were the one for me. That was four years ago.'

'Four years ago, Sergeant, I was not married. And I wasn't an officer.'

'And now you're both. Man-made rules, ma'am. They just have to be broken.'

'You're getting out of your depth, Sergeant. But I'll assume your sentiments are genuine, so I'm not going to do anything about it, if you take me home right now. If you're not prepared to do that, get my bike out of the back and we'll part company. And if you turn up at Hillside again, I'll remind Rufus he hasn't had lunch.'

Still he made no move to turn on the ignition. 'So you aim to be the faithful wife type.'

'I am a wife, Sergeant. And a mother.'

'You left out the word *faithful*. And you reckon your British flyboy husband is faithful too?'

Jolinda smiled, despite her growing irritation with this ridiculous situation. 'He doesn't have much time to be anything else. He flies all night, and sleeps most of every day.'

'What about when he was in France last year? Four months, wasn't it?'

Jolinda frowned at him. 'How the hell do you know about that?'

'Let's say I know a lot about a lot of things. Do you know how he got out?'

'I do not know, and I've never asked. It's top secret.'

'Well, let me tell you. He got out by pretending to be the husband of a gorgeous chick named Liane de Gruchy. She's big in the Resistance over there. You ever heard of her?'

'No, I have not.'

'Well, I can tell you that the Gestapo certainly have: she's inclined to leave her calling card, from time to time, so they know all about her. Their problem is they've never been able to get hold of her. They will eventually, of course. They always do. But meanwhile, she's proving a right pain in the ass.'

'How do you know all this?' Jolinda was interested, despite herself. 'And why are you telling me?'

'Because I reckon you should know. One of this dame's specialties, when she's not blowing people up or shooting them, is getting downed airmen through France and into Spain. Acting as their wife, right? Only she don't do too much acting. Now tell me, you notice anything different about hubby's love-making since he got home?' He paused to stare at her, and she knew she was flushing.

'I have never heard such a ridiculous load of rubbish in my life. Just what do you think you're playing at?'

'I'm trying to bring you into the real world, ma'am. Jolinda. Like they say, what's sauce for the gander is sauce for the goose, right?' She had unbuttoned her greatcoat in the warmth of the cab. Now he parted it.

'Do you mind?' she snapped.

'Just looking at the best-filled tunic I have ever seen. Let's see what you got under there.'

'That's it,' Jolinda said. 'I'll get my own bike. And you, soldier, are going to find yourself on a charge.'

She turned away from him to open the door, and had her shoulders seized and jerked backwards with tremendous force. Her head fell into his lap, while her feet kicked against the door. Nothing like that had ever happened to her before, and for a moment she was too confounded to do more than gasp, while her head spun in a mixture of outrage and indecision. She had never had to use her unarmed combat training skills away from the mat.

She tried to sit up, but he had a hand on each shoulder, pressing her down; the handbrake was eating into her back. As she had estimated on their first meeting, he was very strong. 'Let me go, you bastard,' she panted.

'Gee, you're pretty when you're mad.'

'You,' she said, having got her breath back, 'are gong to spend the next year, at the very least, in the stockade.'

'You still reckon you're on top of the game,' he remarked. 'Well, as the saying goes, first find your stockade.'

He moved, again with startling suddenness, tightening his grip on her shoulders and twisting violently, so that she tumbled off his lap to find herself kneeling on the floor, her face now buried in his trouser leg, while her bun collapsed and her hair fell to either side of her face. She considered biting him, but didn't think her teeth would penetrate the thick serge, and before she could get her breath back her arms had been pulled behind her and she felt the cold steel of the handcuffs.

'There we go,' he said, pulling her up and thrusting her into her seat. 'Now we can have a civilized conversation.'

Jolinda blew yellow strands of hair away from her mouth and eyes, took deep breaths to try and get her emotions under control. Her skirt had ridden above her knees, and she just knew her stockings were laddered. But she was determined to keep calm. If she was about to be raped, the important thing was to survive it so that she could have this lout dealt with afterwards. But she couldn't prevent herself asking, 'Do you really think you can get away with this?'

'Do you really think your big house, your rank, your famous husband, your powerful father-in-law – even your big dog – are gonna help you? Right now, they're actually working against you, baby. They're all the things you're gonna lose, if you don't play ball. Now, you and I are gonna take a drive together, to some place we can be alone and get to know each other real well.'

'You . . .'

He shook his head. 'Right now I don't think you have anything to say that I want to hear.' He opened the glove compartment and took out a billiard ball and a roll of tape. 'Open wide.'

Jolinda clenched her teeth together, but she knew it would be a futile exercise; he merely closed his hand on the base of her jaw and squeezed, very hard. Her mouth opened and he thrust the ball in. It just about filled the space between her teeth, and although she immediately tried to use her tongue to force it back out, before she could do so he had passed a length of tape across her lips. This he now cut with a pair of scissors that had also been waiting in the glove compartment, and smoothed it down on her cheeks.

'There we go. Now, come along.'

He got out of the cab, came round to her side, and opened the door to drag her out. Her knees gave way, and he had to hold her up and again drag her round to the rear. There he let her slump to her knees, while he opened the door, pulled out her bicycle, and threw it into the bushes. Then he pulled her upright again and bundled her into the interior, following her in to kneel beside her. There were some lengths of rope waiting, and he used one of these to secure her ankles. 'I have to say,' he remarked, sliding his hands up her calves and then her thighs, underneath her skirt, 'these legs are really something. Getting between them is going to be an experience.'

'Mmmmm,' Jolinda moaned in futile protest as his fingers slipped underneath her drawers.

'Yes, sir. Something to look forward to.' The fingers moved

away, but only to loop another length of rope round her ankles. Then she was rolled on to her face while the rope was carried up to her wrists and passed round the handcuffs, then drawn tight, so that her legs were pulled up behind her to leave her trussed and unable to move. 'Can't have you rolling about and thumping on the floor, right? But we'll make you as comfortable as we can.' He rolled her on to her side and bunched a piece of sacking to put under her head. 'OK? I'm afraid we have a fairly long drive, as I don't want to get caught up in no town traffic. But I guess you'll survive. Still . . .' He unbuttoned her tunic, pulled her tie down, and opened her shirt. 'Ain't that more comfy? I ain't never seen tits that big. I'm gonna hurry, baby. You and me have a date with a bed. Just for starters.'

Mark Bayley got out of the Rolls and slapped his gloved hands together. 'Brrrr. Good night for a whisky, Jim. Join me.'

'That would be very nice, thank you, sir,' the chauffeur said. Jim Bearman had been Mark Bayley's mechanic in France in 1917, and therefore had known him longer than anyone, save Cecil Hargreaves and his sister Joan. Nor could Jim ever forget that Mark had rescued him from the demobbed and unemployed fate of selling matches on street corners when he hired him to be his driver. But he never allowed either familiarity or gratitude to impinge on the proper relationship between employer and employee.

He also understood Mark's determination never to allow the fact that he was a cripple to get in the way of his life, and carefully waited while he followed his tapping stick through the early-winter darkness to the door. This was opened for him by Clements, who had heard the car, as had Rufus, who came bounding out of the kitchen to greet his master.

Bearman followed Mark into the hall and closed the door, then fielded the dog. Clements helped Mark out of his coat. 'Nasty night, sir,' he ventured. 'And after such a fine day.'

'No cloud,' Mark reminded him. 'So the temperature is dropping like a lead balloon. They're talking about snow tonight. Mrs Bayley home?'

'In the study, sir.'

Mark nodded. 'Come through, Jim.'

He limped through the drawing room, pausing for a moment, as he always did, before Karolina's portrait, before going into the study. Helen was on her feet for a hug and a kiss. 'God, your face is cold. Hello, Jim.'

'Evening, Mrs Bayley. It's perishing out.'

'You must feel like a drink.'

'Never was a truer word spoken.' Mark was already pouring three whiskies. 'Here's to a quiet weekend. Joly joining us?'

'I don't know. I haven't seen her.'

'I'll give her a shout.' Mark always liked to see his daughter-in-law, and he felt she reciprocated.

'I meant, she's not home,' Helen said.

Mark, already at the door, checked. 'Wasn't she due home this weekend?'

'That's what she said. She must have changed her mind.'

Mark remained standing in the doorway. 'And she didn't phone to let us know?'

'Well . . . you know what Joly is like.'

Mark considered for a moment. What he did know was that Helen had never been able fully to accept the American girl, whose background, manners and mores – not to mention moral outlook – were so completely different to her own. He limped through the drawing room and stood at the foot of the stairs. 'Penny!'

'Yes, sir, Mr Bayley.' The nurse appeared on the landing.

'Did Miss Jolinda call?'

'No, sir.'

'But you were expecting her home today?'

'Yes, sir. She telephoned yesterday, and said she'd be home for the weekend.'

'Hmm. Baby all right?'

'Oh, yes, sir.'

'Thank you, Penny.' Mark limped back into the study.

'You don't really suppose something has happened to her, do you?' Helen inquired.

'If she said she was coming home today, then she was coming home today.'

'It's a woman's privilege to change her mind,' Helen pointed out.

'Agreed. But she usually has a reason. It would have to be

a pretty strong reason to keep her away from spending time with Baby Mark.'

'Well . . .'

'Come on, old girl. You know something I don't.'

Helen cast an embarrassed glance at Bearman, who was looking anxious; like every male member of the Bayley household he was very fond of Jolinda. 'I know nothing at all about what Jolinda does when she's not here, or what she thinks at any time. But I do know she's a lovely young girl who is virtually a grass widow. You couldn't blame her if she occasionally accepted an invitation to . . . well, to have a drink in the pub.'

Mark stared at her, surprised at her defending whatever Jolinda might have done, and she flushed. 'Well . . . I mean . . .'

'One should try to look at it from her point of view,' Mark agreed. 'But that doesn't explain why she hasn't come home, or at least telephoned to say she'd be late.'

'If you think Miss Jolinda might have had an accident, sir,' Bearman said, 'I could go and have a look.'

'Hold it a moment.' There was a telephone on the desk, and Mark sat down and picked it up, giving the number to the exchange. 'Ah. Squadron-Leader Browne? Mark Bayley. Very well indeed, thank you. Look, I'm sorry to bother you at this hour, but could you tell me if Section-Officer Bayley is still in her office? Say again? Before lunch? I see. Did she have company? Of course she would not. Riding her bicycle, yes. No, not right now. Thank you very much, Squadron-Leader. I'll come back to you if we need a full-scale search.' He hung up. 'Jolinda left the station at eleven o'clock this morning. She had a two-day furlough, and was coming home for lunch.'

'Then she's had an accident,' Bearman said. 'I'll get the Rolls.'

'Oh, my God!' Helen said. 'If she had an accident at eleven o'clock this morning . . .' She looked at the clock on the mantelpiece. 'She could have been lying out there for six hours, in this cold.'

'Yes,' Mark said grimly. 'I'll come with you, Jim. And we'll take Rufus.'

'But,' Helen protested, 'it's dark, and you don't know where to look.'

'Joly always uses Carter's Lane. It's the most direct route

to and from the station. And if she's anywhere around there, Rufus will find her. He loves her as much as anyone.'

The Rolls left the road and proceeded slowly along the lane, behind the legally required dimmed headlights. The two men had not spoken since leaving the house, each concerned with his own thoughts; the only sound above the engine had been the panting of Rufus on the back seat. He might not know what exactly, but he knew that something was up: he was not usually allowed into the Rolls, nor was he often taken out at night.

Now Bearman said, 'This lane was never intended for motor traffic.'

'You mean she would hardly have been knocked down by a hit-and-run driver.'

'It's very unlikely, sir.'

'She could have over-balanced and fallen off her bike.'

'And not come home, sir? It's only a couple of miles to the house.'

'She might have hit her head.'

'And stayed unconscious for six hours?'

'Just what are you trying to say, Jim?'

'I don't think we're going to find her on this lane, sir. Not in the car, at any rate. I think we should stop and have a prowl on foot. Look over there. That's a gap in the hedge. You stay here. I'll take Rufus.'

'You think she left the lane, with her bicycle? Why should she do that?'

'Well . . .'

'You mean she might have been assaulted and dragged into one of these fields? By God. We'd better get on to the station and get some additional manpower.'

'Just let's give Rufus ten minutes to cast about. If anyone can pick up Miss Jolinda's scent, he's the one.'

'Ten minutes,' Mark said.

Bearman took a powerful flashlight from the glove compartment and opened the rear door. 'Come on, Rufe. Find, find, find.'

The dog gave a growl of anticipation and leapt from the car, disappearing into the darkness, followed by the chauffeur. He had switched off the car lights, and Mark stared into the darkness, arms folded across his chest. The heater had also been switched off, and it was growing steadily colder. The thought of Jolinda lying out there for six hours . . . To have done that, she would have had to be too badly hurt to move. Or be dead. But that led to quite unthinkable thoughts. To consider Joly being murdered was bad enough. To allow oneself to imagine what might have happened to her before death was impossible.

He reminded himself that, statistically, one stood more chance of being struck by lightning than of being assaulted and murdered on a Sussex country lane. But people *did* get struck by lightning.

When he thought of all the happiness she and John had shared, all the sunshine she had brought into his own life . . . He listened to the sound of Rufus barking, opened the door, and got out, leaning on his stick. 'Anything?' he shouted, not knowing what he wanted the reply to be.

'We've found the bike,' Bearman called.

Mark made his way towards them, carefully prodding the ground in front of him. 'Where did you find it?' he called.

'In these bushes.' Bearman was now waving the light to and fro to guide him.

Mark pushed the hedge aside and got through. 'You mean it was hidden?'

'It doesn't look hidden to me, sir.'

Mark came up beside him; Rufus was still snuffling around. 'I see what you mean.' The bicycle lay half in and half out of the bushes; in daylight it would be clearly visible to any passer-by.

'Shall I take it to the car?'

'No. Leave it right where it is. Have you looked around?'

'Rufus has. But I'll check it out. What kind of radius?'

'Jolinda is a big, strong girl. I don't think anyone could have dragged her too far, without . . .' He paused.

'Coshing her.' Bearman was on his hands and knees, peering at the ground by the light of the flash. 'There doesn't seem to be any blood. Rufus barked when he found the bike, but he hasn't shown any excitement since.'

'Have a look anyway,' Mark said. 'See if there's a group of trees together, or even a copse. The sort of place a rapist would likely drag her. I'll be in the car.'

But he waited for several seconds, staring at the bicycle. It had been thrown into the bushes with some force, not leaned against them while its owner went off to do something. Jolinda had either discarded it in a hurry, or she had been pulled or knocked off and then taken away . . . but where?

'Hey!' Bearman had not got very far. Now he was waving the torch again.

Mark limped towards him. 'What have you found?'

'I'll swear these are car tracks. Recent, too. The ground's fairly soft. Someone was parked here for some time.'

Mark followed the direction of the beam.

'I reckon this is a job for the police,' Bearman said.

'The station first,' Mark decided. 'She's one of theirs. We'll let the RAF MPs tackle it. If they decide to call in the local bobby, we'll have to go along with it. But until they do, we don't want what has happened to be screamed all over the neighbourhood unless it's absolutely necessary.' He snapped his fingers. 'Come along, Rufe.'

Bearman walked beside him, shining the flashlight on the ground. 'You reckon she may just have gone off with someone? Abandoning her bike?'

'Yes. The question is, did she do it of her own free will, or was she kidnapped?'

'Either way . . .' Bearman gave a low whistle. 'You going to tell Mr John?'

'Let's see what the MPs can find. And what they have to say.'

And let's pray, he thought. But which of the two possibilities would be the most difficult for Johnnie to bear?

Gentlemen-at-Arms

'The fact is, Mr Bayley,' Inspector Carden said, 'the young lady seems to have done the most complete disappearing act I have ever come across.'

It was the middle of the morning, and the MPs had just completed another search of the area around where the bicycle had been found. Now Carden, a stocky man who liked to be considered a disciplinarian, stood in the hall of Hillside House, looking distinctly apprehensive. Quite apart from the rather overpowering presence of Mark Bayley himself, he was also surrounded by Helen Bayley, Jim Bearman, Clements, Cook, two housemaids, and Penny, not to mention a panting Rufus.

'You are sticking with the theory that she has disappeared of her own free will?' Mark said.

'Well, sir, there is no evidence to the contrary. We have the discarded bicycle, we have the wheel tracks of a vehicle parked only a few feet away and then driving towards the road . . . and nothing else.'

'And you don't think she could have been knocked off her bicycle and forced into the vehicle?'

'Well, sir, that *could* have happened. But there is no evidence that it did. There is nothing to suggest any kind of a struggle. I mean, sir, Section-Officer Bayley is a, well . . .' He glanced at Helen. 'She is a well-built young woman, and she had received full training in unarmed combat. I am bound to say, sir, that if she got into that van, all the evidence we have indicates that she did so of her own free will.'

'So what are you deducing from that?' Mark asked, his voice deceptively quiet.

'Well, sir, that would seem to suggest that the vehicle was

being driven by someone she knew, who perhaps offered her a lift.'

'To a house that was only two miles away, and to which she was returning, as she did virtually every day, on her bicycle. She had a further ten minutes to ride, the sun was shining, and at that time of the day it was not very cold. Yet she not only accepts a lift, but carelessly throws her bicycle into the hedge. She must have been very anxious for that lift, Inspector. And having done that, she promptly disappears.'

'Yes, sir,' Carden agreed unhappily.

'So your theory is that she met someone she knew very well, either by chance or by assignation, and went off with him, abandoning her home, her clothes, her position, and above all, her baby and her husband.'

'Absolute rubbish,' Helen declared.

'Do you intent to post her as absent without leave, Inspector?'

'She is not at this moment absent without leave, sir. As I understand it, she had a two-day furlough. But if you are certain that a crime has been committed, well, it is my opinion that we have to involve the civil police.'

'Hmm,' Mark muttered. 'That meant newspapers, publicity . . .'

'May I ask, sir, what is Wing-Commander Bayley's opinion on all this? I would say it should be his decision as to what steps we take. Or has he been able to shed some light on the situation?'

'I have not informed my son as yet, Inspector. As you may know, he flies night-fighters, a job which requires one hundred per cent concentration at all times. I was hoping this business might have been cleared up by now.'

'I appreciate that point of view, sir. But . . .'

'Yes. As it hasn't been cleared up, he will have to know. Leave that with me.'

'Yes, sir. But in all the circumstances I feel I must either wait until Monday, by which time, if Section-Officer Bayley does not appear for duty, she *will* be absent without leave . . .' He paused, indicating that this would be his preferred course of action. 'Or immediately inform the civil police. I don't think we have any other choice, if you feel a civil crime has been committed.'

'I do feel that,' Mark said, 'so you must do as you think best in the circumstances.'

'Very good, sir.' The inspector looked around the anxious faces, gave a brief nod, and left.

'How are you going to handle it?' Helen asked as she poured them each a whisky. 'Will you go up to Hatfield?'

'I may have to. It's not the sort of thing one discusses over the telephone.' He drank deeply. 'But there is one last avenue we can try first. Carden seems pretty certain Joly went off on her own, having arranged to meet some man.'

'That's dreadful. Joly? I can't believe it.' But her tone suggested that she could indeed believe it, for all her earlier dismissal of Carden's suggestion.

'I agree it's a little hard to swallow. But it is a possibility. I mean, none of us know her very well. I don't think even Johnnie entirely understands her, and I know Cecil doesn't, because he's told me so. What we do know is that she lived a pretty wild life before returning to England. Who can say—'

Helen suddenly snapped her fingers. 'The American!'

'What American?'

'Oh, Mark, you must remember. He was here, a couple of months ago. Joly said she'd met him while out walking Baby, and she actually brought him back here. For tea, she said. I found that a bit odd at the time. I mean, do Americans drink tea?' Mark stroked his chin, and she hurried on. 'And do you know something else? I am positive that she didn't intend to mention it to anyone. She looked quite fed up when I told you and Johnnie how I'd seen this character in the lane.'

'But surely Clements served them tea?'

'Well, yes, I suppose he did. But there was no reason for him to mention it. Does he tell you every time one of my friends comes here for tea? He assumes I will tell you myself.'

'You usually mention it.' Friends coming to tea was one of the few highlights of Helen's life.

'But if I didn't, you wouldn't know.'

Mark finished his drink. Conversations with Helen were inclined to become more convoluted the longer they went on. Of course, she might have a point. But the possibility of Jolinda falling for some itinerant GI . . . although he remembered that she had acknowledged knowing him from her time in the

WAACs. But if they had gone off together, they would both be posted AWOL, and would have a prison sentence waiting for them. And to abandon her job, of which she had always seemed so proud and to which she had always seemed so dedicated; to abandon her baby, whom she adored – or appeared to adore, just as she appeared to adore her husband. But as he had said to Helen, did any of them know the girl well enough to be certain of any of those things? When one remembered her mother . . . *Shit*, he thought. *Shit, shit, shit.*

Helen was watching him anxiously: she knew when he was arriving at a decision. 'What are you going to do?'

'Some investigating of my own. If the police turn up, answer their questions with complete honesty, but please don't offer any opinions of your own.' He limped to the door. 'Jim!' he shouted. 'We're going out.'

'Will you be home for lunch?' Helen asked.

'Probably not.'

'Mark Bayley! This is an honour, sir.' Group Captain Browne hurried from his office.

The arrival of a Rolls-Royce on the station forecourt had the whole place in a buzz, but Browne had known who it must be; he was well aware that his MPs had been out most of the night as the report had been on his desk first thing this morning. He had given their endeavours his blessing, and then decided to await events. As Section Officer Bayley had been on a furlough, free to do as she wished as long as she turned up to work on Monday morning, there still remained twenty-four hours for her to return and explain everything. Certainly before he needed to take official action. But if Mark Bayley had actually come to the station . . .

Mark shook hands and limped into the office, then sat down. Browne went behind his desk. 'You do understand that from our point of view it's not official yet?'

'It's official now, Group Captain. It's the opinion of your man Carden that if she's been kidnapped, then it has to be a police matter, and I have agreed to this.'

'Ah. Very good. So there is evidence that she was coerced?'

'No, there is no evidence that she was coerced. In fact Carden seems to feel that all the evidence points the other way.'

'Ah. But in that case, aren't you . . . well, risking opening a can of worms? I mean . . .'

'That is why I'm here. I'd like to talk to her close friends.'

'Ah. Tricky. Jolinda doesn't actually have any close friends.'

'Oh, come now, Group Captain. All women have close friends. Confidantes. They can't exist without them.'

'Well . . .' Browne was not married himself. 'She is rather a withdrawn person. The only women with whom she comes into real contact here are those she works with and, frankly, they are all terrified of her. She is rather a strict disciplinarian. I really find it impossible to believe that she would confide such a scheme as . . . well . . . running off with someone to any of her staff.'

Mark had to accept that he was probably right. But there had to be someone . . . 'Bob Newman!'

'Eh?'

'Bob is Johnnie's best friend.'

'Well, yes. They don't see much of each other since John was posted to Hatfield.'

'But Newman is still here, isn't he? Just as Jolinda is still here. I mean, *when* she's here. He's probably her closest friend as well. He was best man at her wedding.'

'With respect, sir, he was best man at John's wedding. I can't really believe that if Jolinda was considering eloping with someone she'd discuss it with Newman. In fact, I would say he'd be the very last person she'd discuss it with.'

Mark's shoulders slumped. 'I suppose you're right. Well, thanks for your time, Group Captain.' He stood up.

'Where are you going now, sir?'

Mark sighed. 'Hatfield. I have no choice. I've been clutching at straws. But that never works, does it?' He opened the door, limped across the outer office, watched by the anxious Despatcher.

Browne waited until he had left the building, then picked up his phone. 'I want a person-to-person call put through to Air-Vice-Marshal Hargreaves. Tell him it's me, and tell him it is most urgent.'

Mark and Bearman stopped for lunch at a country pub, and reached Hatfield at four o'clock. Mark had visited the station before and knew that, as the Mosquito squadrons were mainly employed in night flying, during the day there was a general air of somnolence. This afternoon there was a considerable amount of . . . he did not suppose it could be classified as activity, but there were a lot of men, mainly ground crew, standing about the various machines, muttering at each other. None of them seemed very pleased to see the Rolls.

'The natives do not appear to be friendly,' Bearman remarked, coming to a halt before the Dispersal Office.

'There's a flap on,' Mark said, suddenly feeling distinctly uneasy. To lose both his son and his daughter-in-law within twenty-four hours of each other was surely too grotesque a coincidence to be possible. He opened the car door and got out with his stick.

A flight-lieutenant promptly appeared in the office doorway. 'Can I be of assistance?' Then he took in both the car and the man standing in front of him. 'Oh, I beg your pardon, Mr Bayley. Ah! You've come to see . . . ah . . .'

'My son,' Mark said, deducing that there had to be *quite* a flap on to have reduced this young man to such a nervous wreck.

'Quite,' the flight-lieutenant said. 'Yes, indeed. Perhaps you'd care to have a word with Group Captain Hastings.'

'If you think that is necessary,' Mark said, his stomach now filling with lead.

'Through here, sir.' The door was held open for him, and he limped through to the inner office, the flight-lieutenant hurrying in front of him, while two WAAF secretaries blinked at him.

The flight-lieutenant gave a gentle tap on the door and then opened it. 'Sorry to bother you, sir. But Mr Bayley is here.'

'What? Now look here, Bayley, I told you—'

'*Mr* Bayley, sir.'

'Eh? Good lord!' A chair scraped and Hastings hurried forward, hand outstretched. 'Mr Bayley! I do beg your pardon, sir. Good to see you.' This was clearly the most blatant lie. 'Come in, sir. Come in.'

Mark was just getting his breath back; whatever had happened, Johnnie was clearly still alive and apparently unhurt. He entered the office, took the offered chair. 'I seem to have come at an inopportune moment.'

Hastings also sat down. 'When is an entirely opportune moment in war, eh, sir?'

'Well, I'm not going to ask you precisely what the problem is, Group Captain, as long as it's nothing to do with my son. I need to see him on a very urgent matter.'

'So I gather. Well, it's been released to the media anyway, and will be on the news this evening. This morning we carried out a daylight raid on Berlin.'

'Your lot? Good God! And . . . ?'

'Oh, the raid was a success, in terms of what we set out to achieve. Unfortunately, we lost one.'

'Who?'

'Wing-Commander Hoosen, and his navigator. Our people are pretty upset. He's our first casualty. I suppose we have become rather complacent over the past year, begun to feel we were invincible.'

'Do you know what happened?'

'It's a bit hazy. John was his wing man, and was preoccupied with what he was doing. As was his navigator. Then they looked up and saw Hoosen going in. Hoosen was John's best friend in the squadron.'

'Damn!'

'So he's more upset than most. I've sent him off to his quarters and excused him duty for the time being. I just thought you should know.'

'Thank you. Unfortunately, I still need to see him. It's a domestic matter, but it won't keep.'

Hastings nodded. 'Of course. I'll ask him to meet you in the mess. There won't be anyone there at this hour.'

John Bayley peered at his father. 'Dad? I thought I saw the Rolls. Sorry, I was asleep.'

'And I'm sorry to have woken you up.' Mark glanced around, but as Hastings had promised, at half past four in the afternoon the officers' mess was deserted. 'What time did you get in?'

'Just after eleven. Do you . . . well . . . ?'

'Hastings filled me in. Quite a show.'

'I hope so.'

'I'm sorry about Hoosen.'

'Yes. Odd, isn't it? When I was flying Spits, one expected that someone was going to buy it, every sortie. I suppose it was even more like that in your day. But these machines . . . it must have been a lucky hit.'

'Yes,' Mark said.

John was frowning at his father's expression. 'Something's happened at home.'

'Can we have a drink?'

'Of course. Champagne?'

'Ah, no.'

'Oh. Right. Harry, two pints.'

'Coming right up, sir.' The barman had been doing his best to appear not to be listening to the muttered conversation on the far side of the room.

'So,' John began. 'Nothing's happened to Rufe, I hope?'

'No, nothing's happened to Rufe. Thank you.'

Harry placed the two foaming tankards in front of them and withdrew.

Mark drank. 'I would like you not to say anything, or interrupt me, until I have finished.'

'All right.'

Mark spoke for some ten minutes, never taking his eyes from John's face. But the younger man's expression changed very little, apart from a slight tightening of the jaw muscles. When Mark was finished, John asked, 'When do you expect to hear from the police?'

'I imagine they'll be at the house now, wanting to go over all the facts again, in so far as we know them. I've left Helen to cope until I get back.'

'How is Helen handling it?'

'Remarkably well. So far. If you can get leave right away, you can come back with me.'

John finished his beer. 'With what in mind?'

Mark had never been so surprised in his life. 'It's your wife who has gone missing.'

'My wife,' John said thoughtfully, and Mark knew he was thinking of his close friend who was now dead. 'You say a very detailed search has been made for her, without success.'

'Ye-es,' Mark said slowly.

'So what will be my contribution by coming home?'

'Well . . . Baby—'

'Dad, Baby cannot have a clue what's going on. He's not yet two years old.'

'Kids can understand a hell of a lot at two.'

'Has anyone told him Joly's missing?'

'Well, no. Up to this morning we were still hoping she'd turn up. But he's bound to realize . . .'

'Why should he? Joly is at the station at least five days in every seven. And most evenings she gets home, unless there's a flap on. All right, this time she doesn't get home for a couple of nights. Unless this is pointed out to him, he won't even notice. But he *would* notice if I were hanging around, without his mother.'

'It's a point,' Mark said thoughtfully. 'Even if it's a rather, well, cold-blooded approach.'

'Dad, we are fighting a war. I don't let my crew's personal affairs interfere with the carrying out of their duties. The same rule has to apply to everyone. I have a mission to fly tomorrow night, and a lot to do before then. Spencer has called a meeting for this evening to see if we can deduce what happened to Hoosen, and if there is anything we can do to stop it happening again. I can't just run off for what may be a storm in a tea cup.'

'And suppose it isn't a storm in a tea cup? You think that with this on your mind you will be able to carry out your duties – fly in combat – successfully?'

'Yes, I do.'

'I see. Would this be because you are pretty damned sure Joly *has* run off with someone? I don't suppose there is any secret you'd care to share with me?'

'I have never had any secrets from you, Dad. Save where, for security reasons, I have been forbidden to share one.'

Mark considered for a few moments, then nodded. 'Then I'd better leave you to it.'

He went outside to where Bearman was patiently waiting and got into the car. 'Mr John not coming with us?' Bearman asked.

'No, he's not.'

From both the tone and the expression on his employer's face, Bearman realized it would be unwise to pursue the matter, and instead started the engine.

John returned to his room and lay on the bed. It seemed pointless to attempt to go back to sleep: the squadron meeting was in an hour. And then it would be time for dinner. But he did not think he could stand the ebullient chit chat of the mess, which would be the more effervescent this evening because that was the traditional way to react to a fatality.

So he would just return here and brood. And attempt to get his thoughts under control before tomorrow. Poor Langley would have no idea of the emotional timebomb he was flying with.

He had never seen his father so angry. They had only actually quarrelled once before, when he had found out the truth of his parentage. But then they had both been guilty, he because he had known his father had had nothing to be ashamed of, had behaved exactly as he himself would have done, and Mark because despite all, he still felt responsible for the tragedy of Patricia Pope.

This was different, if, he hoped, temporary. Right this moment Dad could not understand why he was not rushing around like a chicken with its head cut off. But he would surely come to realize how absolutely futile that would be. And this time the guilt was all his. Try as he might he could not get the memory of Liane de Gruchy – a woman he had only actually *known* for less than a week – out of his mind. And although he had tried, he had obviously been unable to conceal his sexual preoccupation from Jolinda. So had she just upped and left? That sort of decision was entirely in keeping with her character – and exactly what her mother seemed to have done, even if he didn't know those circumstances.

What was not in keeping with Jolinda's character was to abandon the baby she adored. That indicated that her mood was sheer pique, and that she would come back, sooner rather than later. He had to believe that.

'He wouldn't come home?' Helen was aghast. 'But that's terrible. They must have quarrelled, and he won't admit it.'

'I suppose that's possible,' Mark said wearily, stroking Rufus's head. He had actually had the dog before Helen had moved into his life, and regarded the animal as his closest friend. 'But I find it difficult to believe. John hasn't been home for ten days, and when he was here they seemed as close as ever.'

'No one knows what really goes on in the marriage bed,' Helen said darkly, and flushed as she glanced at him.

'Well . . .' Mark finished his drink. 'I'll tell you what's going to happen in our marriage bed very soon. I am going to sleep. Let's eat.'

To his surprise he did sleep, very deeply. It had been two of the most exhausting days of his life, since flying Sopwith Camels over the German lines in March 1918. A business that had ended in his being shot down, and had changed his life forever. He had been the luckiest man alive, then, and for fifteen glorious years. He wondered if John would be so fortunate, or if his glorious years were to number just two, and those already behind him.

He awoke to find winter sunlight streaming through the window; the curtains had just been drawn. Helen stood by the bed, fully dressed. 'I'm sorry to disturb you. But . . .'

Mark looked at his watch. 'Good God! Ten o'clock?'

'I felt you needed the sleep. But Cecil is here.'

'What?' He tumbled out of bed, put on a dressing gown, and picked up his stick.

Helen followed him out of the room and down the stairs. Air-Vice-Marshal Hargreaves stood in the front hall, while Clements hovered solicitously; he had just been given the Marshal's greatcoat and cap. Hargreaves was a strongly built man on whom the delicate features seemed even more incongruous than on his daughter. He wore uniform.

'Cecil!' Mark reached the floor and shook his hand. 'Sorry I was still in bed. Yesterday was a pretty exhausting day.'

'I can imagine.'

'But you?'

'Browne telephoned me, yesterday afternoon, after you had left.' Hargreaves's tone was only slightly accusatory.

'Yes. I had hoped it wouldn't be necessary. That she'd have come back by now. Have you breakfasted?'

'I had a cup of coffee at the station.'

'I haven't even had that yet. Clements . . .'

'It's on the table, sir. For two.'

'Good man.' Mark looked at Helen.

'I've already eaten.' She escorted them into the dining room, sat at the end of the table, while Clements served from the hotplates on the sideboard.

'I'd like to know exactly what you know,' Hargreaves said.

Mark related the events of the past two days. 'Unfortunately,' he concluded, 'John's lot are so busy he couldn't get leave.'

'Not even for something like this? I never knew Hastings was such a martinet.'

'They've actually just completed something very big. I'm surprised you didn't know of it.'

Hargreaves drank some coffee. 'If you mean the raid on Berlin, I gather it was a great success.'

'They lost one.'

Hargreaves frowned. 'A Mosquito? How?'

'No one seems to be quite sure. But they're all pretty upset. John more than any. Hoosen was his best friend in the squadron and . . . well . . .'

'He feels that Jolinda has taken off with some friend of hers. That is something I could never imagine her doing. Something very big must have happened between her and Johnnie.'

'I don't believe anything of the sort,' Mark said. 'That is the police theory. You know what they're like. They want irrefutable evidence that a crime has been committed, and lacking that, they'll always look for the simplest solution. I don't suppose you can entirely blame them. I mean, women do leave their husbands from time to time.'

He gave them both a guilty glance.

'Yes,' Hargreaves said thoughtfully, obviously wondering if mother was like daughter in this case. But Deborah had taken her daughter with her.

Helen sniffed. 'Harry knocked me about when he was drunk. Johnnie has never laid a finger on Joly except in love. Nor does he ever get drunk.'

'Ahem,' Hargreaves said, embarrassed. 'Well . . .'

'There's the post,' Mark remarked.

Clements hurried into the hall, returned a moment later with a large manila envelope. 'For Mr John, sir.'

The people round the table exchanged glances. 'Give it to me,' Mark said. Clements held it out, and Mark looked at it, then handed it to Hargreaves.

'That is not Joly's handwriting,' the Air-Vice-Marshal said.

'Hmm.' Mark took the envelope back and shook it. 'There's more than just a letter inside. Sounds like some kind of cardboard.'

'I think we should open it,' Helen said.

Mark and Hargreaves looked at each other.

'It's almost certainly about Joly,' Helen argued. 'And if John isn't interested . . .'

'Open it,' Hargreaves said.

A last hesitation, then Mark used a knife to slit the envelope. A sheet of paper and four photographs slid out. Mark picked up the first, turned it over, and gasped. 'Jesus Christ!'

'Mark!' Helen protested.

Mark ignored her, looked at the other photos.

'What are they?' Helen asked. 'Are they of Joly? Let me see.'

Again Mark ignored her, slid the photos across the table to Hargreaves while he read the brief letter.

Squadron-Leader Bayley, these images will prove not only that your wife we have but that we mean business. If you wish to spare her further torment, or even to see her again, you will us meet at Burden's Wood at six o'clock this evening, Sunday, 31 January. You will come alone, into the wood drive, and for us wait to come to you. Remember that we can overlook the approach to the wood, and if you are accompanied, or if there is any sign of police or military activity in the neighbourhood, we will abort the meeting and your wife will have to endure another busy night. The next photographs may even be of her dead body.

There was no signature.

Hargreaves had finished looking at the photographs. 'The bastards,' he muttered.

'Let me see,' Helen begged.

'I don't think that would be a good idea,' Mark said, and gave the letter to his friend.

'But . . .' Helen protested. 'They're of Joly!' she guessed. 'She's dead!'

'No, she's not dead,' Mark said. 'But she's been kidnapped, and is not in good shape.'

Hargreaves had finished reading the letter. 'What are you going to do?' He might be an air-vice-marshal, but Mark had been his commanding officer during their fighting days, and he had no doubts as to either his capability – crippled leg or not – or his powers of decision.

'Analysis,' Mark said. 'Reason?'

'Ransom,' Helen said. 'If Joly has been kidnapped, it has to be for money.'

'There is no ransom demand.'

'They're obviously not English,' Hargreaves remarked. 'That is German phraseology. And they want to see Johnnie personally.'

'But they don't know much about either the RAF or our domestic arrangements. They are apparently presuming that Johnnie operates from here.'

'Joly will have told them that,' Hargreaves claimed. 'Hoping to mess them about.'

Mark nodded. 'Therefore they may not know that John habitually drives a motorbike.'

'But if they do . . .'

'I think we have to chance that, Cecil. If they want to see John badly enough to kidnap his wife, it can only be for one of two reasons. Either it's something to do with Max – although I cannot believe Max would be involved in anything as sick as this – or it's to do with the Mosquito. My money is on the Mosquito. That being so, and having gone to all this trouble, they are not going to abort unless they feel they are in danger. *That* being so, the fact that Johnnie turns up driving a Rolls rather than a Harley-Davidson is not immediately going to put them off. Providing, as I say, he is alone and there is no suspicious behaviour on his part.'

'Risky.'

'If you have a better idea, Cecil, let's have it.'

'No, no. But can you possibly get Johnnie down from Hatfield in time?'

'No, I can't. But I don't think these people know what he looks like, and I can still get into my old uniform.'

'Now, wait a moment,' Hargreaves protested.

'That's a crazy idea!' Helen cried. 'You'll be killed.'

'A whole lot of Germans spent a whole lot of time trying to kill me twenty-five years ago. They didn't make it then, and they won't make it now. I want the buggers who took these photographs, and who did this to Joly.'

Helen snatched the photographs and stared at them. 'Oh, my God!' she gasped. 'Oh, my *God*!'

'But I wouldn't say no to some back-up,' Mark said, looking at Hargreaves.

'You have it. If you'll tell me how, if they're watching the approaches to the wood.'

'The Rolls is a big car. We'll take Bearman as well. It's been too long since he had a scrap. Just give me ten minutes to get dressed. I don't suppose you brought a weapon with you?'

'Well, no.' Hargreaves snapped his fingers. 'But I know where we can get all the hardware we need.'

'Will he go along with it?'

'What's the point in being an air-vice-marshal if you don't pull rank from time to time?'

Browne goggled at the two uniformed officers. But he was even more concerned at what they had to say. 'With respect, sir,' he protested, 'don't you think we should let my people handle it? They can surround the wood, and . . .'

'No one would turn up,' Hargreaves pointed out. 'And if anything were to go wrong, my daughter's life would be in danger. Your Section Officer,' he added.

'Yes, sir. But . . . well . . . I mean to say . . .'

'Look here, Group Captain. Neither Mr Bayley nor I are yet fifty, and we are both as fit as fiddles. Well . . .' He glanced at Mark apologetically. 'Fit enough to take on a pack of Jerries, anyway.'

'What we would like,' Mark said, 'is to have the use of a walkie-talkie, so that we can be in touch with your men to come in and pick up the pieces.'

'That can be arranged . . . ah . . . sir.' He was clearly uncertain how to address this distinguished middle-aged gentleman who was wearing the out-dated uniform of a World War I flight-lieutenant. 'But did you say "pieces"?'

'We'll need some things from your armoury,' Hargreaves explained.

Browne gulped. 'This really is . . . well . . .'

'Most irregular, I agree. But we intend to get my daughter back, without turning out the entire country.'

'Yes, sir.' He pressed his intercom. 'Maureen, ask Captain Carden to step in here, will you?'

The MP officer listened to what Hargreaves had to say with an increasingly pessimistic expression. 'May I say, sir—'

'Don't,' Hargreaves recommended. 'We are going ahead,

with or without your assistance, Captain. But your help would be appreciated.'

Carden glanced at his chief, and received a brief nod. 'Very good, sir. What exactly would you like?'

'What have you got?'

'Within reason . . . it might help if we had any idea what sort of hardware these people might be carrying. And how many of them there are likely to be.'

'They are German agents,' Mark said. 'I would expect there to be at least four of them, but for them to be equipped with pistols, nothing more.'

'Probably Lugers,' Carden mused. 'As regards side-arms, we only have revolvers.'

'But forty-five calibres,' Browne observed. 'As opposed to—'

'Nine millimetre, sir. The difference is not that great, certainly at close range. And the Luger carries at least nine shots to a Smith and Wesson's six. In affairs like this, it is always preferable to possess overwhelming firepower. If it is a matter of you two gentlemen against four Nazis – presumably all skilled in the use of firearms, and with the greater fire power . . .'

'It won't just be us two,' Hargreaves explained. 'We have Bearman with us.'

'Sir?'

'My chauffeur,' Mark explained. 'He is also ex-RAF.'

'Yes, sir. You do realize that it is against the law to engage in an exchange of firearms, certainly in a public place? You should obtain a warrant from a magistrate before considering such an action.'

'Mr Carden,' Hargreaves said, 'there is no time to go looking for a magistrate, much less to persuade him to grant us a warrant. He would certainly wish to involve the civil police, which, with respect, would be a catastrophe. Not only is the life of my daughter at stake, but these men are German agents, who are at the very least guilty of both kidnap and rape, but are also attempting to obtain military secrets. We shall endeavour to apprehend them, but if that proves impossible, it may be necessary to shoot one of them.'

'Or even two,' Mark remarked.

'Without being shot yourselves.' Carden sighed. 'Well,

gentlemen, if you are determined on this course, and in view of the fact that it involves service personnel, we shall of course help you in every possible way. In this regard, I strongly suggest that you let me drive the car, with one of my men in the back.'

'I can't allow that,' Hargreaves said. 'If anything were to go wrong, you'd be cashiered. No, no, this has to be our show. It's our family involved.'

Carden again looked at Browne, but the Group Captain was looking totally bemused. 'Very good, sir. Well then, for the actual confrontation, you need everything we can give you. May I suggest that in addition to revolvers you equip yourselves with tommy-guns.'

'You can let us have a tommy-gun?'

'I have a fully equipped armoury, sir. I can let you have three tommy-guns. One each. Providing of course they are returned here when the . . . ah . . . action is completed.'

'Good man!'

'May I also suggest, however, that you take with you some grenades of tear-gas? As I understand your meeting with these people is to take place in the open air, these will not be as effective as in an enclosed space, but they will still be off-putting to your opponents if thrown with any accuracy.'

'*Very* good man! I am going to recommend you for promotion, Captain.'

'Thank you, sir. If we come through this without being locked up.'

Burden's Wood was an isolated copse some ten miles from the main road. 'We'll stop in the village here,' Mark said, prodding the map. 'It's as close as we can get; they are obviously going to have the area near the wood under surveillance; that's open country. It won't be all that bad. What do you think, Jim? You'll be in the boot.'

'Not a problem, sir. If you're sure you can manage.'

'Ten miles? I think so. If necessary, I can use my stick.'

'Ah . . . yes, sir.' Bearman's tone indicated his doubt as to whether the accelerator on the Rolls, or any car, could be controlled with a stick.

'Do you actually have a licence?' Hargreaves asked.

'I'm afraid not. But I know how it's done. I've watched Jim here often enough.'

'Bit of a turn up if you're arrested for dangerous driving with us armed to the teeth.'

'If that is all we have to worry about, Cecil, we have nothing to worry about.' He looked at his watch. 'Five fifteen. Let's get started.'

It was now quite dark, and this far from civilization there was little chance of their being overlooked. Jim got out from behind the wheel, opened the boot, and crawled in, taking with him a revolver, a tommy-gun, and two tear-gas grenades. He closed the hatch, but could open it from the inside. 'Can you breathe all right?' Mark asked.

'I'm fine, sir.'

'Cecil?'

Hargreaves, also fully armed and with two grenades, got into the back and lay on the floor. In the darkness he would be invisible provided nobody opened the car door.

Mark got behind the wheel. His revolver was tucked into his belt, and he rested the tommy-gun and his two grenades on the seat beside him, covering them with a blanket. Bearman had left the engine running, and it was simply a matter of engaging gear. Declutching with his left leg was simple enough. Biting his lip he rested his right foot on the accelerator and pressed. To his relief the car moved forward, gradually increasing speed. He had exercised as much as possible over the years, and the bones in the leg, broken by the German bullets, had gradually knitted together, even if they had never regained any straightness, but his muscular reaction remained weak and uncertain. Before he knew it the car was travelling at over thirty miles an hour, and he hastily took his foot from the pedal and allowed it to slow.

'Problem?' Hargreaves asked.

'Just getting the hang of it.'

He drove at just over twenty-five miles an hour along the main road. One or two cars passed him, but he ignored them, concentrating on following the down-turned beam of the head-lamps. Even so, the sign to Burden's Wood took him by surprise, and he braked violently so as not to overshoot the turning.

'Talk to me,' Hargreaves suggested.

'Relax. We're just about there.'

Mark turned the wheel and they were soon on the track,

immediately starting to bump and bounce. 'You fellows all right?' he asked.

They grunted their assent. Now he could make out the trees, looming out of the gloom. As instructed, he continued to follow the track into the copse, and then stopped, switched off the engine, and thrust his hand under the blanket to rest it on the tommy-gun.

He was aware of the adrenalin flowing through his arteries, but that was excitement rather than apprehension. Events had forced him to step from vigorous young manhood into premature middle-age, without warning and without any period of adjustment. He had accepted that, alleviated as it had been by the stimulating support of Karolina. But his misery over what might have been had always lurked.

He had sought solace in the youthful exuberance of his two sons, envisaged them enjoying the career that had been his for the taking. But he had not foreseen the catastrophe of Max. The real tragedy was that Max, inheriting both Karolina's spirit and his own ability, was clearly an outstanding pilot in a way that Johnnie, for all his dash and superb courage, had never been. Now he was a general, and famous, and apparently happily married, and yet doomed. While Johnnie . . . He supposed these episodes had hardened his hatred for the Germans, at least after the Nazis had come to power. But the hatred had started with them, from the moment Karolina had turned her back on them and removed her fortune to England; not enough of it had been centred in Germany for any important sequestration.

They had declared war on him long before the British Government had declared war on them. They had seized the opportunity of a visit by his sister Joan to Germany in 1938 to arrest her as a spy, and inflict both pain and humiliation on her before they had been forced to drop the absurd charge. And they had engineered the seduction of Max.

Now they had targeted him and his again. But this time they had ventured into his back yard, and he was determined that they would pay for it, whatever the consequences.

Five minutes passed, and then ten. He could hear the occasional distant growl of engines on the road.

'You reckon they're coming?' Hargreaves asked.

'They're just being cautious.'

'Well, I wish they'd get a move on. This floor isn't getting any softer.'

'Stand by.'

An engine noise was getting closer, and now, looking in his rear-view mirror, he could see the shaded lights coming down the track behind him. 'Bingo,' he muttered. The lights came up to the back of the Rolls, and were then doused. He could make out a white van. The front doors opened, and two men got out. 'Two visible,' he said. 'But it's a van with a good deal of space in the back. Your end, Jim. When I say, go.'

'Wilco.'

'Just remember that we have to have one of these characters alive. You awake, Cecil?'

'And waiting.'

Mark thrust his hand beneath the blanket to find the trigger of the tommy-gun. The two men surveyed the Rolls for a few minutes, then came forward, separating to be one on each side. 'Yours is on the left,' Mark said, and rolled down his window.

The men appeared. 'Some car,' the man at Mark's window commented. 'You John Bayley?'

'I am Mr Bayley, yes.'

'Hoity-toity. OK, fella. I guess you know we have your wife, and I guess you also know that if you don't play ball, she's gonna suffer a lot of grief.'

'Where did you get that American accent?' Mark asked.

'I lived there for a while. What's it to you?'

'I like to know who, or what, I am dealing with.'

'Yeah, well, right now you're dealing with me.'

'So what part of Germany are you from?' Mark inquired, speaking the perfect High German he had learned from Karolina.

'Who's a bundle of surprises,' Kesten remarked. 'Enough chat. You get out of this hearse, and go to the back of the van. There's a guy waiting for you. You get in and we'll take you to your wife. And we'll have a little chat about airplanes.'

'Just a guy waiting for me,' Mark mused. 'That's what I wanted to know. Thank you. But you still haven't told me where you come from in Germany.'

'What the fuck is that to you?'

'Well, you see,' Mark explained, 'when you're going to kill someone, I do feel you should know something of his background.'

'What?'

'And I feel that you should know that I have killed thirty-seven German officers. That is, thirty-seven confirmed. Time to make it forty, don't you think?'

As he did not really want to commit murder, he had been watching Kesten's hands while he taunted him. Now Kesten reached for his pocket at the same time as he shouted, 'Herman!'

'Go!' Mark snapped, bringing up the tommy-gun and firing through the open window. Kesten disappeared with a gasp. Mark heard the report of Hargreaves' gun from behind him, and the chatter of Bearman's as the boot was thrown open. 'Grenades to the van,' he shouted. Then he opened his own door and got out, the tommy-gun tucked under his arm.

Kesten lay on his back; he had obviously died instantly. 'Cecil?'

Hargreaves was opening the offside rear door and getting out. 'This chap is dead.'

'Snap. Jim?'

Bearman had got out of the boot and hurled his two grenades; the van was so close he couldn't miss, and the vehicle was shrouded in a white mist; the acrid tang of the tear-gas was even seeping back to the Rolls. 'There's been no shot. But you said you wanted him alive.'

As if to contradict what he had said, a shot rang out and there was a crump as the bullet struck the car.

'Holy shit!' Bearman exclaimed; the Rolls was his pride and joy.

'Take cover,' Mark commanded, and limped round the car to stand beside Hargreaves. 'You in there,' he called. 'Your two boys are both dead, and there are three of us armed with sub-machine guns. Unless you wish to join your friends, come out with your hands on the top of your head. We'll give you five seconds.'

There was only a brief delay, then Wolfert emerged with his hands up; he was still coughing.

'A sensible decision,' Mark said. 'Come here.'

Wolfert approached slowly.

'Did you really think you could take on the RAF?' Mark asked. 'Even the retired RAF?'

'I do my duty,' Wolfert said stiffly.

'And that includes raping helpless young women?'

'We had to convince you that we meant business. It was for the Fatherland.'

'For whom, like your pals, you would cheerfully die, of course.'

Wolfert gulped.

'However,' he continued, 'it may be possible to keep you alive, if you are prepared to cooperate. We will use your van, and you will take us to wherever you are holding my daughter-in-law.'

Wolfert blinked at him. 'You are not Wing-Commander Bayley?'

'Sadly, I never got that far. Still, I'm his father, which is the next best thing. And this gentleman is Mrs Bayley's father, so you will understand that we both have a vested interest in this business.'

'If I take you to Mrs Bayley, what will happen to me?'

'We will hand you over to the police.'

'They will hang me.'

'That depends on whether or not you have adopted British nationality. If you are simply a German spy, they will probably just lock you up for the duration. However long that may be. They will also wish to ask you some questions.'

'They will roast my balls.'

'Sadly, I don't believe they go in for that sort of thing on this side of the Channel,' Mark said. 'But I do recommend that you cooperate. Starting now. Because, of course, *we* don't have any restrictions on things like roasting balls.'

Wolfert looked from face to face. 'You understand that whatever I did was for the Fatherland.'

'Of course, my dear fellow. We will make that point.'

'And my people?'

'How many are waiting for you?'

'There is just Frieda.'

'Would she be the woman in the photograph? I look forward to meeting her. We shall not harm her, unless she attempts to harm us, or has already harmed Mrs Bayley in any permanent way.'

'And these men?'

'You do worry about your people. I appreciate that. I'm sure they will have a civilized burial. Maybe you should call Carden, Cecil. Then we can be on our way.'

The Missing

John Bayley brought the Harley-Davidson to a stop, switched off the ignition, and put down the stand. But he did not immediately dismount. He needed a few minutes to compose himself, as if he hadn't been trying to do that all the way from Hatfield.

He was not used to being so entirely on the defensive. He had felt guilty when he had broken his engagement to Avril Pope. That ungallant act had been justifiable because he had just discovered that, as the daughter of his mother's brother, she was in fact his first cousin, a fact that had not been obvious from looking at the pretty young ATS private he had met in a bar when just out of flying school, even if he had thought her last name an unfortunate coincidence. But the justification had been flawed, on two counts.

The first was that he had already slept with her – innocently, certainly: he had not yet known who she was, and she had wanted it. But she had wanted it on the understanding that they were going to be married. The second was far more damning: while he had still been involved with Avril, he had met Jolinda. Had that not happened, would he now be married to Avril, incest and all?

He felt guiltiest about the fact that he had never been able to bring himself to tell her why he was ending the engagement. He had been afraid to risk hurting, or even destroying, the fragile personality he had come to know. So she was left believing him to be the biggest heel she had ever known. He supposed that was fair enough.

And now he had been an even bigger heel. Again, excuses were easy to find. He had been both mentally and physically exhausted by the events of the day, almost distraught at the sight of Hoosen going in. They had been close friends, certainly: Hoosen had introduced him to flying the new machines. But there had been a far less noble reason. Over the past year the Mosquito pilots had come to regard themselves as immortals, their speed and firepower putting them beyond the reach of any enemy interceptor or anti-aircraft fire.

Easy to say that going in low, and with the Germans already activated by the first wave, a lucky shot had always been a possibility: the incident had still blown the myth of invincibility apart. He had wanted to do nothing save hit back at the enemy as soon as possible – and come home safely. Just like coming off a horse, one had to remount as quickly as possible and resume one's gallop, or one might never remount again. He had therefore been totally unprepared for a domestic crisis, and certainly one which, in his bones, he had felt was looming in any event.

Obviously he had not been thinking clearly. The idea that Jolinda might follow her mother's example and do a runner was by no means impossible. The idea that she would abandon her child to do so was so absurd as to be obscene. That he should have so instinctively turned his back on her, in effect accepted her decision that their marriage was over, merely compounded his own guilt. As for what she must have suffered . . . He had none of the details, but on the telephone Dad had made it sound fairly horrendous.

At least the old man was home now, waiting for him: the Rolls was parked in the garage. John got off the bike and went to the front door, which as always opened for him; Clements had heard the noise of his engine. Rufus was there as well, wagging his tail. 'Cold out, Mr John,' the butler commented.

'That is the truth.' John spoke with difficulty; his lips were frozen, despite wearing his heavy scarf. He handed the scarf to Clements, along with his cap, and then stripped off his gloves. Then he removed the leathers he was wearing over his uniform, while Rufus nuzzled him.

'They're in the library,' Clements said helpfully.

'Ah . . .'

'Mr and Mrs Bayley, sir. Air-Vice-Marshal Hargreaves has returned to his base.'

'Of course.' There was relief in his voice. 'And . . . ah . . .'

'Miss Jolinda is in her room, sir.'

'Oh. Right.' John looked at the stairs, then turned to the drawing room. He paused as he passed Karolina's portrait; how he wished it could be her waiting to greet him. Then he squared his shoulders and continued to the library.

Mark was on his feet, standing beside Helen's chair, almost as if *they* were posing for a portrait, John thought. 'You look quite blue,' Mark commented. 'Cold trip?'

'Yes.'

'Then you must feel like a drink.'

'Yes. I'll get it.' He went to the sideboard, glancing at his parents, who already had half-filled glasses.

'Joly is upstairs,' Helen remarked.

John poured. 'Clements told me. How is she?'

'According to Parkinson, she's all right,' Mark said. 'Physically at least. He muttered something about having a psychiatric examination, but she isn't keen, and I certainly felt she should see you first.'

'Does she want to see me?'

'Don't you want to see her?'

That was not an answer, John realized. 'Yes, I do. But I'd like to be fully up to date first.'

'She was raped,' Mark said. 'Several times. And photographed while it was happening. The police have the photos, but I don't imagine you'd want to see them, anyway.'

'What about the police? I mean, as regards you and Cecil?'

'We took two of them alive. One was the commander of the exercise; the other was a woman who was acting as Joly's jailer. They were both happy to talk when they discovered that if they spilled the beans they wouldn't be hanged. So the official line is that Cecil and I stumbled on a spy plot, tried to make a citizen's arrest, and found ourselves engaged in a shoot-out. Fortunately, we happened to have some weapons with us, and we defended ourselves. Everyone has been very helpful.'

John took a deep breath. 'You know I can never thank you enough. Or apologize enough for my behaviour.'

'Then do neither,' Mark recommended, and held out his hand. 'Just remember that she loves you.'

John grasped the proffered fingers. 'Did these people confess who put them up to it?'

'They were Abwehr.'

'Yes, but even the Abwehr has to have the necessary information in order to plan an operation like this.'

Mark frowned. 'Just what are you driving at?'

'Dad, there are some sixty Mosquitoes in service. That is a hundred and twenty crews. And out of all of those, I am the one that is targeted. My wife is the one that is kidnapped. Tell me why.'

Mark's frown deepened. 'You think Max could have put them up to this? I can't believe that.'

'It seems very logical to me. It is something I'm going to remember, when next we face each other.' He finished his drink and left the room.

He paused outside the bedroom door, mentally bracing himself for what he might find, then knocked.

'It's open.'

He turned the knob, stepped inside. Jolinda sat in a rocking chair by the window, Baby Mark at her feet. She was wearing her favourite casual slacks and slippers, her hair tied in a loose bow on the nape of her neck. It was as he remembered her best, when not in uniform.

The boy had been playing with his blocks, but now he crawled towards the door. 'Da!'

John scooped him from the floor and into his arms. 'We're going to have to watch your weight.' He kissed him, then looked at his wife.

'We heard the bike,' Jolinda said. 'It must be brass monkeys out there.'

'You could say that.'

They gazed at each other, then she rang the bell on the table beside her chair. Penny immediately appeared.

'Time for Baby's bath and supper,' Jolinda said. 'You can play with Daddy after, sweetheart.'

The boy allowed himself to be transferred from his father's arms to those of the nurse, and she carried him from the room, carefully closing the door.

'I'm glad you came down,' Jolinda said.

She showed no sign of leaving her chair, so John pulled up the other chair to sit opposite her. 'Didn't you expect me to?'

'Dad told me how busy you've been. How successful. And how upset you were at losing Hoosen.'

'And you didn't think I'd be equally upset at losing you?'

She gazed at him. 'I think it's up to you to convince me of that.' She gave a quick smile. 'Or maybe you reckon you have anyway?'

His intake of breath was harsh. 'Because . . .'

'I was raped, Johnnie. I can't really remember how many times.' He reached for her hand to squeeze it, but she withdrew it. 'I couldn't fight them, because I was tied to a bed.' Now she raised her hand, and he saw the rope burns on her wrist. 'So I guess I just tried to shut my mind to what was happening, and waited for it to stop. It always does, you know. One way or the other.'

'Jolinda . . .'

'But do you know, I'm not sure I cared. There were too many other things . . . things they told me. What was her name? Liane de Gruchy?'

John had been leaning forward. Now he sat straight. '*They* told you of Liane?'

'They seemed to know a lot about her.'

'Oh, my God! If . . .'

'Relax. They haven't captured her. Although they expect to do so in the near future. But as I said, they seem to have a pretty good idea of her . . . methods.'

'She saved my life.'

'Does gratitude equal love? I suppose it can do, providing the woman is beautiful enough. Was she as beautiful as they say? Is she?'

'Joly . . .'

'So forget it. She's history. Or she can be history.' She paused to stare at him.

'Joly, you don't have to bargain with me. I know what happened to you. I understand.'

She raised her eyebrows. 'Can you? Can any man understand what it is like to be tied to a bed and raped?'

'I'm trying to explain that I know there was nothing you could do about it. That it wasn't your fault—'

'Save that at the back of your mind there will always be a little blister. Because it always *is* the woman's fault, isn't it?'

'Joly . . .'

'And you know what, Johnnie?' Her eyes were blazing even as they filled with tears. 'You'd be absolutely right. I befriended that so-called Yankee, believed his story that he had known me in training camp, even if I couldn't remember him, because I wanted to. I may not have heard of Liane de Gruchy then, but I knew there was someone. I was so goddamned lonely. Even with Baby and Rufe, and Dad and Helen, and Clement and Jim Bearman, and everyone here, I had nothing without your love.' Now the tears were rolling down her cheeks. 'So I let him pick me up. And when we met on the lane on Friday morning, I accepted a ride in his van, even if every instinct in my body told me that something was wrong, wrong, wrong.'

Again he reached for her, and this time she did not withdraw or resist, but allowed him to lift her from her chair and bring her on to his lap. He held her close while he kissed her hair. 'It's over. You have nothing to reproach yourself for. I'm the one at fault. Nothing is ever going to come between us again. I swear it.'

She raised her head to stare at him. 'Nothing? Johnnie, I've been—'

He laid his finger on her lips. 'History, remember.'

'But can you . . . ?' She blinked away her tears to stare into his eyes.

'We are going to start again,' he said. 'Whenever you are ready.'

She licked her lips. 'Could we . . . ?'

'Of course. Let's join Dad and Helen.'

'I should change . . .'

'Not tonight. Come as you are.' He escorted her to the door. 'Penny,' he called, 'bring Master Mark down when he's had his supper.' They went down the stairs. 'Clements,' he called. 'The Bollinger. Two bottles.'

'Is it Stalingrad?' Hildegarde asked as they walked the baby in the park. It had snowed in the night and it still lay underfoot; all three of them were well wrapped up.

'Is what Stalingrad?'

'Your mood, since you came back.'

Hildegarde was a strongly built young woman, no more than medium height but with wide shoulders and powerful legs. Max had first encountered, and fallen for, her obvious strength of both body and character when he had joined the army preparing for the invasion of Russia. She had been secretary to one of the generals, and as he had been leading a fighter wing under that general's overall command, they had come into frequent contact. He remembered having been extremely wary of her at first, both because of her position, which seemed to put her beyond the reach of a mere major, as he had then been, and because of that obvious strength, which was in such enormous contrast to the yielding weakness of Heidi. He had in any event still been suffering from the mental effects of that catastrophe.

He had been even more wary when the so attractive young captain – who was actually two years older than himself – had set her cap at him; that had been too suggestive of Erika. But he had soon discovered that she was not a woman who indulged in passing fancies, although she was certainly experienced. And suddenly he had realized that here was the woman he had sought, subconsciously, all of his life, a woman who was at once handsome and earthy, who knew her own mind and was yet willing to submit to the man of her choice, a woman to love, and most important of all, a woman to love him.

The course of their romance had been the opposite of smooth. They had been fighting a war, and although they were both in the same army, the increasingly widespread course of the conflict as the Wehrmacht, and its essential air support, had driven ever deeper into Russia, meant that their meetings had been seldom and often stolen. And any long-term prospects for them seemed to be lost when Max had been virtually cashiered for striking an SS officer. Erhard Milch had come to their rescue, restored Max's career, arranged for Hildegarde to be transferred to his own staff so that they could be together, and then overseen their marriage.

Then finally there was happiness, after so much trauma. But in war, especially as waged by Nazi Germany, the trauma always lurked. The quarrel with the SS officer had occurred because the SS had executed a Russian woman – admittedly a partisan in league against the Reich – who had helped Max when his engine had caught fire and he had come down in a remote forest. He had promised Galina (he had never learned her last name) safe conduct if she would guide him to safety; the SS detachment that had come to his rescue had been under orders to execute any partisans captured on sight, regardless of age or sex, or promises. He did not suppose he would ever forget the look Galina had directed at him as the rope had been looped around her neck, even if she must have known, from the fact that he was under arrest, that he had done his best for her.

Now he could not help but worry that the same situation might arise again, in reverse as it were. And all because of his absurd weakness for helping women in distress. But that was not something he felt he could share with his wife. So now he said, 'It is damned depressing, my darling. An entire German army, just swallowed up. But I suppose we knew it was going to happen, some time ago. I'm sorry I've been so tense. I've had Heinrich on my mind.'

'He wasn't in Stalingrad, was he?'

'Good lord, no. But when we were ordered to leave Kharkov we were told to fly out, immediately. The ground crews were to follow by whatever transport could be arranged. That was more than a month ago, and he hasn't turned up yet.'

Hildegarde frowned. 'You mean none of them have come out?'

'Oh, yes. A batch arrived safely. But they were strictly ground crew and technical staff. I did give instructions before I left that Heinrich and . . . ah . . . another servant – a Russian I had taken on – were to be given priority, but apparently this was over-ruled by some general, who decreed that non-combatant personnel should remain until all fighting men had been evacuated.'

'Oh, poor Heinrich. But he's quite safe in Kharkov, isn't he? I mean, we still hold it, and it's five hundred kilometres west of Stalingrad. Anyway, he's a tough old bird. He'll survive.'

'Five hundred kilometres isn't all that far considering the way we have been retreating. But I'm being senselessly pessimistic. As you say, Heinrich can survive anything.' *And can make sure that Rena does too*, he thought. 'Look, I still have three days' leave left. Let's go down to Bitterman. It's only fifty kilometres from here. And it's time the family met you.'

'Oh,' Hildegarde said. 'Will they really want to meet me? I mean, my family isn't a von or anything.'

'But this is Nazi Socialist Germany, darling. Vons are quite irrelevant. I suspect they've become a handicap. Anyway, don't you realize that our Max is in line for both the title and the estates? And what's left of the family fortune?'

'Good lord! But . . . didn't you tell me you had a cousin?'

'Erika, yes. But she's not in contention, for two reasons. One is that she's never had a child, and now that she's split from her husband, there isn't going to be one, at least on the right side of the blanket. The other reason is that legally it all belongs to me. Milch worked it out for me. My mother was the daughter of the founder of the family fortune. Uncle Max only took over after Mother's death, when he quarrelled with my father. And of course he had the support of the Party. But I am still the direct heir.'

'Good lord!' Hildegarde said again. 'I never knew I was married to an aristocrat. But you've never claimed your rights.'

'Well, I've been rather busy these past few years, wouldn't you say? But they have to be nice to me, because they know I am going to claim my rights some day – and certainly for Little Max.'

'Max! How good to see you.' Count Max von Bitterman shook his cousin's hand vigorously. He was a tall, heavily built man, and with his bald head – for which he attempted to compensate by wearing a thick Bismarckian moustache – and the rather coarse features he had bequeathed to his daughter, he in no way suggested a close relative of Karolina. 'And this is . . . ?'

'My wife, Hildegarde.'

'Your wife! Ah, I did not know you were married.'

He was obviously taken aback, and Max had to wonder if, in view of the collapse of Erika's marriage, he had hoped that the cousins might at last get together.

'And my son,' Max added for good measure; Hildegarde was carrying the baby in her arms.

'Good heavens! But I am forgetting my manners. Frau Bayley, this is both a pleasure and an honour.'

'And for me, Herr Count.' Hildegarde was impressed, not by her host, but by the castle rising above her – the twin towers, the castellated battlements, the huge entry hall with its suits of armour.

'And you have come to stay?' Bitterman eyed the suitcases that had been placed on the steps by the taxi driver before he had departed. 'How splendid. Herman!' he bellowed. 'Come and fetch these bags. Oriane! Oriane! You'll never guess who's come to visit.'

'This place is unreal,' Hildegarde remarked, standing at the bedroom window and looking out at the rolling parkland beyond which the majesty of the Alps could be viewed.

'I know they are a bit extreme.' Max stood behind her and put his arms round her waist; the baby had been placed in the centre of the bed. 'But as they say, you cannot choose your own relatives – at least, the ones who were there before you turned up.'

'I was not talking about the Count and his wife, although she is an odd little thing. I was referring to the schloss. I've never been in a proper castle before.'

'Don't you like it?'

'I think it's fabulous. You grew up here?'

'No, no. I think I was born here, but I grew up in England, although we came here every summer until Mother died.'

'I think you adored your mother.'

'Everybody adored my mother. Except for Cousin Max and his lot. They never forgave her for marrying an Englishman.'

'But you intend to throw them out and live here yourself, when the war is over.'

'*We* are going to live here, ourselves, when the war is over, my dearest girl.'

Hildegarde turned in his arms. 'I will have to get used to that idea. But it is something to look forward to.'

'I hope that crib is all right,' Oriane von Bitterman said at dinner. She was a tiny, bird-like woman – less than half the size of her husband – who, like a bird, was inclined to twitter. 'I know it's very old, but do you know, it belonged to Erika. My daughter. But of course, you know Erika.'

'I'm afraid we've never met,' Hildegarde confessed.

'Oh!' Oriane looked at Max for an explanation.

'The three of us have never been in Berlin at the same time,' Max confessed. 'How is Erika?'

'Ah . . .' Now Oriane looked to her husband to answer.

'We don't see much of her nowadays,' Bitterman said. 'She's very busy. War work, you understand. And frankly I don't think she ever really recovered from . . . Oh, I do beg your pardon, Frau Bayley.'

'Oh, please do call me Hildegarde.' He would not know that she liked her friends to call her Hilde.

'Thank you. But—'

'Hildegarde knows about Heidi,' Max said.

'Such a tragedy,' Oriane said.

'I am sure neither Max nor Hildegarde wish to go into that now,' Bitterman said severely, and poured wine. 'It is best forgotten. Yes, Herman?'

The butler, having served the entrée, had withdrawn to his pantry, but was now standing in the doorway. 'I am sorry to interrupt, Herr Count, but there is a telephone call.'

'Perhaps it's Erika!' Oriane cried. 'She must have found out you're here.'

'The call is for General Bayley, personally, Countess.'

'There! I knew it.'

Max and Hildegarde exchanged glances.

'It is from the Air Ministry,' Herman added.

'Oh.' Max pushed back his chair and got up. 'You'll excuse me.' He gave Hildegarde a quick squeeze of the shoulder and followed Herman; the telephone was in the hall. 'Bayley.'

'Max! Jeschonneck here. I've been trying to get hold of you all afternoon.'

Colonel-General Franz Jeschonneck was Field-Marshal Milch's Chief of Staff. 'I tried the hotel and they said you'd left. But the beggars wouldn't tell me where you'd gone.'

'I instructed them not to,' Max pointed out.

'My dear fellow, you really must always keep in touch.'

'I wanted to enjoy the last three days of my leave in peace and quiet. What is the problem?'

'The Field-Marshal wishes to see you. Immediately. Can you come back tomorrow?'

Max sighed. 'I suppose I can, if I must. As I do not have an aircraft with me, I shouldn't think I can get there before tomorrow night. Do you have any idea what this is about?'

'The Field-Marshal will explain when he sees you.'

'Very good. But while I have you on the line, Franz, what is the situation regarding my people from Kharkov?'

There was a moment's silence, then Jeschonneck asked, 'You had people in Kharkov?'

The choice of tenses did not immediately register. 'Of course I do, as you well know. When we were pulled out I had to leave my ground crews behind. They were to come out by truck.'

'Oh. Yes. They have been re-assigned.'

'The ground crews, I know. What about the admin staff, the officers' servants, my man Heinrich. He should be back by now.'

'I will check for you and have the information when you get to Berlin.'

Something in his friend's tone made Max frown. 'Franz,' he said, 'you can confirm, now, that they are out.'

'I cannot do that, off the cuff, Max. I know that there were a great number of difficulties with transport. And of course, as I am sure you appreciate, fighting personnel had to be brought out first.'

Again Max, his mind entirely concerned with finding out about Rena, did not immediately pick up on either the tense or the choice of words. 'Surely you can get through to Kharkov and ascertain whether they are still there?'

'Max, Kharkov fell to the Russians, two days ago.'

Max stared at the phone.

'Of course we are going to take it back,' Jeschonneck said. 'The counter-attack is being prepared now. But it will take a week or so. And I'm afraid, well, any of our people who did not manage to get out will have been taken prisoner.' He paused, waiting for a response, and when there was none, he went on, 'Believe me, I know what it is like to lose a good and faithful servant, but—'

Max hung up. *A good and faithful servant*, he thought. What he had most feared had come true. Rena, pinned to a door by bayonets, left to hang, and die. For the second time he had promised a woman her life, and had been unable to keep his word.

'Max?' Bitterman asked, as he returned to the dining room. 'There is bad news?'

'I am to return to Berlin immediately. Tomorrow morning.' Max forced a smile. 'So you won't have to put up with me for more than one night.'

'Oh, what a shame!' Oriane said. 'But . . .' She looked at Hildegarde.

'We will come with you, of course,' Hildegarde said.

'I have no family accommodation. We can't go to the Albert.'

'My dear girl, you are welcome to stay here, until something is sorted out,' Bitterman smiled.

'Baby and I will go with Max,' Hildegarde said, her tone leaving no room for argument. 'The Albert is not the only hotel in Berlin. Anyway, I have friends there. And surely you will be allotted married quarters immediately.'

'Yes,' Max said absently. 'I would like to have you with me. But it will be exhausting for the baby.'

'I shouldn't think so. He will sleep the whole way.'

She waited until they had reached their bedroom after dinner. Then she asked, 'Is it very bad?'

Max sat on the bed. 'I don't know. Milch wants to see me urgently, so something must have come up.'

She sat beside him, put her arm round his waist. 'But you are upset.'

Max sighed and rested his head on her shoulder. 'The Russians have taken Kharkov.'

'Your base? Oh, lord! They're not sending you back again?'

'I don't know. They chop and change their minds so often. But that's not important. They don't think Heinrich got out in time.'

'Heinrich? Oh, my God! But he's not a fighting soldier. He'll only have been taken prisoner.'

'I don't think the word "only" applies to the Russian front. You must know what we did to their people. What we are still doing.'

'Oh, Max.' She hugged him. 'Is there anything we can do?'

'Not a damned thing, apparently. Unless we recapture the city very rapidly.'

'You mean before they can move the prisoners out? Surely we can do that. We must believe that.'

'I don't think it can possibly be in time for Rena,' Max said, without thinking.

'Rena?'

'Oh.' He raised his head. 'I told you I had taken on a Russian servant as well.'

'Rena. Isn't that a girl's name?'

'It's a woman's name, yes.'

He expected her to let him go, braced himself for a crisis.

But she continued to hold him, her arms tighter than ever. 'I would like you to tell me about her.'

'Oh, shit! She was presented to me, as a bed-warmer, by the SS in Kiev. She was such a helpless little waif. When we moved to Kharkov, I took her with me. She was half starved and being used as an SS whore. So . . . can you forgive me?'

'Of course I can forgive you, you silly man. I know what it's like to be in constant combat, the strain of it. If she gets out we'll take her in. But you don't think she's coming out?'

'I left instructions that she was to be brought out with Heinrich. But if he wasn't given priority, it isn't very likely she was.'

Hildegarde hugged him in silence for several moments. 'What would they do to her?'

'They lynch those citizens suspected of collaborating with us.'

'What a foul world this is,' she said, and released him. 'I'll just get Baby up for his last feed.'

Max watched her sitting on the bed, Little Max sucking vigorously. She was so splendidly built, a woman specially created for motherhood, and for so much more. Rena had been nothing more than a wisp of humanity. He had no idea what she had actually thought about her situation, whether she had had any affection for him, or whether she had actually hated him as an enemy, albeit one who was providing her with a little bit of comfort in a comfortless world. He wondered what she had thought as she was being dragged to her execution. But that image was suddenly overtaken by another, of Hildegarde being in a similar situation, were the Russians ever to get into Germany. He got up to sit beside her and put his arm round her naked shoulders.

'Max!' Erhard Milch grasped his protégé's hand. 'I would say that you had a good holiday. Hildegarde is well, and the baby?'

'They are both very well. And I did have a good holiday, Herr Field-Marshal. Up to the night before last.'

Milch returned behind his desk and sat down, gesturing Max to a chair. 'I am sorry to have to break in like that, but there are some problems, and we need you.'

'Kharkov?'

Milch raised his eyebrows.

'Jeschonneck told me . . . Actually, I asked.'

'You knew about it? The news hasn't been released yet.'

'I did not know it had fallen. I was inquiring after the people I had to leave behind when we were recalled a couple of months ago. I was worried since they did not appear to have been brought out yet.'

Milch nodded. 'And now they are gone. It is a damnable business.'

'I had promised them they would be brought out.'

'As I say, a damnable business. That front is in real danger of total collapse.'

'Jeschonneck said a counter-attack is to be mounted. Am I to be part of that?'

'There is a more serious matter closer to home. Did you know that we have managed to bring down a Mosquito?'

'I did not. Who managed it?'

'To be honest, it was a fluke. A lucky shot. But the event is causing waves. There were only six of them, and they flew the length of Germany, in broad daylight, to bomb and strafe Berlin. Oh, the damage was slight. The physical damage, that is. The morale damage, now, I would say it has been greater than Cologne. Not least amongst our superiors. The Reich-Marshal is furious. He was about to make a major speech to tell the people that what happened at Stalingrad will have no effect upon the outcome of the war, when the Tommies turned up. He had to take shelter, and spoke several hours late, by which time most people had stopped listening anyway. But the military implications are the most serious of all. If that raid was just a trial run, well . . .'

'But you say we got one. Haven't we been able to learn anything from the wreckage?'

'It came down in flames and was almost completely destroyed. Both the crew were killed. The engines were burned out, although our experts tell me they are certain they were super-charged Merlins, as used by the Spitfires, so there is obviously something else that gives them their exceptional speed. Apart from their weight, of course.'

Max frowned. 'Their weight, Herr Field-Marshal? Aren't these twin-engined, two-seater machines, armed with bombs as well as cannon, and obviously carrying an enormous fuel load . . . ?'

'Agreed. But we did learn something from the wreckage. The Mosquito is made of wood.'

Max's head jerked. 'Sir?'

'That is fact.'

'But you cannot fly a wooden machine at more than six hundred kilometres an hour. It would disintegrate.'

'This one does not. Our engineers have been unable to find any trace of metal in the wreckage, apart from one main strut. There are no bolts, no rivets. The machine is made entirely of a very light wood – they think it is balsa – which is apparently laminated together using a special glue, under tremendous pressure, which gives it an enormous strength. Obviously such a machine is more vulnerable to opposing fire than a metal one. The problem is, flying so fast, it is nearly impossible to hit the damned thing, except by chance, as happened in this instance.'

'Well, sir, at least we have some idea of what we are up against, at last. If Abwehr can add to that knowledge—'

'The Abwehr operation has collapsed.'

'Sir?'

'They are refusing to release any details of what went wrong, but there is a rumour going about that all of their agents engaged in the operation have either been killed or captured.'

'My God! Then we must hope for a few more lucky shots. Am I being returned to Belgium?'

'You are. But not specifically to combat the Mosquitoes. Another potentially more dangerous threat has suddenly appeared.'

Max waited. He felt there were already too many dangerous threats, on land as well as in the air.

'Three days ago,' Milch continued, 'something very strange happened. Very sinister. You remember from before you went to Russia last time, that the Americans were coming over virtually every day, in broad daylight, usually with some Spitfire protection?'

'I remember. And when they persisted in flying beyond the escort range, we made a meal of them.'

'Quite,' Milch said drily. 'Now, three days ago, a flight of heavy bombers crossed the Channel and flew for Essen. They were clearly using this new British navigation system, the one they call Oboe. However, to the surprise of our observers, they did not appear to have an escort. So when they entered our first Kammhuber box the fighter wing went up to deal with them. This wing was about to engage the enemy when another enemy flight was reported. This flight had apparently previously been flying so high it had not been spotted by our radar, but now it was coming down. However, strangely, there were only six machines in this flight, to protect something like a hundred bombers. Major Peltzer, commanding the interceptor squadrons, therefore detached two of his flights to see off this limited escort. He then engaged the bombers, and was fully occupied for the next ten minutes. During that time he heard an exchange between his flight commander and a section leader, which went as follows: "Those are not fighters, Helmuth; they are light bombers. I leave you to disperse them." He then returned to the main combat. Peltzer had neither the time nor the inclination to question his decision. He made two passes at the main force, shot down three, then the weather closed in so completely that he had to break off the attack and return to base. The bombers had to return as well. But the section commanded by Senior-Lieutenant Todt was not heard from again.'

'What do you mean? That they just vanished?'

'No, we found their wreckage. But the crews were all dead. They had literally been shot to pieces before they could bail out or use their radios.'

'And the enemy?'

'There was no enemy wreckage in the vicinity, save for the three heavy bombers brought down by Peltzer's command.'

Max frowned. 'You are saying that three of our –what were they? 210s?'

'No. Gustavs. Still superior, in aerial combat, to any bomber.'

'Who commanded the other flight? The one that did not engage?'

'Captain Mannheimer.'

'He must have had a good look at these machines.'

'He reports that they were single-engined, had been flying very high, and were about a third the size of a heavy bomber.'

'Obviously they were Mosquitoes,' Max said. 'And he only saw one engine?'

'Mannheimer says they were not. He has encountered Mosquitoes before. He is positive that there was only a single engine, and they were twice as big as any fighter he had ever seen. That is why he put them down as light bombers. But they also seem to have had exceptional range, for either a light bomber or a fighter. And they weren't British, they were American.'

'You are absolutely sure he did not lose his head?'

'There was no reason for him to,' Milch pointed out. 'He saw six enemy aircraft, which were definitely not heavy bombers but which were too large to be fighters. He therefore deduced that they were light bombers that had become detached from the main body and were trying to rejoin, and sent Todt to disperse them, while he rejoined the main battle. There is nothing either negligent or unorthodox in that decision. You or I would probably have done the same thing. What is a mystery, and is disturbing everyone out there, is that whatever happened to Todt's planes, it happened so suddenly and so overwhelmingly that none of them got off any sort of message. This has had a bad effect on morale.'

Max nodded. 'I can believe that. Do we have any idea what kind of aircraft the Yanks are working on? I mean, those Mustangs of theirs were pretty hopeless.'

'Agreed. And we know they have been working very hard on improving their fighter capability, particularly after the mauling they received from the Japanese Zeros last year. But we haven't seen too many new designs over here. The principal one seems to be the P 38 Lightning. Several of these have been active in North Africa. They are very fast, very well armed, and seem to have a good range, although nothing like the Mosquito. Frankly, they are proving a bit of a handful for our 210s. But they are no bigger than any conventional fighter. So this is something entirely new. We want one on the ground, Max. But more important, we need it proved to those boys that they can be shot down.'

'Yes, sir. What have I got?'

'You have command of the entire Channel coast interceptor fleets. I am giving you carte blanche. You have about four hundred planes. Frankly, that's not as many as I would have liked, but they are all we have available, what with everything else that is going on, and there are more coming off the production line every day. Use your people as you think best. Fly whichever machine suits you best. Most importantly, restore morale. The whole nation needs a boost since that Stalingrad catastrophe. That is not truly your province, although some spectacular victories in the air would of course help. But our concern – yours and mine – is the Luftwaffe. Our pilots have definitely been shaken by the appearance of machines like the Mosquito. Now, I happen to know that we are developing something which will be far superior to anything possessed by the Allies, but it is not ready yet, and I would prefer you not to ask me about it until it *is* ready, which may be a few months yet. Right now we are confronted with another mystery machine, which may pose an even greater threat than the Mosquito. The idea that there is something else out there which cannot be beaten has to be nipped in the bud. I know you will not let me down in this.'

'Of course I will do my best, sir. If you approve I will return to Ostend and make my headquarters there. Am I allowed to take Hildegarde and the boy?'

'You may take whoever you choose. I am continuing Langholm as your chief of staff.'

'Thank you, sir.'

'As for Hilde, of course you must take her – if you feel it is safe to do so.'

'If the RAF can reach Berlin at will, I would say she will be as safe in Ostend as anywhere else. There is just one more thing. Is there any news at all of our people in Kharkov?'

Milch frowned. 'We have no people left in Kharkov.'

'I know that, sir. But when I was pulled out, I had to leave some of my personal staff behind, and no one seems to know what happened to them.'

'I'm afraid, Max, that if they did not get out before the city fell, you will have to forget about them. Were they close to you?'

'Two of them, sir. My personal servants.'

'Not old Heinrich?'

'Yes, sir.'

'God, what a fuck up!' Milch sighed. 'I know he was a good friend. But that is what happens in war, Max. Good friends get killed. Those of us who survive must enjoy our good fortune and get on with the job. As I know you will get on with yours. Heil Hitler!'

PART THREE
WHIRLWIND

'And, pleas'd th' Almighty's orders to perform,
Rides in the whirlwind, and directs the storm.'

'The Campaign'
Joseph Addison

The Future

'General Bayley, sir! Heil Hitler!' Colonel Peltzer saluted his new commanding officer, who had just climbed out of his 210. He was the older man, but they had served together before, and it was not his place to resent Max's youth. 'Welcome to Aachen.'

Max returned the salute, took off his helmet and gloves, then shook hands. 'It is good to be back.' He turned to a hovering sergeant. 'Have my machine refuelled immediately.'

'Immediately, Herr General.' He hurried off to summon a bowser.

'I understand Frau Bayley is accompanying you,' Peltzer said anxiously as the two men walked towards the headquarters building. The station looked in remarkably good shape, with very little visible damage. 'I have taken the liberty of preparing married quarters, which I hope she will find satisfactory.'

'I am sure she would, Peltzer. However, my wife has not yet arrived. She is coming by train. And she will not be staying in Aachen. I am moving headquarters to Ostend.'

'Sir?' Peltzer was aghast. 'But that is . . .'

'As near to the enemy as we can get?'

'Well, it is the front line. It nearly always takes a few hits, every time they come over.'

'It is where they should be met and, if possible, broken up. That is our task.' He entered the office, and the secretaries hastily stood to attention. 'At ease.' He led the way into the colonel's office. 'So you will prepare your people to move out, tomorrow. You will leave a skeleton staff here, as back-up.' He smiled. 'Just in case we all get in the way of a bomb. I am going there now. Colonel Langholm has gone on ahead of me.' He smiled at the expression on the colonel's face. 'But I will have a cup of coffee first.'

'Of course, sir.' Peltzer gave instructions through the open doorway, while Max sat behind the desk.

'Now, tell me about these new machines. Sit down.'

Peltzer sat, anxiously. 'They are definitely fighters.'

'You have brought one down?'

'No, sir. Not as yet. But there have been some engagements. The aircraft are very large, for fighters, but they are also very fast. I would not care to guess at the horsepower of their engines. They are also very heavily armed. But they do not appear to carry a bomb load; they have never been seen to drop anything.'

'What sort of numbers do they fly in?'

'We have encountered groups of up to forty at a time.'

'Simply protecting their bombers.'

'Yes, sir. They fly at ten thousand metres, using their radar, and when they see our interceptors rising to meet the bombing force, they come down.'

'That makes sense. So, what are your tactics for dealing with them?'

Peltzer looked embarrassed as he waited while a female secretary placed two cups of coffee on the desk, then withdrew. Max stirred his coffee. 'Well?'

'We attack the bombers, do what damage we can, and when the fighters get down to us, we withdraw.'

Max sipped. 'My God! This is real coffee.'

'Yes, sir. There is still some available in Belgium. We turn up little hoards of it every so often.'

'I see. Now, would you repeat what you just said? I am not sure that I heard you correctly.'

'Ah . . .'

'I thought you said that when you are attacked by these new fighters, you disengage and withdraw.'

Peltzer licked his lips. 'Yes, sir.'

'I would like you to explain to me why you adopt a strategy that is a clear dereliction of duty.'

'Well, Herr General, it is a matter of morale.'

'Say again?'

'Our pilots know that their machines are inferior to the Americans, and that if they engage them they run the risk of being shot down.'

Max could hardly believe his ears. 'Are these tactics also employed at night?'

'Well, no, sir; the Americans do not come over at night.'

'But the British do. Aren't they escorted?'

'By Spitfires for part of their journey.'

'Not by Mosquitoes?'

'Not as a rule, sir. I don't think they have that many. They seem to be using the Mosquitoes mainly as pathfinders, preceding the main force and illuminating the target with incendiaries.'

'I see. Are your main squadrons based here?'

'And the other airfields in Belgium and north-west France. We are echeloned in depths.'

'And you are still using the Kammhuber system?'

'Indeed, sir.'

'But it is not doing you much good if you are afraid to engage these new American machines.'

Peltzer flushed. 'The truth of the matter, sir, is that they seem more able to afford losses than we can. We shoot down ten, perhaps twenty bombers on every raid, but they still keep coming. Every plane we lose, I apply for a replacement, but I do not get it for a month. As for pilots, they either don't arrive at all, or if they do, they are straight out after a few weeks at training school. They are hardly fit to fly, much less to fly in combat.'

Shades of Russia, Max thought.

'Do you know, Herr General,' Peltzer went on, detecting a glimmer of sympathy, 'several of my squadrons are down to eight machines each?'

Max frowned. 'I was told, by Field-Marshall Milch, that I had four hundred operational aircraft at my disposal.'

'Well, yes, sir. We have forty-five squadrons in the command.'

'Very good. Well, Colonel Peltzer, before I continue to Ostend, I wish to address all of your squadron commanders. Will you assemble them, please?'

'Yes, Herr General.' Peltzer stood up, and turned to the door as the alarm bell jangled.

The secretary appeared, looking breathless. 'Yankees!' She looked from face to face, as if uncertain which of the officers she should be addressing. 'A hundred-plus, over the coast.'

'Escort?' Max asked.

'None visible, sir.'

'That is because of the height at which they fly,' Peltzer pointed out.

Max nodded. 'Is A Box airborne?'

'Yes, sir,' the woman answered.

'Very good. We will have to delay my talk, Colonel Peltzer. How many squadrons have you got on stand-by?'

'Four, sir.'

'Which is?'

'Thirty-six aircraft, sir.'

'You will take two squadrons and attack the bombers as they enter this box. I will take the other two and cover you.' He picked up his helmet and gauntlets and left the office, Peltzer at his heels. The adrenalin was flowing; he had not seen action for over a month and the thought of what might have happened to Rena was still burning holes in his brain, together with the excitement of encountering the unknown.

The pilots were already assembled by their machines, muttering at each other. The knowledge that they had received a new CO was starting to spread, as well as whispered speculation as to who it might be; they had already identified the waiting 210 as having well over a hundred bars painted on its fuselage. Now they stared at the youthful figure in consternation.

'Gentlemen,' Peltzer announced. 'Our new commander, General Bayley.'

The pilots came to attention; they had all heard of Max Bayley.

'At ease,' Max said. 'I had hoped to get to know you before leading you into action, but that will have to wait. LG 47.'

'Sir!' A tall man stepped forward. 'Senior-Lieutenant Leitner.'

'LG 49.'

'Sir.' This man was shorter and more solidly built. He was also somewhat older. 'Captain Mannheimer.'

This rang a bell. Mannheimer was the name of the man who had first encountered the mystery machines, and had made the decision that a single flight could deal with them. But Max decided against raising the matter now. Instead he said, 'Your squadrons will follow me. We are going to engage the enemy escort, when it appears.' The pilots gulped. 'I will

lead; LG 47 will be on my left, LG 49 on my right. We fly
in close formation, and we maintain that formation. The enemy
must fight on our terms. If either squadron is split up, it will
immediately reform in close order. Understood?'

They clicked to attention.

'Very good. Colonel Peltzer, good hunting.'

'Yes, Herr General.' Peltzer had suddenly found some
enthusiasm.

The Despatcher appeared in the doorway. 'Enemy one
hundred and twenty kilometres, entering Box B.'

Max was tempted to ask if there were any results from Box
A, where Gunther would certainly have engaged. But again
he decided that might be counter-productive with these still-
nervous pilots. The Despatcher helped him out. 'They appear
to have suffered several casualties, Herr General.'

'Thank you, Heinemann. Well, gentlemen, let us see what
we can do. Eight thousand metres. I will see you at lunch.'

He went to his machine, where the mechanics were waiting
to adjust his straps and settle him into his seat. The engine
was already warming up, and a few minutes later he was off
the ground and climbing into a clear spring day. There was
hardly a cloud in the sky, and at eleven in the morning the
sun was still behind him, just, but that very slight advantage
would soon be lost.

A glance to left and right as he climbed told him that his
two squadrons were in position, nine machines to either side.
Peltzer's force was some three thousand metres below them.
He reached eight thousand metres, levelled off, strained his
eyes, and made out the cluster of enemy aircraft in the distance.
However many casualties they had suffered, there were still
a great number of them.

He heard Peltzer giving last-minute instructions over the
radio, but was concentrating on what was happening above
him. And soon there they were, dropping out of the sky, a
dozen aircraft, single-engined but certainly larger than any
fighter he had ever seen, and travelling at startling speed.

'Stay close!' he said into his mike, and then switched
frequency as he went up. There was some static, and he
was within range before he found the right band. Then he
was head to head with the American machine. Tracers raced
towards him and around him, and he knew he had been hit,

but it really was a case of who would blink before the collision, and the American did so, pulling his stick back to climb above the oncoming Messerschmitt.

Max had held his fire to that point. Now, at hardly more than fifty metres' range, he loosed two rockets into the belly of the enemy, watched it explode into a thousand pieces, and hurtled through the disintegrating debris, feeling a succession of shocks. Then he was out the other side and turning sharply, while checking both his instruments and his wings. There were holes, but his engine was functioning.

'Christ Almighty!' a voice said. 'That guy just blew Sammy apart.'

'You see those markings?' another voice asked. 'That guy's a big one. *Jesus!*'

Max was checking his squadrons, and spoke absent-mindedly. 'And you're next, old buddy.'

His pilots had followed him as directed, and had smashed through the centre of the enemy planes, but at least three had gone down. On the other hand, another of the Americans was falling earthwards. The others were not coming back, but were racing towards Peltzer's squadrons, intent on defending their bombers.

'Go, go, go!' Max shouted.

His pilots responded with a will, but the Americans were faster, and were up to the second German group before Max could catch them up. But Peltzer was already into the bombers, and three of the huge planes were falling in flames.

'Look out!' someone shouted. 'That bastard is behind you!'

Max squeezed the trigger, and again the American plane burst into flames. This time the pilot managed to get out, but as he was over German-occupied territory his war was over.

Max had no time to see him go down as he was fastening his sights on his next opponent, but then someone said, in German, 'I am out of ammunition, Herr General.'

'And I also,' said another pilot.

Max sighed. The price of nerves and over-anxiety, firing too soon and in too prolonged bursts. 'Break off the engagement,' he said. 'Return to base. Box C will have to take over.'

'Max!' Milch's voice on the telephone was excited. 'A triumph on your first day!'

'I wouldn't exactly call it a triumph, Herr Field-Marshal. We brought down two of them, but they got three of ours. That is not a good rate of exchange.'

'*You* brought down two of them, Max.'

'I think we took them unawares, Herr Field-Marshal. They did not expect us to attack them.'

'Again, your doing, Max.'

'The bombers got through, sir.'

'Well, you cannot be everywhere at once. I am proclaiming this a victory. The Fuehrer will wish to see you when next you are in Berlin. I will arrange it. Now tell me, are you settled in?'

'Well, yes, sir.'

'And is there anything you need?'

'Yes, sir. I need planes, and I need men. Experienced ones if possible.'

There was a brief silence. Then Milch said, 'I will see what can be done. You realize that the situation in Russia is critical. We are staking a great deal, perhaps all, on the offensive we are undertaking to pinch out the Kursk salient, and for that we need just about every plane we have.'

'With respect, Herr Field-Marshal, would you not describe the situation on the Channel Coast as critical? If these rumours we hear are true, that the Allies are planning an assault on France . . .'

'At this moment those are rumours, Max, unsupported by our agents on the ground. Indeed, our agents report there is no question of an invasion being launched this year. The Russian situation is fact, and our ability to win this war may depend on a victory at Kursk. For the time being, we hold in the west, as we are being forced to hold in the south. I will see what I can do about replacements for your losses. But you are doing a magnificent job, showing your men that even the best American planes can be defeated. I rely on you to continue the good work.'

'Yes, sir.'

'Very good. Now, before I go, I have two pieces of news for you. I'm afraid they are not very good.'

Max waited, his mind in abeyance.

'The first is more interesting than bad. Our people have dissected that second kill of yours, which came down in marshy land and was not totally destroyed. They say it is something called a P47 Thunderbolt. The interesting thing is that they estimate it must weigh something like seven tons. Can you imagine a seven-ton fighter aircraft capable of flying at more than six hundred kilometres an hour?'

'I probably could not imagine it, sir, had I not seen it.' Max reflected that a Messerschmitt weighed only just over two tons. 'Do they know what sort of engine is being used? There was only one.'

'They are working on it now. The second piece if news is a bit grim. Our people have retaken Kharkov. I know that would normally be good news, but what they found there was disturbing.'

'Heinrich?'

'There was no sign of Heinrich, or any Germans. I would say that those who were not killed in the fighting have been taken away as prisoners. Which is not good news. I'm sorry, Max. As the French would say, *c'est la guerre.*'

'Yes, sir. You spoke of disturbing discoveries.'

'Ah, yes. It was what the Russians had done to those of their people who had been convicted of collaborating with us. Rows and rows of men hanged, women crucified . . . it makes the blood run cold.'

'Yes, sir. My other servant was a woman.'

'My dear fellow. I am so sorry. Was she important to you? I mean, like Heinrich?'

Important to me, Max thought. But he doubted the Field-Marshal would, or could, understand. Milch was one of the most honourable, straightforward of men, but he was a Nazi to the tips of his toes. He believed in the Fuehrer, and the Fuehrer's philosophies, one of which was that anyone of non-Aryan stock had to be a sub-human, and that the Slavs ranked only one degree above the Jews in that regard. So he said, 'I had promised her that if she worked for me she would come to no harm.'

'As I think I have told you before, Max, it is highly dangerous to make promises you cannot guarantee. Now you must forget the past. You have a very important job to do, and you are doing it magnificently. Keep up the good work, and I will send you whatever replacements are available.'

* * *

Clements hovered in the study doorway. 'Excuse me, sir, but there is a gentleman here to see you.'

'At this hour?' Mark looked at Helen. They had heard the car, but had assumed it was Jolinda, who had telephoned to say that she would be late, and had obtained a lift. Although the days were both longer and warmer than a few months before, she seldom used her bicycle nowadays. But unexpected callers in the early evening always created tension. 'You'd better show him in.'

He stood up to face the doorway as the tall, thin, hatchet-faced officer wearing the uniform and the insignia of a colonel in the United States Army Air Force advanced across the drawing room. Now he paused as he saw Mark waiting for him. 'Mr Bayley?'

'Correct.'

'Colonel Stephen Renfrew, sir. I'm sorry to appear out of the blue, and so late.'

'Not at all. Come in.' Mark shook hands. 'My wife, Helen.'

'Ma'am,' Renfrew gave a brief bow. 'I guess I sure am butting in.'

'Not at all,' Mark said again. 'I'm sure it's important. Will you have a drink?'

'That would be very nice, sir.'

'Scotch?'

'On the rocks, thank you.'

Mark poured. 'Well, sit down, and tell us what brings you down to Sussex.'

Renfrew sat down, took the glass, half raised it to his lips and then changed his mind. 'It's kind of embarrassing. One of our generals suggested it might be a good idea to have a chat with you.'

'I'd say that was a compliment.' Mark raised his glass. 'Your health. In what connection?'

Renfrew also drank. 'Would I be right in assuming that your son is a pilot?'

'You would be right, yes. My son John flies Mosquitoes.'

'He's shot down forty-nine German aircraft,' Helen said proudly.

'Is that a fact, ma'am? That's going some.'

'Most of those were during the Battle of Britain,' Mark pointed out.

'He's still our number one ace,' Helen insisted. 'Just as you were, in the Great War.'

'Now, darling,' Mark said, 'you know I was never remotely close to being our number one.'

Renfrew had been looking from face to face. Now he said, 'Well, I sure seem to have got my numbers crossed. The guy I'm looking for has a son named Max.'

'Oh, dear,' Helen said.

Renfrew raised his eyebrows.

'I have two sons, Colonel Renfrew,' Mark said quietly.

'Holy— I beg your pardon, ma'am. You saying you have one son in the RAF and another in the Luftwaffe?'

'His mother was German.'

Renfrew looked at Helen.

'His mother was my husband's first wife,' Helen explained.

'And he opted for her nationality, as he was entitled to do,' Mark pointed out.

'Yeah. But doesn't that kind of make him . . . well . . .'

'A traitor? As I said, he was entitled to make that choice. I should point out that the choice was made in 1938, when Great Britain and Germany were at peace.'

'Yeah. Like you say, sir, it's a point of view. But he sure seems to have done well for himself. Shooting down your planes. Our guys reckon there are something like a hundred victory bars painted on his machine.'

'I think it was a hundred and thirty, when last we heard,' Max said.

Renfrew scratched his neck. 'And no hard feelings?'

'Those victories were all gained in open combat, man to man. And incidentally, more than half were in Russia. Did you come down here to make inquiries about my son?'

'Well . . .' Renfrew flushed. 'In a manner of speaking, I guess I did, Mr Bayley. I guess you know that we've been taking heavy casualties in our sorties over Germany.'

'Because you will persist in daylight raids. That is meat and drink to any competent interceptor.'

'Maybe. But our brass decided to do something about it, and not by turning to the inaccuracy of night bombing.' His tone suggested that he regarded the RAF tactics as faintly yellow. 'So we brought over some squadrons of P 47s.'

Mark nodded. 'The so-called Thunderbolt.'

'Say, you know about that?'

'It's my business to know about that.'

'Is that a fact? Well, the Thunderbolt made a whole lot of difference, till a few days ago. It's a class act, far superior to anything the Krauts have. We had them on the run; they were afraid to engage. Until, like I said, a few days ago, when they got this new CO. This guy didn't seem to be scared of nothing. He just tore into our people like there was no tomorrow, or if there was, it sure didn't matter to him. And like I said, this plane was covered in those little black bars. What's more, he actually spoke to them, in English, before he shot them down.'

'How many did he get?'

'Two. So when they came back and reported, our people started to find out something about this whizz kid. Meanwhile, another sortie, another encounter with this character, and boom-boom, two more of our boys have gone in.'

Helen, who had put down her glass, involuntarily gave a little clap, and then flushed. 'Let me freshen your drinks,' she volunteered, getting up.

'OK,' Renfrew conceded. 'You have every right to be proud of your own flesh and blood. But he's become a problem. I mean, here we are with the better machine, but it seems like they've got the better pilot. That's bad. That's bad for business, and it's even worse for morale. Maybe you remember, in the First War, the Krauts had this guy called Richthofen.'

'I remember him very well,' Mark said. 'I had the great pleasure of meeting him.'

'You don't say. How'd you do that?'

'I was in a German hospital, and he came to see me.'

'Jesus!' Renfrew commented, clearly getting more and more out of his depth. He accepted another drink from Helen. 'The point is that your guys became scared of him, didn't want to engage him.'

'Some of them,' Mark said modestly.

'Yeah. Well, our brass is worried that the same syndrome may be setting in here. We want this guy. So we're wondering if you could give us any info on things like his technique, his weaknesses in the air . . .' He paused as he gazed at Mark's expression.

'The answer is no,' Mark said.

'Because he's your son? Shucks, Mr Bayley, he's an enemy of your country. Of my country too. Of the whole goddamned free world. He's a renegade in anybody's book.'

'I cannot give you any information about my son's technique, his strength or his weakness in the air for the simple reason that I do not know what they are. My son left England to live in Germany in 1938, before he had ever flown an aeroplane. He learned all his flying skills with the Luftwaffe, and I have no idea what he was taught, and what tactics he may have learned for himself. However, I can offer an opinion as to the reason for his enormous and continued success. As you have suggested, I believe that he does not care whether he lives or dies, and goes into every action on the basis that it will be his last. That gives him an immediate advantage over any opposing pilot who may wish to return from his mission.'

Renfrew studied him for several seconds. Then he said, 'You do admire the guy.'

'As you just said, should a father not admire his son? My only regret is that he's flying for them and not for us.'

'Yeah.' Renfrew finished his drink and stood up. 'Thanks for your hospitality, Mr Bayley, Mrs Bayley. I won't take up any more of your time.' He went to the door, but paused. 'We are going to get him. It's been given top priority.' He left the room.

'I see them,' Gunther said. As always, his eyes were the keenest in the wing. 'A hundred plus. No escort.'

'They'll be around,' Max said. 'Usual tactics. 47, 51, 53, follow me. Close formation. 36, 48 and 56, take the bombers. Good shooting, Gunther.'

'Wilco.'

The twenty-eight Messerschmitts dropped through the scattered clouds. Only twenty-eight, where there should have been thirty-six. But then, he had only twenty-three following him, again out of thirty-six. Milch had only been able to provide twelve replacements for the six squadrons of the wing, and the pilots were utterly green. All because of Russia, that immense wringer into which the Wehrmacht, and the Luftwaffe, were being fed like an endless sacrifice to some horrific pagan god.

So they had to make do with what they had. Which was

why he was here. Because he never argued, never recriminated, just got on with what he did best.

'I see them,' Heinemann said. 'Twenty-plus.'

The Thunderbolts came down with their inevitable rush. Max supposed their only weakness, apart from the inexperience of their pilots, was that they never changed their tactics, relied on their speed and their immense firepower to scatter the opposing flights. No doubt that inflexibility was forced on them *by* the inexperience of their pilots.

Not that he was any better off in that respect. He knew, without any sense of hubris, that the only advantage his wing possessed was himself – and, to a lesser degree, Gunther – to lead it into action. Their immense reputations – Gunther was himself close to a hundred kills now – their boldness and their utter contempt for death were the wing's main advantages. 'Close up out there,' he said. 'Straight at them.'

Again the American pilots blinked first, and started to scatter as the 210s hurtled at them, the more daunting because he had at last got the message through to them, and they were holding their fire until the last possible moment. There was a gap in front of him now, and he held his course, but swung away at the last moment to fasten on the nearest Thunderbolt, loosing two cannon shells into its fuselage and seeing it burst into flames. Then he was in open air, turning to rejoin the combat, only realizing as he did so that there were three planes with him, following him round.

As was his usual practice he had switched his radio to the American wavelength immediately before engaging, and now a voice said, 'Stick with the bastard, Benjy. We're gonna get him this time.'

A stream of tracers passed just over his head. Max dived, rolled, lost consciousness for a moment, and came to behind the Thunderbolts who had been surprised by his sudden manoeuvre.

'Shit!' someone cried.

Max fired at close range. The enemy was travelling so fast that only one of the shells struck, but immediately there was a plume of smoke.

'I'm hit,' the pilot said. 'Get some more planes over here, Joe. We gotta get this guy.'

Max's aircraft shuddered as bullets slammed into it. This

time he climbed steeply, rolling again, but knowing an odd
sensation as he realized he personally was the target. Then he
heard Heinemann's voice. 'The skipper's in trouble. With me,
Keppel.'

Two Messerschmitts detached themselves from the mêlée
to join the private battle. Max got off another burst and hit
his target, but was then hit again himself. The 210 continued
to respond to the controls, and there was no sign of any fire,
but its movements now became sluggish. 'I must go down,'
he said. 'Break off the engagement.'

'Of course you did the right thing,' Milch agreed over the
phone. 'If we lose you we lose everything.'

'If we don't get more planes, or something better than the
210, we are going to lose anyway,' Max said.

'I know how you feel. But I ask you to continue, only for
a little while. We have something very big coming along,
something that will revolutionize air warfare. Listen, Galland
will be paying you a visit in a few days' time.'

'To replace me?'

'Good God, no. He has something to show you. Call me
again after you have seen him.'

Max replaced the phone and went outside, surveyed the
parking apron. It was crowded with machines being serviced
by the ground crews, but not as crowded as it should have
been. He had begun the day with fifty serviceable aircraft.
Now he counted forty-three, and several of these were
damaged. They could be repaired, of course, but the numbers
were still dwindling at a frightening rate.

'Mueller,' he said to the Despatcher, who had followed him
out. 'Get on to the other boxes. I want a full casualty report.
Pilots as well as aircraft.'

'Right away, Herr General.'

Max walked to his own plane, which was somewhat separated from the others, surrounded by mechanics, and also by
Gunther, and Hildegarde who, as was her custom, had driven
over from their quarters when the planes began to return. Now
she held his arm. 'It's full of holes.'

'But you are not,' Gunther said. 'Only a consummate pilot
could have brought her down in this condition.'

'I'm not quite sure how I did it. Well, Steiger?'

The sergeant – who had fought with him in Russia – clicked his heels. 'Twenty-four hours, Herr General, and she will be as good as new. My people will work right round the clock.'

'Thank you, Steiger. Heil Hitler!'

Steiger saluted and hurried off.

'How many did you get?' Max asked Gunther.

'Four.'

'And?'

'We lost one.'

'And I lost six.'

'But you got three. Heinemann got one.'

'Yes, he did. He is a very good man.'

'So we broke even.'

'I don't think that is a sustainable rate of exchange, Gunther. I am going to have some lunch.'

Hildegarde held his hand as they walked towards the mess. 'What did Milch say?'

'He was upbeat as usual, talking about new and better machines coming off the production line. I don't know whether he believes it himself.'

'Gunther was saying something about how the Yanks seemed to be targeting you more than anyone else.'

'That could be true. Three of them concentrated on me, and when I got one, they called in more.'

'But why? Can they know who you are?'

'I doubt that. But they can see from the markings that I am commander of a wing, and they can also see that I have quite a few victories to my credit.' They entered the mess, and a steward hurried forward to escort them to their seats and proffer the menu.

'I think it's terrible,' Hildegarde commented, when they had ordered.

'It is the price of success.'

'Well, can you not fly an unmarked aircraft? Then they would not know either that you are an ace or that you are a commanding officer.'

'Now, really, Hilde, would that not be to concede a moral defeat even more serious than being shot down?'

'If anything were to happen to you . . .'

He reached across the table to squeeze her hand. 'They

haven't got me yet. Even though I've been shot down twice. I'm still here.'

'Is not the third time the fatal one?'

'Some say it's the lucky one.'

She finished her meal, sipped her wine. 'What is going to happen to us, Max? To Germany?'

He gazed at her. 'I suspect only Hitler knows the answer to that, and I'm not even sure about him.'

'But can we still win the war?'

'It doesn't look too likely. But perhaps we can avoid losing it. If Milch is right about these new planes, and there are rumours of secret weapons in the pipeline that will bring the Allies to a halt, well . . .'

'Do you believe there are any such weapons?'

'We have to believe it, Hilde. Otherwise, to continue fighting is madness.'

'The machine is ready for your inspection, Herr General,' Sergeant Steiger said.

'That is very good work, Sergeant. Let's have a look.' Max followed the mechanic out of the Headquarters building and across the tarmac. It was only eight o'clock, too early for the Americans, and he had left dealing with the RAF during the night to his subordinates. He had in fact had a very good night's sleep. His body still glowed from lying with Hilde in his arms. Now he felt ready for anything.

He walked round the machine. The various patches were very evident, but they all looked and felt solid enough, the guns were in perfect order, and the engineer assured him that the engine was also in perfect working order. 'Then I congratulate you all,' he told them, and turned to frown at the sky as he heard a huge booming sound. 'What the devil . . . ?'

'There, sir!' Steiger pointed.

The machine, invisible up to a few moments before, had come out of the clouds and already passed over the airfield, which was why they were only now hearing the sound of its passage.

'Jesus!' said one of the crew. 'If that was an enemy bomber—'

'He would have dropped a bomb,' Max pointed out.

'But what was it, sir?' Steiger asked.

The strange aircraft had already disappeared. Max had had several unsuccessful encounters with Mosquitoes, which were the fastest airplanes he had ever seen, but this seemed to be travelling at almost twice the speed. The very idea gave him a prickling sensation at the nape of his neck.

Other people had also seen or heard the phenomenon and were now clustering on the apron, staring at the sky, shouting at each other. Max was joined by Gunther. 'Did you see it?'

'A glimpse. That was all any of us got.'

'I never saw it at all,' Gunther complained. 'I was inside. But I certainly heard the noise. What do you think it was?'

'I have absolutely no idea,' Max said.

'If it was a Tommy, or a Yank . . .'

'He surely would have strafed us at the very least, rather than just demonstrate what he can do.'

'Should we report it?'

'I think we have to do that.'

'There he is again!' Steiger shouted.

The speck was approaching very fast, and gradually developed into the shape of a plane.

'Should we take cover?' Gunther asked. 'Or scramble?'

There had been no warning, either from Central Radar Control or by telephone. 'Let's see what he plans to do.'

The Despatcher emerged from Dispersal, panting. 'Pilot requesting permission to land, Herr General.'

'Who is he?'

'He wouldn't give his name, sir.'

'He's one of ours,' Gunther said, pointing at the now visible wing markings as the strange plane reduced speed.

'Give permission to land,' Max said.

The Despatcher hurried back inside while the aircraft, now travelling relatively slowly, circled the airfield as the pilot awaited the necessary permission.

'It's got no propellers!' someone shouted.

'No engines, you mean,' Steiger said.

'And look at those wings!'

They were certainly smaller than any Max had ever seen before. Like his men, he stared as the aircraft came down at the far end of the runway, its perfect landing being engulfed in the huge roar of reverse thrust to slow it down, while masses of white vapour surrounded it, rising from what Max

could now make out were two huge barrels, one under each
wing.

It needed almost the entire runway to come to a halt, then
it turned and slowly taxied towards the waiting group of men,
which had now increased to include almost everyone on the
base, even the various secretaries. The machine stopped, and
Max went forward as the cockpit canopy was pushed back,
only to check as the stocky man in the black flying suit dropped
to the ground, taking off his helmet to reveal his somewhat
broad features, neatly split in two by the thick black moustache. 'Adolf?'

'Max.' Adolf Galland shook hands.

'Milch told me you were coming to see me, but . . .'

Galland turned to look at the machine. 'What do you think
of her?'

'I don't know what to think.' Max glanced at his men and
women who had gathered in a semi-circle around the two
generals, at a respectful distance. 'Gunther,' he said. 'You
know Gunther Langholm, Adolf?'

'Of course.' Galland shook hands.

'So what exactly is this?' Max asked.

'This,' Galland said proudly, 'is the ME 262 jet-propelled
fighter.'

'Adolf!' Hildegarde presented her hand for the famous airman
to kiss. 'As debonair as ever.'

'As you are as beautiful as ever, Hilde. And the boy?'

'He's well. Come and sit down. Dinner in ten minutes.
Champagne?'

'Thank you.' Galland raised his glass. 'Heil Hitler! And
damnation to the Tommies, and the Yanks.'

The men sat down, round Hildegarde. 'Are you going to
tell us the secrets of your machine, sir?' Gunther asked.

'Actually, there are no secrets, just a simple – and perhaps
obvious – truth. Ever since the Wright brothers, flying has
been based upon the principles of the internal combustion
engine. This means that the vehicle is dragged forward,
whether by the movement of its wheels over a solid surface,
in the case of an automobile, or by the rotating of propellers
at colossal speed, to create a forward surge in the air far greater
than the downward pressure on its wings. Now, over the past

forty years we have improved and refined this principle a hundred times, and improved and refined its exhaust systems, to obtain the maximum forward pull. One could say that the British Mosquito is the ultimate in the use of this principle. But that's just the point, it's the ultimate. There is a finite point, which we have just about reached, beyond which we cannot go, on the drag principle. Oh, we can try using new materials to lessen the weight, or we can try new exhaust systems to add to the impetus, but the overall result is not more than a few – a very few – additional kilometres per hour.'

He looked from face to face, but every expression was one of rapt attention. 'Until someone, it was actually an Englishman named Whittle, I believe, came up with the obvious solution. If our only hope of real advance is by use of the exhaust system, why not use *only* the exhaust system, so that the machine is *propelled*, rather than dragged.'

Once again he looked round their faces, which were now showing traces of scepticism. 'As you can imagine, this did not go down very well with those conservative elements that run our air force. Fortunately, this applied on the British side as well. It has taken nearly ten years for the idea to come to fruition. But now we lead the field. We understand that the British are working on a jet fighter of their own; I think it is called the Gloster Meteor. But they are several months behind us. That plane out there is ready for combat. It is as heavily armed as any 210, any Spitfire or Mosquito, even any Thunderbolt, but it can fly at over eight hundred kilometres per hour. It can seek and destroy any Allied aircraft in existence, and it cannot be caught by any Allied aircraft in existence. Think of it, Hilde. An air fleet composed of 262s will completely change the course of the air war by re-establishing our superiority.'

'Sounds too good to be true,' Gunther remarked.

'But it is true, Gunther. It is there on the tarmac for you to look at. You may fly it if you wish. But for God's sake be careful. It is the only one we have, at the moment.'

Max put down his champagne glass. 'Would you repeat that?'

At this point some of the animation finally left Galland's face. 'These things take time. There are so many calls upon our stocks of steel, upon our top skilled labour. I mean, there would be very little point in regaining our supremacy in the air if we then lost it on the ground. Our new Tiger tanks, well, they are unbeatable, but they use a great amount of high-quality steel. So we have to share our resources. But at least we have the prototype in the air, and we have proved its qualities. When it is mass-produced—'

'When will that be?' Max asked.

'By the end of the year, certainly.'

'That is nearly eight months away,' Gunther said.

'So, for the time being we must maintain our holding pattern. Have we not been doing this successfully enough for the past few months?'

'On the basis of one of them for one of us,' Max said. 'But I think there are more of them than there are of us. And we are not getting sufficient replacements, of either men or machines.'

'I know,' Galland said sympathetically. 'It is a matter of hanging on, and waiting for things to improve.'

'But they will improve?'

'Absolutely. I have said that these new aircraft will be coming off the assembly line in increasing numbers by the end of this year. But that is not all. Our scientists have been applying this principle of jet propulsion in other directions, and they have come up with the ultimate weapon.' He looked around the still somewhat sceptical faces. 'Can you envisage a bomber that will carry a payload of several thousand pounds, for a thousand miles, at nearly a thousand kilometres per hour? That is faster than any Allied interceptor is capable of. It will be quite untouchable, the ultimate aggressive weapon.'

'And we have such an aircraft?' Gunther asked.

'It is not an aircraft. It is a rocket, fired from a ground base.'

'A rocket?' Max's sense of disbelief grew. 'Who is going to pilot this thing?'

'No one.'

'Eh?'

'That is the beauty of it.'

'But . . . how does it come back?'

'It doesn't. Again, that is the beauty of it. It is launched with a gyroscopic compass designed to take it to its target.

The distance from launch site to target is calculated, and the rocket is loaded with just sufficient fuel for the journey. When the fuel is exhausted, the engine stops, and the flying bomb just drops from the sky. It is calculated that we can destroy London in a matter of weeks, and without the loss of a man or a bomber, or the necessity to employ a single one of our fighters as an escort.'

'And these things are in service?'

'Well, no, not yet. The launch sites have to be created and prepared. The bombs themselves are in production, but of course they cannot be used until we have enough of them stock-piled. There would be no point in sending them over one at a time. They need to be launched en masse to produce the destruction, the despair, that we need.'

'So when are we talking about?'

'Oh, next summer, certainly.'

'Next summer.'

'Just a matter of twelve months, Max. I can tell you, the future is bright, and victory is certain.' He raised his glass. 'I give you the Third Reich! Heil Hitler!'

Fire Storm

'Do you think he is telling the truth?' Hildegarde asked in bed that night. 'Do we really possess such weapons?'

'Adolf Galland is as honest as any man I have ever met,' Max said. 'And he is actually flying a 262, so we know that we certainly possess such weapons. As for whether they can be produced in time – or enough of them, at any rate, to change the situation – that is another matter.'

Hildegarde held him close. 'What's going to happen to us, Max? I mean you, me and Baby.'

'I don't think, right now, that we can do more than aim to survive, and pick up the pieces afterwards.'

'Will there be an afterwards, if the Russians invade us?'

'The Russians are still a long way away, and we still have a couple of million men between them and us. I think we need to worry more about what the Allies may be thinking of doing.'

'Are they going to invade?'

'Oh, certainly. When they're ready. And until then, they're going to continue trying to soften us up.'

'Can they do that?'

He smiled into her hair. 'Not if we can help it. But it's been some time since their last massive raid. I wonder when they'll try another?'

'Gentlemen!' Air-Vice-Marshal Harris surveyed the several rows of pilots seated in front of him. 'It's been too long since we met. But I am delighted to say that you have again been seconded to Bomber Command for an op, only this time it will be somewhat different from the last.'

He paused to beam at them. He was a short, pudgy man,

with a round, somewhat pudgy face; even his moustache suggested pudginess. He always made John think of a bank manager, prosperous and at peace with the world. That beneath the placid exterior there lurked the most ruthlessly acute brain in the Air Force was always hard to accept – until he started speaking.

'When last year we attacked Cologne,' Harris went on, 'in our first thousand-bomber raid, you and your Mosquitoes flew in a diversionary role, distracting the Nazi defences by raiding Holland and Belgium. You did a magnificent job. Unfortunately, the actual raid was not a great success, certainly not the success we had anticipated. It was impossible to imagine that a thousand bombers could not obliterate a city the size of Cologne. But the fact is that the damage done was minimal. A lot of houses were knocked down, and a few thousand people were killed or wounded. The factories, which were our actual targets, were virtually untouched. As for the devastating blow to German morale that we anticipated, that simply has not happened. In that direction, you fellows accomplished more, caused more alarm and despondency in the enemy's minds, with your six-plane raid on Berlin at the beginning of this year.'

He paused to take a sip of water. 'So, we need to do better. Now, the principal causes of our failure to accomplish our objective at Cologne were the inaccuracy of our bombing, and the inexperience of a large number of our pilots; the two are closely linked. In order to make up that magic figure of a thousand machines with their crews, we had not merely to scrape the bottom of the barrel, but to scrape it clean. That meant using novice pilots and navigators who had only just begun their training, much less just completed it. And we had to use aircraft that were barely serviceable. This desire, the determination, to attain that magic figure, so important for propaganda purposes, was perhaps a mistake. I am prepared to admit that. But I do not think the situation in that direction, even with our new bomb sights and radar beacons, can be greatly improved. The evidence of the last few months does not suggest this. However, there was a third factor that militated against our achieving the success we sought, and that was the reverse side of the propaganda coin.'

Now he stared at them, looking from face to face. 'Our

superiors were concerned that we be seen to continue to conduct the war in as honourable and justifiable a manner as possible. It has taken them some time to understand that when fighting a foe like the Nazis that is a contradiction in terms. If we are going to beat these people, we are going to have to inflict more death and disaster upon them than they have upon us, or upon France, or are currently doing upon Russia. This means raining destruction upon the German people, as well as upon the German army and their Nazi masters.

'Now, I know this idea is distasteful to you. We have endeavoured to fight our war in the air according to those principles of honour and gallantry – of chivalry, if you like – that are such a part of our heritage. Sadly, the time for that is past. I have been given permission to inflict upon the Reich the most severe, the most grievous blow ever delivered in the history of war. Gentlemen, we are going to obliterate the city of Hamburg.'

Another look around their faces; no one moved and there was not a sound in the large room.

'Now, I have to tell you that we no longer have the capacity, even after scraping the bottom of the barrel, to send over a thousand heavy bombers. We have about seven hundred and fifty available. So we are going to use them in successive waves, night after night. The Americans are going to help us with a daylight raid on one of the intervening days. Our bombers will be armed with both high explosive and incendiary devices, and our aim is to hit them a second and third time before their emergency services can cope with the first and then the second waves. Our aim, as I have said, is the complete destruction of the city, regardless of the casualties that may result. However, let me make one thing perfectly clear: Hamburg was not chosen at random, with a map and a pin. As perhaps Germany's major seaport, it is a legitimate – and can even be considered a vital – military target.

'Now, your task, with your Mosquitoes, will be to lead the first attack as pathfinders, as you have been doing so successfully over the past year. Again, as usual, you will go in an hour ahead of the main body. But this time you will be armed with nothing but incendiaries, and you will be given specific target areas. You will go in low, and drop your bombs as accurately as you can. You will also be equipped with our latest anti-radar device, something we call Windows.' From a box on the table in front of him he scooped a handful of thin strips of metal. 'These have been tested and they work. Dropped from your aircraft when at height – that is to say, before you begin your bombing run – they will float slowly and gently downwards, and will totally distort the enemy radar signals. The fires you start will as usual guide the bombers behind you to their targets. The bombs they drop on your fires night after night will, I have no doubt, complete the destruction of the city, and thus play a major part in the destruction of the enemy morale, and in his capacity to continue waging war. Thank you, gentlemen. Your exact schedule and the date of the attack will be given to you in due course. What I have said today is, of course, confidential.'

'So, now we are to become mass murderers,' Evans remarked as they were driven back to Hatfield.

'I think the old boy has a point,' Squadron-Leader Wilson suggested. 'You cannot win a war by flapping at the foe with powder puffs. And every day this war lasts, thousands more lives are lost.'

'So we have to do our bit, or we'll be left out of the history books.'

'We have to do our duty,' Spencer said. 'No matter whether we like it or not. But you can all have a two-day furlough. Just remember what the man said: don't talk about it. I would suggest you don't even think about it. It's a job of work that we have to do, and that's it.'

'What about our crews?' John asked.

'They fly where we're sent. They must accept that.'

'I mean, do we tell them?'

'No. From their point of view, it's an op like any other. We'll let the brass, and the politicians, and the historians, argue about the rights and wrongs of it. Just remember that if we don't win this war it'll be the wrong set of brass, politicians and historians doing the arguing.'

'Well,' Mark said over dinner, having told John about Renfrew's visit, 'they haven't come back to me again.'

'I think they had a bloody cheek in coming to you at all,' John said, and glanced at Jolinda.

'Oh, I agree with you,' she said. 'But that's the nature of

the beast. They may have been reluctant to get involved in this war, but when they do get involved in something, they get very serious about it.'

'So you think they are definitely targeting Max.'

'I would say so,' Mark agreed.

'I find that creepy,' Helen said.

'It does seem a little unsporting. So, Johnnie, tell us what's on your mind.'

John raised his eyebrows. 'Is there something on my mind?'

'Yes,' Jolinda said.

'I'm surrounded by psychoanalysts. Sorry, no can do. Not right now.'

'It's something big, isn't it?' she asked as they got into bed.

'Yes.'

'Don't tell me you're going back to Berlin in daylight.'

He kissed her. 'I'll tell you about it when it's over.'

'What a perfectly glorious day,' Hildegarde said as she entered the bedroom, Baby Max in her arms. 'Do you know what I would like? To go for a drive in the country. Do you think we could do that?'

Max stretched. 'That depends on what Uncle Sam has in mind. But I tell you what: tomorrow Gunther can command for a few hours. We will have a picnic.'

'Could we? Oh, that will be marvellous. I will write it in my diary in red ink: Saturday twenty-fourth July, 1943. Picnicked with Max and Max.'

Max grinned and got out of bed to kiss them both. 'It hasn't happened yet, you know.'

But it was impossible to feel anything less than happy on such a glorious summer's day. Max stood on the tarmac and gazed up at the blue sky, the scattering of white puffball clouds driven by the gentle breeze. Outside the Dispersal office his pilots lounged. There were far too few of them, and indeed he knew, Uncle Sam willing, that he would have to spend the rest of the morning making up lists and re-allotting squadrons, or parts of squadrons, to other boxes to maintain as even a spread as he could across his command, just as he knew that when they were next summoned into action they would once again be facing the fearsome Thunderbolts.

But he felt they were slowly getting the measure of the American machines, and even if the P47s were undoubtedly superior to the 210s, their pilots still lacked the experience to beat the best German pilots. If only he had more of *them*. It was the future, the promise held out by Galland, that was so important. He had flown the 262, and it had been an experience beyond his wildest dreams. To lead a squadron of those jets into battle would, he thought, be the culmination of his career. And it was surely drawing nearer. All he and his men had to do was hang on, as if they were besieged – not such a wild fantasy – and wait for relief.

Senior-Lieutenant Leuthen was standing in the doorway. 'Yankees, two hundred-plus. Entering Box E.'

The pilots scrambled to their feet.

'Stand down,' Max told them. 'We may have some later.' But two hundred was a sizeable force, and it would undoubtedly have fighter escort. 'Telephone Lille and find out if they require assistance,' he told Leuthen.

Gunther joined him. 'They will ask for it. What do you propose?'

'I will take 47 and 49 if they call for it. You'll have to hold the fort here.'

Gunther grimaced. 'You are the one who should stay here. You are the CO.'

Max grinned. 'I feel like a scrap today, especially as I am leaving you in command tomorrow.'

Leuthen reappeared. 'Radar Control reports intruders are through F and appear to be making for the Elbe. It is considered possible that they are heading for Brunsbuttel, or even Kiel.'

Gunther whistled. 'That's a long way.'

'Colonel Schaffer, Box H, requests assistance. He has only two operational squadrons, and these are only at two-thirds strength.'

'Very good,' Max said. 'Tell Colonel Schaffer that we are on our way, but we will need to fuel before we return. He must have this facility waiting for us. I will take 47, 49 and 52, Gunther. Now, listen. Brunsbuttel is surely at the limit of any possible fighter escort, even these Thunderbolts. That means they will be coming back. If I find them, I will engage. If I do not find them, then it is up to you. By the time they regain the coast they will be watching their gauges. We could do well out of this.'

'Yes, sir, Herr General. Good hunting.'

'Yankees!' Heinemann said. 'Two o'clock.'

Max looked in the required direction. The broad snake of the Elbe was visible below and behind the approaching aircraft, with Cuxhaven, virtually at the mouth of the river, clearly to be seen to the west. Ahead of them was the little port of Brunsbuttel, at the western end of the Kiel Canal, and way over to their right was the huge seaport of Hamburg. There was smoke rising from Brunsbuttel. Presumably the lock gates had been the target, but the cloud of bombers had passed on, and were just visible in the distance; they were indeed heading for the great naval dockyards of Kiel.

And their escort was only just returning, to the east. 'They'll be low on fuel,' Max said. 'Draw them out.'

He switched wavelengths. 'Blast through them,' a voice said in English. 'Don't hang about.'

'Say, skip,' said another voice, 'you see what I see?'

'That guy with all the markings,' said a third voice. 'Ain't he the Kraut we want?'

'You got it,' agreed the Flight-Commander. 'Just watch your fuel levels.'

'Well, gentlemen,' Max said. 'Tally-ho.'

'Shit!' the American replied.

The range was closing fast. Max stuck to his usual tactics, flying straight at the lead Thunderbolt, hand hovering above his firing button. But this American was not blinking. Instead he shouted, 'Jerusalem!'

The impact took Max by surprise. An even greater surprise was the realization that he had not expected it to happen, so confident had he been in his greater courage, his lack of thought for whether he lived or died, which until now had been his greatest asset in combat. But that was history. Now he had every reason, every desire, to live and find happiness with Hildegarde and his son. And now it was too late.

That realization dawned on him while his ears were still ringing. To begin with he felt no actual pain, but he knew that was shock. For a brief moment he found himself staring at the American pilot, who was staring at him, mouth open, perhaps amazed at his own suicidal temerity. Then the planes fell apart, both plummeting earthwards.

I must get out, Max thought. But when he tried to release his belts his arms felt curiously heavy. Gritting his teeth he freed himself, then reached up to push back the cockpit canopy. It would not move. Sweat pouring down his face, he strained every muscle, without success. And now pain was seeping upwards, from his legs and lower back. *I have broken something*, he thought, *and I am going to crash in this machine and be killed, if I am not burned alive.*

But I *am* still alive, he reminded himself. And amazingly, as yet there was no fire. Perhaps the machine could still be flown. The cockpit windows were cracked and distorted. Peering forward, he could not see a propeller, but when he pulled back on the stick some of the frightening downward movement was slowed; his flaps were still working, at any rate. He peered downwards, could see nothing, and realized that he was in the middle of thick cloud. He scanned his instruments. Three thousand metres and descending very fast, but still high enough for a parachute. He gave another tug on the canopy, and this time it moved back. Gulping fresh air into his lungs he fell out of the aircraft, and pulled his ripcord. The jerk tore through his body like the cut of a sword, and he fainted.

Endless pain, tugging at his consciousness. And yet, moments of comfort, a softness beneath him, soft hands wiping sweat from his forehead, soft voices whispering about him. Heaven, or hell? He did not believe that a Luftwaffe pilot could ever assume he was in heaven.

And if he were dead, he would surely not be in such pain. He opened his eyes, and there was a flutter of activity about him. His throat was parched, and when he tried to lick his lips he could not. But his effort had been observed, and a glass was held to his lips. He did not know if it was simply water or not, but it tasted like nectar. And the face above the glass seemed that of an angel. It was not a particularly handsome face, long and solemn, and over-exposed because any hair on the head was invisible behind the huge white headdress. But the solemnity was relieved by a gentle smile as she took the glass away. 'Dr Coupars is here,' she said.

The doctor wore a moustache and, inevitably, a stethoscope, but he used his fingers to take Max's pulse. 'This is good. You are a strong young man, General Bayley. Are you in pain?'

This time Max managed to lick his lips. 'Yes.'

Coupars nodded. 'There is a limit to how much morphine we can give you at the moment. You will have to be completely sedated for the operations, but once that is done, you will start to feel better.'

'Did you say operations? What operations?'

'You have broken both your legs, Herr General. They are not good breaks. And there is damage to your lower vertebrae. The impact must have been tremendous. But we will do the best we can.'

This reminds me of Father, Max thought. Mark Bayley had refused to allow the surgeons to operate, and had settled for being a cripple rather than lose his leg. 'You will not take my leg,' Max said now.

'I have said that we will do the best we can, Herr General. Now, you must not be agitated. The orderlies will be in soon. Nurse.'

The doctor's face disappeared and was replaced by that of the nurse. 'Would you like something else to drink? I'm afraid you cannot eat until after the operation.'

'I am not hungry,' Max said. 'But I am very thirsty.'

The glass was held to his lips, and then taken away again. 'Where am I?'

'You are in Hamburg, Herr General. You were seen to come down a few miles away, and a recovery team brought you in.'

'My wing . . .'

'We are informing Ostend now, sir.'

'My wife . . .'

'She will also be informed that you are alive and will survive. Ostend is not so very far away. She will be here tomorrow.'

'No!'

'Sir?'

'She must not come here until after the operation.'

'The operation will be carried out within the hour, sir.'

'Yes, but . . .' He drew a deep breath. 'I do not wish to see her – for her to see me – until after we see how it turns out.'

She regarded him for several seconds, then nodded. 'I will tell Dr Coupars.'

'What is your name?'

'Elena, sir.'

He sighed. For a moment he had supposed it would be Karolina.

'Why, Gunther. How nice to see you.' Hildegarde sat in her rocking chair watching Baby Max's repeated attempts to stand. 'Don't tell me: Max has been delayed.'

Gunther held his cap in both hands, as if protecting himself. 'Max is in hospital, Hilde. In Hamburg.'

Hildegarde stopped rocking and slowly sat up. 'What has happened?'

'Apparently this lunatic American pilot flew straight into him. Both planes went down. The American was killed, but Max jumped. He will survive, but he is badly injured.'

'How badly?'

Gunther swallowed, but remembered that this woman had served with the Wehrmacht in Russia: she was no stranger to catastrophe. 'Both legs. It seems one was broken in the impact. The other was broken when he hit the ground. He was unconscious, you see. He had fainted from the pain.'

Hildegarde stood up. 'Will you arrange transport for me, please? And I will need someone to look after Baby while I am gone.'

'Ah . . .'

'Yes?' Hildegarde could be quite imperious on occasion.

'The hospital said that Max has specifically asked that you should not visit him before tomorrow.'

Hildegarde regarded him for several seconds. 'You have not told me the whole truth.'

'Yes, I have, Hilde. It is just that the operations are taking place today, I would say right now, in fact, and he does not wish you to see him until . . . well, until it is possible to see how they have turned out.'

'Operations?'

'To see if they can straighten the legs. You know, put them back together.'

Hildegarde sat down again. Baby Max was also sitting, staring at his mother. If he did not know what was going on, he could tell that she was agitated. 'You mean he could lose them,' Hildegarde said. 'The legs.'

'Oh, no.'

She gazed at him.

'Well, certainly not both of them. They really are quite optimistic.'

'Not both of them,' Hildegarde said, half to herself.

'There'll be transport waiting for you tomorrow morning. Unless . . . well, unless we hear from Max to the contrary.'

'Unless . . .' Hildegarde said.

'Straight in,' Spencer said over the radio. 'Windows first.'

John glanced at Langley, who was still concentrating on his beacon signal. The flight-sergeant had made no comment when informed of their mission, but then he had not yet been told the whole story. This was a raid, and they were path-finding, as they had done so often before. 'Let them go,' John said.

He looked out of his window at the surprisingly bright night sky, suddenly filled with a million flashing pinpoints of light. Then they had faded into the darkness, and Langley was saying, quietly, 'Target in sight, sir.'

Flying at thirty thousand feet, they had as usual zoomed through the various German boxes before any opposition could be sent up to intercept them, and now, looking down through the clear night sky, they could make out the Elbe. Hamburg was of course blacked out, but such a large city was un-mistakeable once the river was reached.

'Going down,' Spencer's calm voice came through again. 'All together. Bombs only, at five thousand.'

'All ready, sir,' Langley said.

The six aircraft dropped from the sky. The defence, although it must have had them on radar for some time, clearly had been confused by the strips of steel, and had not deduced their target; it seemed to be assuming they were a follow-up to yesterday's American diversionary attack on Kiel. And besides, six aircraft, even if their speed had identified them as Mosquitoes, could be no more than a pin-prick; the Germans were more interested in the very large formation of heavy bombers which was at that moment crossing the coast with its Spitfire escort.

'Seven thousand,' Langley said.

Now at last the anti-aircraft batteries opened up, but John ignored the puffballs appearing to either side. Only a lucky shot would hit him, as had happened with poor Hoosen.

'Five thousand,' Langley said. 'Target dead ahead.'

John levelled off. They, along with Evans, had been given the dock area, now easily identifiable. The two planes went in together, the river seeming very close; they could make out the ships lying alongside. To their left there were already plumes of flame rising from the incendiaries dropped by Spencer and his companion.

'Bombs away,' Langley said.

John pulled the stick back and the machine soared into the night, still closely followed by Evans. He looked back and saw the exploding red of the eight 250-pound incendiaries they had dropped between them.

'That'll burn for a few hours,' Langley commented.

Spencer apparently thought so too. 'Time to go home,' he said. 'We've done our bit.'

Max realized he had been staring at the ceiling for some time without actually seeing it. But now the view was interrupted by Elena's smile. 'Herr General! How do you feel?'

Max gazed at her. *How do I feel?* he asked himself. Still in considerable pain, but now it seemed once removed, thanks to the anaesthetic, which was still controlling his brain and his nerves. As for the situation below his hips . . . 'Tell me how I should feel,' he suggested.

'Dr Coupars will be in tomorrow morning to bring you up to date. But I can tell you that he is very pleased.'

'You mean I still have two legs?'

'Of course.'

Relief flooded his system like a physical force. 'So when can I get out of bed?'

'Oh, that will not be for some time. There is still a lot of healing to be done. But we will start on the physiotherapy course in a few days. The doctor will explain it when he sees you.'

'What time is it?'

'Eleven o'clock.' She half turned her head as wailing sounds could be heard. 'In here, Rudolph.'

Two men appeared beside the trolley bed.

'What is happening?' Max asked.

'It is an air raid. This is the first we have had for some time. That is bad luck, eh?'

Max attempted a smile. 'They must know I am here.'

'That is possible,' she said seriously. 'The news has been released. But they will not get you. We will just move you down to the cellars.'

'Will you stay with me?'

She made a moue. 'I am going off duty now. But do not worry. You will have much company.'

Hildegarde was ready at nine. To her surprise, Gunther himself was in the car. 'Are you coming with me? I am so glad.'

'Hilde, you must be patient.'

'What do you mean?'

'We cannot go today. There was a heavy raid on Hamburg last night. Incendiaries. Several parts of the city are in flames, and the area has been cordoned off until the fires can be brought under control.'

'Oh, my God! Max!'

'He is all right.' He held her hands. 'I have spoken with the hospital. There are still a few lines working, and I pulled rank. The hospital was not hit; it is actually situated just outside the town, on the banks of the river. But, Hildegarde, I have great news: the operations were a success.'

'You mean . . .'

'He has both his legs, and in the course of time the doctors anticipate they will function properly again.'

She gazed into his eyes. 'You would not lie to me, Gunther.'

'I was told this by the doctor himself.'

'Oh, thank God! But you said in the course of time. How much time?'

'Well, it may be a few months. There is a lot of tissue that has to regenerate . . .'

'Will he fly again?'

'Ah . . .'

'You are telling me that he is a cripple for life?'

'Now, Hilde, that is by no means certain. And even if he is, has he not done enough for glory? And did not this same thing happen to his father? And he is still alive, and thriving.'

'His father,' she muttered. His father had had the help of the famous Karolina. *Well, then,* she thought, *I must be as supportive as Karolina.* But Karolina had been in the hospital with Mark Bayley when he had been at his lowest ebb. 'Gunther, I must get to Hamburg! I must be with him.'

'And you will be with him, just as soon as it is possible. I will take you there myself.'

She kissed him.

'Damnation!' Mark Bayley remarked, peering at *The Times.*

'What's the matter, dear?' Helen asked.

'Max has come down again.' *But the last time he was brought down by Johnnie,* he thought. As if that mattered! But it had been kept in the family, and therefore somehow acceptable.

'He was shot down? You mean he's dead?'

'This says: "Berlin Radio has announced that General Max Bayley, commander of Fighter Wing One, crashed yesterday when his Messerschmitt 210 was involved in a mid-air collision with an American P47." At least they couldn't shoot him down.'

'But is he dead?'

Mark continued reading. '"General Bayley managed to escape his aircraft and reach the ground, but he is badly injured and is in hospital in Hamburg. The American pilot was killed." Hmm. I suppose if he deliberately rammed Max because it was the only way he could get him, then that makes him pretty much a hero.'

'That man Renfrew said they were going to get him, no matter what it took.'

'Yes, he did.'

'What are you going to do?'

'There is nothing I can do. I'd better let Johnnie know, I suppose.'

He went into the study to telephone. The operator in Hatfield was reluctant to put him through, but when she discovered that it was Mark Bayley she abandoned her objections.

'Dad?'

'Did I wake you up?'

'As a matter of fact, yes. Is there a flap?' *Not another one,* his tone implied.

'I thought you might like to know that Max has gone in.'

There was a moment's silence. 'When?'

'Yesterday morning. He's not dead. Listen.' He read the newspaper report.

'Hamburg?' John asked. 'Shit!'

'Is that important?'

'It'll be on the news this evening. We raided Hamburg last night. We went in with incendiaries first, to create a target, and the heavy bombers followed, seven hundred and fifty of them, with HE. And if Max came down yesterday morning . . .'

'He'd have been in hospital there when you were over. But if the hospital had been hit I think Jerry would have mentioned it.'

'Yes,' John said slowly.

'What is it? Do you know something about what happened?'

John hesitated. *No*, he thought. *I know nothing of what happened. I only know what's going to happen. Today and tomorrow night.* But instead he said, 'I have no idea what could have happened. As for Max, we'll just have to keep our fingers crossed that he pulls through. Even if he is a swine, I'd prefer to settle that business myself. Thanks for letting me know, Dad.'

He replaced the phone. 'We are going to wipe Hamburg from the face of the map,' Harris had said. 'Tomorrow night.'

'There's the all clear,' said the orderly. 'Let's get you back up top, Herr General.'

'Do you think it's worth the effort?' Max asked. 'You'll have to bring me back down again in a couple of hours.'

'No, no, sir. That is most unlikely. We had the Tommies on Saturday night, and now the Americans today – do you know that half the city is in flames? There is no target left worth attacking.'

His morale – the morale of the entire hospital staff, not to mention the patients – was amazing, despite the fact that as most of them were local, they had to know that their houses were at risk, and had to fear that their families might be amongst the casualties. There must be a lot of casualties.

And there were going to be a lot more. Max lay on his bed and looked through the window at the smoke and the flames. Most of these were in the centre of the city and the dock area;

as Elena had told him, the suburbs were relatively undamaged and the hospital had not been hit at all. But what might
be going on only a couple of miles away did not bear consid-
eration. The noise was tremendous. Early this morning the air
had been filled with the clanging fire-engine alarm bells, the
blowing of whistles. There had been every indication that the
worst of the fires would be brought under control. But then
had come the Americans with their far more accurate daylight
bombing. Not that they had needed a great deal of accuracy
to hit this target; all they had had to do was drop their bombs
in the centre of the flames they could see beneath them,
disrupting the efforts of the emergency services. Now most
of the fires were blazing uncontrollably again.

Max had no doubt that some of the American planes had
been brought down: they always were. But the thought that his
pilots were up there engaged in battle without him to lead them
was frustrating. As was facing the fact that he might not be
able to lead them again for some time. He looked at his legs,
emerging from beneath his hospital gown; both were encased
in plaster from the thigh down to the ankle, incapable of
movement except when assisted, and although he was being
fed morphine on a regular basis the pain was still considerable.

As there was only one telephone line working out of the
hospital, he had been unable to call either Gunther or
Hildegarde; just to hear her voice would have been a balm.
On the other hand Milch, with his position of power, had been
able to phone in to give him not only his own wishes for a
speedy recovery, but those of the Fuehrer himself.

Elena came into the room. 'Do you not wish this window
closed, Herr General?'

'There is no smoke getting in. The wind is the other way.'

'There is still the racket. And the stink. The stink is
everywhere.'

'Is your home involved? Your family?'

'No, no, thank God! My home is in Baden-Baden. I was
seconded here only two months ago.'

'And where is your husband?'

'Husband? I have no husband.' Her tone suggested that the
very idea was absurd.

'Then the young men of Baden-Baden are not very
observant.'

She made a moue. 'Perhaps they are too observant. Now, do you wish to pee?'

'Yes.' He didn't actually, but he wanted to be handled by her. *I am a womanizing bastard*, he thought, *lying here a total wreck, drugged and in pain, and I am having sexual thoughts about this woman.* He wondered how long after his catastrophe Dad had had sexual thoughts about Karolina. From what he had been able to glean over the years it had not been very long. But then, Karolina had been very beautiful, and Dad had not been a married man. And anyway, the Bittermans had always held the opinion that it was Karolina who had done the seducing.

Elena was all efficient disinterest. She folded back his robe, lifted his thighs to insert the pan, and then placed the bottle. 'You must put it in,' she explained.

'I would like you to do it.'

There was a slight hesitation, then she held his penis, very gently, and inserted it into the bottle. There was an immediate, if not very powerful, reaction, and her ears became tinged with red. 'You must control yourself,' she said. 'You cannot pee if you are erected.'

'I have changed my mind. I do not wish to pee. I just wish you to hold him.'

She turned her head to look at him.

'But first, close the door.'

'That is not proper, Herr General.'

'But as you have just reminded yourself, I am a general, and I have given you an order.'

Another hesitation, then she left the bedside to close the door.

'Now come back here and stand beside me.'

'Do you not have a wife, Herr General?'

'Yes, I do. And if she were here, she would do this for me, because I need it done. But she is not here.'

Elena returned to the bed, and stood beside him.

'Now take off your hat. I wish to see your hair.'

She reached up to remove various pins and placed the hat on the chair. Her hair was thick and black and straight, and it slowly uncoiled itself. Shades of Erika. But he did not think this young woman would be anything like Erika.

'Thank you.' He rested his hand on her buttocks, then slipped it down. 'Raise your skirt.'

'Is that an order, sir?'

'Yes, it is. There is nothing to be afraid of. I can hardly rape you in my condition.'

'My sister conceived her third child while her husband was flat on his back, unable to move with a ruptured disk.'

'She must have been very enthusiastic. I just want to hold you.'

Elena raised her skirt, and he slid his hands under her drawers. She gave a little ripple, and her cheeks glowed.

'Now, you hold me, and I will hold you, and we will see what happens.'

Still the fires glowed, made the brighter by the night darkness, but the noise had somewhat subsided. The heat was intense, and the smell of scorched wood and, he suspected, scorched flesh, was everywhere, even if the breeze remained off the river to carry most of it away from the hospital.

Max felt totally relaxed; even the pain in his legs seemed to have subsided. He did not know what Elena had felt since she had revealed very little save the odd murmur. But her fingers had been utterly knowledgeable. And she would be here again tomorrow. There was a delicious thought.

In fact she was here now, even if accompanied by an orderly. 'Time to go down, Herr General.'

'Eh?' He had dozed off, but now that he was awake he heard the sirens. 'Not again.'

Already there was the sound of explosions.

'We must hurry,' Elena said.

'No.'

'Sir?'

'As you have said, they do not attack the suburbs. I wish to see what is happening. You,' he told the orderly. 'Go and help someone else. I will ring if I need you. Elena, you will stay with me.'

The orderly looked at Elena, who shrugged. He left, and she closed the door. 'This is against all the rules.'

'So you said before.'

'I meant to stay in your room during a raid. If you were to be killed, I would probably lose my job.'

'No, you wouldn't,' Max assured her. 'If I am killed in this room, you will certainly be killed with me.'

'You say the sweetest things. What do you want me to do this time?'

'I would like you to take off all of your clothes and get into bed with me.'

'Are you out of you mind, Herr General? If someone were to come in—'

'No one is going to come in. Everyone has gone down to the cellars.'

'Oh . . .' She took off her hat, and then turned to the window. 'My God, listen to them.'

The entire night was filled with the droning sound, punctuated by the *crump* of the ack-ack guns.

'There do seem to be a lot of them,' Max agreed.

'They are saying there were more than seven hundred bombers on Saturday. This is the same noise. You don't remember?'

'I don't think I was too aware of anything that was happening on Saturday night,' Max confessed. 'But two seven-hundred-bomber raids in three nights, with an American raid in between? What is so important about Hamburg?'

Elena didn't reply, but moved closer to the window. 'My God! Look!'

With an effort Max half turned in the bed. The night had been fairly bright in any event, because of the still-glowing fires. Now it had brightened still further as yet more flames seared the darkness, while the heat coming through the open window was intense, and now there were wisps of smoke. He realized that the wind had changed, and was blowing towards the river.

'Everything is burning,' Elena said.

'They are using incendiaries. *Again?*'

Over and above the booming there was a sudden crack, and the panes of glass shattered. Elena gave a little shriek. 'We cannot stay here.'

With an even greater effort Max managed to turn his whole body to look out of the window, and could not repress a gasp of horror. Now the night was as bright as day as enormous sheets of flame shot skywards, accompanied by bangs and crashes, explosions, and the wail of a hundred thousand people expressing their terror. And the flames were now very close. Even if the hospital had not suffered a direct hit, it was clearly going to be consumed in the fire storm that was engulfing the city.

'You're right,' he said. 'You must get out. Now.'

'And leave you? I cannot do that.'

'Elena, be sensible. I cannot walk.'

'You are my patient, Herr General. You are my responsibility. Wait here.'

She left the room, and left him wondering where she had gone. He stared at the glowing night outside the window. Once again he was facing that recurring nightmare of being burned alive, unable to escape the cockpit of his machine.

He realized that the electric bulb above his head had gone out; the hospital had its own generator, but that had either stopped or been turned off. Not that it made a great deal of difference: the room remained illuminated by what was happening outside, even if the light was a hellish red glow.

Elena returned, pushing a wheelchair. 'Come along now,' she said briskly.

'Where are we going?'

'Downstairs.' She held his arms to drag him off the bed, taking his weight on her shoulders as she turned him round to sit in the chair. The pain from his legs was excruciating, but he ground his teeth together to stop himself from crying out. She settled him, then pushed him through the door and along the corridor. This was deserted, and in front of them loomed the elevators. 'They are not working,' she said, unnecessarily. 'But there is a ramp.'

This was a little farther along the corridor. It was a gentle slope, but even so she had to strain to stop the chair from getting away from her, using the brake constantly. As a result she was panting by the time they reached the next level, sweat pouring out of her hair as the heat intensified.

'You are killing yourself,' Max protested. 'I wish to God you'd leave me and get out. If you can reach the river you have a chance.'

'And I wish to God you would shut up, with respect, Herr General. It is my intention to reach the river. With you.'

On the next floor they encountered Doctor Coupars, his white overall stained black with smoke, his hair wild. 'Where have you *been*?' he shouted. 'Don't you realize this building is on fire?'

Max ignored the question. 'Where is everyone?'

'In the cellars. You must get down there right away. The roof is on fire and will start coming down at any moment.'

'You must get them out.'

'What? There is nowhere for them to go. Those cellars are roofed with reinforced concrete. They can withstand the entire building coming down on top of them.'

'Doctor, whether they are buried alive or not, they are going to be incinerated if they are not suffocated first. Your vents are going to be totally blocked in a very little while.'

Coupars hesitated, chewing his lip.

'If they can get to the water,' Max said, 'they have a chance.'

'But most of them are very sick indeed.'

'They will have a *chance*,' Max shouted. 'In those cellars they have no chance at all. They are your responsibility, Doctor. Nurse, get me out of here.'

Elena resumed pushing, but stopped after a few more steps. 'I should help him.'

'To do what? He has a staff, hasn't he?'

She started pushing again.

The hospital was now filled with smoke, and was like the inside of an oven. The night was a mass of creaks and groans and the roaring of the flames, and the heat was increasing by the moment. Anyone who did not get out within the next few minutes was not going to get out at all.

From behind them came a rising paean of screams and shouts as the staff and the patients were alerted to their danger, but Elena had reached the ground floor and now pushed the doors open. They emerged into a reasonable representation of hell. Behind them the city was one huge fireball, driven towards them by a roaring wind such as Max had never heard before; it was impossible to suppose that anyone could still be alive. To their right the docks were also blazing, ships flaming like incandescent candles; even the water was burning where oil had spilled over its surface. Above them the hospital also burned fiercely, and the upper floors were beginning to crumble. And in front of them the Elbe flowed by, dark and silent, although there were several police launches out there, watching helplessly.

'What can we do?' Elena shouted.

'Get into the water,' Max replied. 'Can you swim?'

'I can. But you . . .'

'I can use my arms, and you can help me. If we can reach one of those launches we can survive.'

She hesitated a moment, then unbuttoned her dress and threw it on the ground. She pushed the chair down to the edge of the low wall bordering the river, put the brakes on, grasped his arms to lift him, looked back at the building, and screamed. Max also looked over his shoulder, and saw several people staggering out of the doors they had just left, but these were human torches, their clothes and their hair on fire. Then he looked up, and saw the entire outer wall of the hospital falling towards him.

A Glimpse of Hell

M ark studied *The Times*. 'It says Hamburg has been entirely destroyed.'

'Oh, come now,' Helen protested. 'That's not possible. A whole city? In one night? London was blitzed every night for six months, and it's still standing.'

'London is a bit bigger than Hamburg,' Mark reminded her. 'And it wasn't the bombing, per se.' He read aloud: '"Observers report that the extensive use of incendiaries, dropped on existing fires caused by the previous day's attack, and the inability of the various services to reach the centre of the city because of the damage, created a fire storm that sucked in flaming winds of hurricane force that consumed everything, and everyone, in its path."'

'My God!'

'Max was there.'

'You don't know that!'

'I know he was taken there.'

'After he crashed. That was five days ago. You don't know he was still there.'

Mark's sister Joan came down from London. Two years older than Mark, she had lost her unborn baby at the very start of the London blitz in 1940, and remembered very well what it was like to fall through several floors of a collapsing and burning building. 'I survived,' she said. 'You never know what is going to happen.'

Mark let his hand lie in hers. 'It's the feeling that he deserved whatever happened.'

'Do *you* feel that?'

'Of course I don't. He followed his conscience, and as far

as I know he was an honourable foe, as well as being a great pilot. But it's all around me. Even Helen . . .'

'I'll have a word with her.' Joan and Helen were old friends, and indeed it was Joan who had introduced Helen to Mark and subsequently promoted the marriage. 'But I suppose we are in the middle of the most dreadful war there has ever been. We can't be blamed for hating the men who are trying to destroy us.'

'Do you hate the men who blew up your home in London?'

'I hate them for killing my baby.'

'Then you hate Max. You're happy that he is dead.'

Joan sighed, and squeezed his hand. 'It is very difficult to hate one's own flesh and blood. I only wish things were different.'

This, Mark realized, was not an answer. And now she asked, 'What does John think of it? Was he involved?'

'I haven't seen him since the raid, and no details have been released about the aircraft taking part. We'll have to wait until he comes home on leave again.'

'But he'll know about Max.'

'I imagine he will,' Mark said sombrely.

'As it looks pretty certain that we will be writing the history books,' John said, 'Hamburg will be recorded as a necessary evil to bring victory closer.'

He stood before the fireplace in the library, glass in hand, and faced the family. Joan had remained to be with her brother, and Jolinda was also home, anxiously watching her husband's face. She knew better than any of them just how affected he was by what had happened, what he had helped to do.

'But there's a "but"?' Mark suggested.

'I don't think it's something that any of us can ever be proud of,' John said. 'Do you know, they are estimating that more than forty thousand people died, mostly burned to death. In one night! The estimated deaths in London from the Blitz is thirty-two thousand – over six months.'

'You know that Max was in the city.'

'Yes.'

'If you had known, before the raid, would you have still gone ahead?' Helen asked.

Mark looked embarrassed, but John reacted vehemently. 'Of

course I would. We are fighting a war. I had hoped to get him in my sights again, one day. Now . . .'

'We don't know he's dead,' Jolinda said.

'It seems that just about everyone who was in Hamburg is dead,' Joan pointed out.

'We'll drink a toast to him,' Mark decided. 'Clements—'

'I have it here, sir.' Clements had already uncorked the bottle of Bollinger. Now he filled the glasses and handed them out.

Mark raised his. 'To Max. If anyone could have survived such a holocaust, he will have. You may have him in your sights yet, Johnnie.'

Faces. And pain. Both were everywhere, but while the pain was constant, the faces came and went. He did not recognize any of them, in the beginning, nor was he sure he wanted to. They spoke, and he could not hear them. He tried to speak to them, and the words seemed trapped inside his brain, unable to get out. This was irritating, as perhaps they understood. Someone held up a mirror, and he gazed at a head totally encased in white bandages, with only the eyes exposed. Were they his eyes?

The faces were friendly, sympathetic, anxious, but every so often, far too often, they seemed to find it necessary to do things to him, and then the pain became so unbearable that he screamed in agony. But they kept on doing it, just the same.

Heavily sedated as he was, he had no sense of time. Memory was so vivid that he felt it might have happened ten minutes before – that wall, seeming to hang above him, immediately before he lost consciousness, Elena screaming, the burning people running towards him . . . And then there was nothing.

A face he recognized! Gunther! And Hildegarde? Her face was distorted with grief as she bent over him. He could see her lips moving, knew she was speaking to him. As always, he replied, but she did not seem to hear him. And then there was one of those huge winged headdresses. Elena! It had to be Elena. But it was not.

'I think we can take some of these off,' Dr Berndorff said. His was a bluff face, one with which Max had become increasingly familiar over the past . . . was it days, or weeks, or even months? But recently he had been able to hear, and the pain had started to recede. Or had he become so used to it that it no longer dominated his life? He had certainly become aware of what was happening to him, that he was encased in bandages and plaster from head to foot, was being fed on an intravenous drip, had his involuntary bodily functions attended to by the nurses, who also endeavoured to keep him clean. He had also been aware that Hilde's face had often been hovering above him, more composed with each visit, as she had apparently been convinced that he would live.

But what would become of him? Suddenly he was overwhelmed with anxiety, as gentle hands began to unravel the bandages swathing his face and head. What would she see on her next visit?

Now he could hear quite clearly. 'Where am I?' His voice was nothing more than a whisper.

'You are in Berlin.'

The other side of the country from Hamburg. He had no memory of making so long a journey. 'And what date is it?'

'The fifth of October.'

'But . . .'

'Yes, Herr General. You have been in our care for nine weeks.'

Nine weeks! 'When do I leave?'

Berndorff gave a deprecatory smile. 'You must be patient, Herr General. You are very fortunate to be alive at all. Do you realize just how badly injured you were? Are?'

'I wish you to tell me.'

'Well, let me see. You were taken to the Hamburg hospital with two broken legs and a ruptured vertebra. During your escape from the hospital one of your legs was broken again, and you fractured two more vertebrae. You also broke your arm and several ribs, and suffered a severe head wound. Then you also suffered several second-degree burns. That was the result of debris falling on you.'

'It was a wall.'

'Eh?'

'The wall of the hospital collapsed, and I was under it.'

'There, you see. You have had an even more fortunate escape than we supposed.'

'But what happened to the woman, Elena?'

'Elena who?'

'I have no idea. She got me out. She saved my life.'

'I have no record of anyone named Elena.'

'Then how did I survive?'

'You were picked out of the river by one of the police launches. Even with your broken arm, you were clinging to a spar of wood. You have a very strong sense of self-preservation.'

'But I could not even have been conscious. I remember nothing of it. Don't you see, Doctor? Elena must have carried me into the water, and found me that piece of wood. And then . . .'

'Now, Herr General, you must not excite yourself. I will see if anyone has heard of this woman. Unfortunately, as you can imagine, while we know the hospital employed staff from all over Germany, all the records were consumed in the flames.'

'She came from Baden-Baden,' Max muttered. 'She had family there.'

'A woman named Elena, who had family in Baden-Baden.' Berndorff looked across Max at the waiting Sister, his expression conveying his opinion that they might have a problem with the General's mind. 'We will see what we can do, of course. Now, Herr General, would you like me to call your wife?'

'Of course I wish to see my wife. And my son.'

'She comes every day,' Berndorff explained.

'I know that. I have seen her.'

'But she has not seen you.'

'What do you mean? She has been here, in this room.'

'Indeed. But until today you have been bandaged. She has not been able to see your face.'

Max stared at him, and he snapped his fingers. Sister held a mirror in front of Max's face, and he caught his breath. He was looking at a skull, the bones clearly visible through the paper-thin skin stretched across it, and the skin itself was discoloured in places, almost black.

'This is a temporary condition, of course,' Berndorff explained. 'As you start eating proper food, and drinking lots of milk, your flesh will fill out.'

'Those marks . . .'

'Are where you were burned. They will fade. But these things take time.'

'Can you not warn my wife?'

'Of course I will, Herr General. But . . .'

'I still wish to see her, as soon as possible.'

'Yes, sir. And the boy?'

Max considered. 'I will leave that up to her.'

Sister spoke in an arch whisper. 'The Field-Marshal is here.'

Max could feel his muscles involuntarily contracting into attention, even lying on his back. But he had known this moment had to come, and that it was going to be a defining moment.

Milch stood above the bed, Sister having tactfully left the room. 'I am told you are improving every day.'

'I believe I am, Herr Field-Marshal. They tell me I am putting on weight, and I am soon to start a limited physiotherapy programme to get some strength back into my legs.'

Milch nodded, and sat down. 'The things they can do nowadays. But it will take time.'

'I am afraid so, sir. But not a day longer than is necessary. I want to get fit to fly a 262.'

A shadow passed over the Field-Marshal's face. 'That is unlikely to happen for the foreseeable future.'

'The doctors say a few months . . .'

'The development and production of the 262 has been put on hold until further orders.'

'But . . .'

'That is a directive from the Fuehrer, Max. As we have discussed before, our supplies of high-quality steel are limited, and it is a matter of priorities, of deciding where that steel can best be employed for the protection of the Reich, and indeed for the achievement of ultimate victory.'

'But surely victory can only be possible if we regain air superiority?'

'That is the view of any airman, certainly. The Fuehrer thinks otherwise. His priorities are more Tiger tanks, and more U-boats. There are sound military reasons for that decision. We have suffered severe casualties in the east, and we need to double the size of our Panzer armies if the Russians are to be stopped. And starving Great Britain into surrender promises a quicker victory than shooting down their planes. And of course, our rocket programme must also have high priority. You see, it is all a matter of urgency, and we have had to make some hard decisions. Once we are in full production, we can turn out a hundred flying bombs a week. It takes not less than a year to produce a hundred 262s, and two years to train the pilots to fly them. That is not a practical timescale in our situation. When we resume blasting their cities, and if at the same time we can cut off their supplies from the United States, we can still force them to a negotiated peace.'

'Despite what Roosevelt and Churchill said at Casablanca? Unconditional surrender or nothing?'

Milch waved his hand. 'Rhetoric, to appeal to their masses.'

'And you genuinely believe we can still come out of this with a negotiated peace? A nurse said yesterday that there is a rumour the British and the Americans have landed in Italy. That Italy is out of the war.'

'That is perfectly true.'

Max stared at him.

'Oh, let us be honest, for once, Max,' Milch said. 'The Italians have always been a complete liability. If the Fuehrer has made one serious mistake in this war it is his almost slavish loyalty to Mussolini. So what is the result? Rescuing the Italians from that debacle in Greece cost us a vital month in 1941. Not even the Russians deny that had we invaded in May instead of June we would have taken Moscow before the weather broke. Rescuing the Italians from that debacle in North Africa cost us men and materiel which would have been invaluable in Russia and has now cost us an entire army, and God knows how much prestige. So now they are definitely out of the war. Good riddance. There is even talk that they may decide to come in on the Allied side. That will make life simpler for us, and more difficult for the Allies.

'But if the Allies are in mainland Italy . . .'

'They are not going to get very far. We have constructed a series of defensive lines across the boot, each one stronger than the last.'

'But we are still committed to a wholly defensive policy, trying to hold the Allies in the south, the Russians in the east, while the Allies blow hell out of us in the west.'

'You are feeling depressed,' Milch asserted. 'I do not blame you, after what you have gone through.'

'I am alive, Herr Field-Marshal. How many died in Hamburg?'

Milch grimaced. 'The latest figure estimates more than forty thousand.'

'In one city, in one night.'

'No, no. It was over the three nights. They are calling it the Battle of Hamburg. I'm afraid we have to concede defeat there. The docks are destroyed, and so are most of the factories.'

'Which is more important than forty thousand people,' Max said with bitter sarcasm. And one nurse named Elena; there could be little doubt that she had died saving his life. And there could be no exculpation from the thought that she would have died anyway, as had everyone else in the hospital, even if she had been sheltering in the cellars.

Milch took the comment seriously. 'I'm afraid it is, in the context of a war of survival.'

'So do you have any idea which city is next on their list for obliteration?'

'Who can tell? We must do the best we can. There is no use in hanging our heads and wailing "woe is me". Jeschonneck did that.'

'Perhaps he is a realist,' Max suggested.

'Was.'

'Sir?'

'Colonel-General Jeschonneck shot himself, last week.'

'Oh, my God!'

'It was not because of Hamburg. It was despair at the cancellation of the 262 programme. He regarded the new machine as the panacea to all our ills.'

'We all did, Herr Field-Marshal. How is Galland taking it?'

'Adolf is, like you, a fighting airman who does the best he can with what he is given. He is disappointed, of course. But he is carrying on. As will you, as soon as you are up and about. I have filled Jeschonneck's place temporarily. The moment you are fit enough, I wish you to take over.'

'Me, Herr Field-Marshal? Surely Galland . . .'

'Adolf is senior to you, certainly. But he is still a combat airman, and we need him in that capacity. You are not.'

Max stared at him.

'I am sorry to have to spell this out, Max. But surely you already know in your heart that you will never fly again? You have suffered the most terrible injuries and yet you have survived. And you still have a great deal to offer the Reich, through your experience, your proven courage, your determination. I want you, Max. I need you.'

'You pay me a great compliment, sir. And you are prepared to wait?'

'Yes, Max. I am prepared to wait. Where will you convalesce when you get out of here?'

'I thought of going down to Bitterman.'

'Ah, yes. In Bavaria. Where your cousin lives.'

'Yes, sir. It is in a remote area, well away from any bombs. It will be good for Hilde and the boy.'

'And you are sure of a welcome there? Does your cousin know anything of the matter we discussed last year?'

'He has never mentioned it. Nor have I. But he must be aware of the situation.'

'Hmm. But you do intend to mention it?'

'I thought perhaps when the war is over, Herr Field-Marshal.'

'Hmm,' Milch said again. 'I wonder if it is wise to wait that long. What of the daughter? The infamous Erika.'

'Is she infamous?'

'She is doing her best to become so. Did you know she is under investigation by the Party?'

'Sir?'

'She has a wide circle of friends, not all of them . . . appropriate. Also, she does nothing, and has done nothing, for the Reich since the war began. Did you know that Haussmann has divorced her?'

'I knew that they had quarrelled,' Max said cautiously.

'The reason given is adultery. But, as you may know, the Gestapo has a long memory, and they remember that Erika was Heidi's closest friend.'

Max felt tension creeping through his body; it was a painful process. 'I was Heidi's husband, sir.'

'Of course. But you were not here during the period she was seeing that British agent. If you had been, you would probably have sued *her* for adultery.'

Max preferred not to answer that. He had been so captivated by Heidi Stumpff's beauty that he doubted he could ever have divorced her. His memory of Heidi – the Heidi who had presented herself to him, as opposed to the real Heidi – was, he had no doubt, mainly responsible for his continued weakness for wishing to get close to women, despite the fact that he now had Hilde genuinely to love and to be loved by. That all the women he had tried to help had met with catastrophe simply renewed his sense of failure as a man. A sense that had now become overwhelming, because of his physical condition.

Milch was studying him. 'I did not mean to upset you, Max. I want only the best for you, as I hope you understand. I simply do not wish you to be drawn into any seditious plots. Or even discuss them. With anyone.'

'You would prefer me not to go to Bitterman.'

'Of course you must go to Bitterman. It is your home.' He peered at Max. 'Does Hildegarde object to, as you put it, being buried in the country? You have just said that it is the best place for her and the boy.'

'I think she would love to live at Bitterman. She found it quite beautiful there.'

'And I would say she is more important than anything, or anyone, else.' Milch got up. 'Well, you will have a couple of months together there, to think about things. Just remember what I have told you, and remember also that if at any time you wish, or find it necessary, to assume full control of the property, you will have my backing. I look forward to your restoration to full health. Heil Hitler!'

The door closed, and Max stared at the ceiling. What the Field-Marshal had really meant, he knew, was that the Gestapo's long memory included him, for his assault upon one of their leading officers when he had learned of Heidi's arrest, and equally, his assault on that SS officer who had hanged the woman Galina. They would never dare touch Germany's leading fighter ace – who was also a national hero – but if his flying days were over, and he would thus sink out of the public eye, even if he were on Milch's staff, he would suddenly become vulnerable, supposing they could ever link him to any other subversive activities.

'Are you all right, Herr General?' Sister asked solicitously.

'Not really,' Max said. 'I think I need a sedative.'

'You will be a Colonel-General,' Hildegarde said as she pushed the wheelchair along the bridle path. Even if it was December, in southern Bavaria the weather was not yet cold, although Max was well concealed beneath a blanket. 'I am so proud of you.'

'Even if I cannot walk,' he remarked.

'You will walk. You are coming along in leaps and bounds. You are so impatient.' She turned the chair to go back; the battlements of Schloss Bitterman appeared over the slight rise.

'Am I being impatient to want to have sex with you?'

'I suppose not. Because you are a man, and men associate sex with loving. Do you think I really care whether you can have sex or not? I am just happy to have you in one piece.'

'Don't you realize that we are living on borrowed time? All of us. You, me, and Baby.'

'Oh, really, sweetheart. You are just twenty-four; Baby is just one. And I am twenty-seven. God, how old that makes me seem. But I don't think I have one foot in the grave just yet.'

'And when the Russians cross the Vistula? They are going to do that, you know, within a couple of months. And when the Allies cross the Channel? That too is liable to happen next year. Not to mention crossing the Alps.'

Hildegarde stopped pushing, and the chair came to a halt. 'Do you really think those things are likely to happen? You were so positive last year, when I was the doubter.'

'Hilde, I have just realized that these things are certain to happen.'

'You have been told this? Milch told you this?'

'No, he did not. I don't know how sincere he is, but he continues to claim that we can still win, or at least force the Allies to make peace. He is relying on things like these new "flying bombs", as they are called. A thousand tons of high explosive delivered with absolute accuracy to any target in the heart of London, or anywhere else we choose. He says a combination of them and the U-boats will bring Britain to its knees, while the new Tiger tanks hold the Russians in the east.'

'And you don't want to believe him.'

'Oh, I *want* to believe him, Hilde. But common sense tells me it isn't going to work.'

She started pushing again. 'You will feel better as your strength comes back.'

'Maybe. But can you blame me for wanting to have sex with you as much as possible while we have the time?'

She kissed the top of his head then looked up as they approached the drive. 'Visitors?'

'Shit!' Max cried. He had recognized the small Volkswagen.

* * *

Oriane stood in the huge castle doorway. 'Max!' she cried, her voice even higher than usual. 'You'll never guess who's come to visit.'

'I already have.' Max looked past her at Erika, emerging from the hall. 'Good morning, Erika.'

'Max!' Erika screamed, half falling down the steps, and then halting in front of him. 'My God! What have they done to you?'

'I think you can probably take your pick. You haven't met my wife. Hilde, this is my cousin Erika.'

'Hildegarde! I have heard so much about you.'

'Have you?' Hildegarde was surprised, but she allowed Erika to take her hand.

'Max and I have no secrets from each other.'

'How nice for you,' Hildegarde said quietly.

'Erika is given to exaggeration,' Max assured her.

'I think we need to get you into the house,' Hildegarde said. 'It has become quite chilly.'

'Let me help you,' Erika said.

'Well . . .'

'Herman!' Oriane shouted. 'Herr Max wants a hand.'

'I'm sure we can manage, Mother,' Erika said, grasping one of the arms of the chair.

'We will wait for Herman,' Max said.

And at that moment the butler appeared. He did most of the work, assisted by Hildegarde, although Erika insisted on retaining her grip. 'Do you have to do this every day?' she panted as they reached the top of the steps.

'It is no hardship,' Hildegarde said.

'Well, I think we all need a drink. Papa!'

Bitterman, who had apparently been in his office doing accounts, hurried in and poured schnapps. 'Well, now,' he said. 'Here is the whole family together. We should drink a toast. To us.'

'Should not Little Max join us?' Erika asked.

Hildegarde shot her a glance.

'Mama took me to the nursery to see him. Such a pretty little boy.'

'You mean you woke him up from his nap?' Max accused.

'No, no. He was awake and playing with his blocks.' Erika giggled. 'That dragon you have looking after him actually shooed us off.'

'That is her business,' Max pointed out. 'Looking after him.'

'I have to go upstairs anyway,' Hildegarde said. 'I'll bring him down.'

She left the room.

'Such a charming girl,' Erika remarked. 'Even if she is a little . . . well . . .'

'What were you going to say?' Max inquired, his voice deceptively low.

'Well, a little bourgeois, wouldn't you say?'

'A toast,' Bitterman hastily cut in. 'We can drink another when Hildegarde comes down.'

'I think,' Max said, 'that before we drink a toast, Erika should rephrase her last remark.'

'Why should I?' Erika inquired. 'I say what I think, when I think it. If people take offence, it is usually because I am telling the truth.'

'If I take offence,' Max said, 'it is because I dislike boors and hypocrites.'

'Oh, dear,' Oriane muttered.

Erika stared at him from beneath arched eyebrows.

'I have brought Hildegarde here,' Max said, still speaking quietly, 'so that she can be with me while I recuperate. And she is going to remain here after I have recuperated and returned to duty. If you intend to continue to visit, I suggest you say or do nothing to upset her. If you are unable to do that, then I suggest that you leave.'

Erika closed her mouth, and then opened it again. 'You . . . I . . .' She turned to her father. 'Are you going to let him speak to me like this? Acting as if this was *his* house.'

'Well . . .' Bitterman looked into his glass as if seeking inspiration, then drank without waiting for the toast. 'The fact is, my dear, that it *is* his house.'

'What did you say?'

'Schloss Bitterman is my property, Erika,' Max said. 'By the terms of our grandfather's will, which left his entire estate to my mother, but which also required her to leave the estate to her eldest son as and when he came of age. I happen to be that son, but as my mother died *before* I came of age, and as she never discussed such matters with me, I did not learn of it until two years ago. I did not do anything about it then, because I happened to be fighting a war for the Reich. I do not intend to do anything about it now, until the war is over. I have no wish to turn Max and Oriane out. But I do intend for my wife to live here, because, as my wife, she is just as much the owner of the schloss as I am.'

Erika continued to stare at him for several seconds before turning and leaving the room.

'That was about the grimmest meal I have ever had,' Hildegarde confessed in their bedroom after dinner. 'Did you have to be so . . . well, brutal about it?'

'Believe me, my dearest girl, people like Erika only understand brutality, although I will admit they prefer to dish it out than to receive it.'

'You were in love with her, once.'

'Yes, I was. And I suppose I still have a soft spot for her. But I am not going to let her upset you.'

'Them, you mean.' Hildegarde hugged herself. 'They all hate us.'

'Darling,' Max said. 'The whole world hates us. Because we're German.'

She raised her head; her eyes were stricken. 'What are we to do?'

'Survive. For as long as possible. And love each other.'

'Come in, John.' Both Group Captain Hastings and Group Captain Spencer were in the office. 'I would say that you have probably flown over north-western France more often than any other pilot in England.'

'I have been there a few times, sir,' John said modestly.

'So tell us if, in the course of your flights, you have seen these before.'

The photographs were spread across the desk. John studied them, frowning. 'I can't say I have. May I ask from what height these were taken?'

'Approximately ten thousand feet.'

'Ah.'

'Why?'

'I was going to say that they look like the entrance to mine shafts. You know, the sort of sloped platforms down which carts can be pushed or dragged. You can just make out the tracks along which the carts would be pushed or pulled. But if these were taken from ten thousand feet, well, they would have to be enormous mines.'

'Quite,' Spencer agreed. 'Do you suppose they could possibly be launch pads? They are certainly sloping down into the earth. But could they not also be considered to be sloping up *out* of the earth?'

'I see what you mean, sir. You think that under the earth there could be some kind of huge gun? A sort of latter day Big Bertha, which can be wheeled up the ramp for firing and then withdrawn out of sight? But if that were so . . .' He picked up one of the photographs to study it more closely. 'If the idea is to bombard us, such a gun should surely be sited near the coast. There is nothing here to suggest the sea or a coastline. From ten thousand feet that should clearly be visible.'

'Absolutely. You have undoubtedly got hold of the right idea. But you are thinking in the past, rather than the future. Or, as I am afraid may be likely, the present.'

'You've lost me.'

'Well, you haven't had access to the secret information that we receive from the French Resistance. This suggests that Jerry is working on some kind of large, unmanned delivery system.'

'Unmanned? Who would control it?'

'The idea is a bit of the Buck Rogers or Flash Gordon variety, I know,' Spencer said. 'But it is actually feasible. You build a rocket and fill it with high explosive, equip it with a gyroscopic compass which will take it in the required direction, and with fuel tanks that will burn for a certain number of hours, and launch it. So it flies along its selected route until the fuel runs out, by which time, if the calculations have been correct, it should be over its target. Then its engine stops, and it drops. If you consider the device as a vast shell, fired from some huge gun, only it's self-propelled, well, as I say, it's quite practical.'

'It doesn't sound too clever to me,' John objected. 'I mean, it's not going to be a shell. You have described it as a rocket. How far can a rocket fly, anyway?'

'As far as its fuel permits.'

'You mean, it could reach London?'

'Theoretically. It could certainly reach the southern counties.'

'Where,' Hastings put in, 'the build-up to D-Day is underway.'

'And you think one rocket can disrupt that?'

'One rocket? Hardly. But if they had a whole fleet of them . . .'

John scratched his ear. 'I still don't see how they hope to get through. I mean, a conventional bomber, when attacked, can try either to fight back or take evasive action. If this machine has no pilot, and a pre-selected course which cannot be varied, well, it would be a sitting duck.' He grinned. 'Will we be allowed to add each one to our tally of kills?'

'By all means,' Hastings agreed. 'But supposing you – even you – couldn't catch it?'

'Rockets, by definition, travel very fast,' Spencer said. 'Faster even than a Mosquito. That is clearly what Jerry has in mind.'

'But when the Meteor comes into service—'

'When. Not for another six months at the very earliest. We have to know how soon these flying bombs may be ready. So it's back to your earliest role: photo reconnaissance. I'm sending your flight because these sites are certain to be protected. But I want you to go in low and get close-ups of what is going on. Photograph anything the least bit suspicious or even out of the ordinary – and, of course, these ramps themselves. Our Intelligence will decipher what you bring back.'

'Wilco,' John said. 'And suppose we see something worth shooting at? Like one of these rockets being transported, or tried out?'

'We're going to have to leave that to your judgement. Please bear in mind that even if you were to hit one of these things and send it up, that is hardly likely to disrupt their programme. It is more important that you come back with the photos. You will leave at dawn tomorrow, and I will expect you back for lunch.'

'That's what the man said,' John told Evan and Lewis. 'It's the photos that matter. We go in as low as we can, take our snaps, and come home. So we enter in single file, me first, you second, Taffy, and you third, Lew. If you're shot at, you may return fire, but not if it in any way interferes with your mission. Understood?'

They did not look particularly happy at the assignment, but John reckoned that might be because they were no longer used to being woken up before dawn on a cold winter's morning. He settled himself into his seat, adjusted his straps. 'All set?'

'Yes, sir.' Langley had his equipment ready.

The tower gave them the all clear, and he spoke into his mike. 'Thirty thousand until we are over the target. When you have completed your run, regain that height and come home. Do not worry about formation. Get home.'

'Message understood,' the other two pilots replied.

'Then go.'

It had just been getting light on the ground, but almost immediately they were in heavy cloud. But at five thousand feet the air was clear, and the sun was already up on the eastern horizon. The day brightened steadily as they climbed as rapidly as possible. But they were only at thirty thousand feet for a few minutes, and then Langley said, 'Time.'

The three Mosquitoes dived steeply, plunging back into cloud. Langley set his camera, and at five thousand feet they were again clear, although below them the day remained gloomy. 'Enough light?' John asked.

'Oh, yes, sir,' Langley said. 'Target in line, distance five miles.'

They had come the whole way on the radio beam, and were down to three thousand feet. John went lower yet, the soggy winter landscape of Flanders opening below him. At a thousand feet he could clearly see traffic on the road, and some agitation as the three aircraft hurtled over the watchers on the ground.

'Bingo!' Langley said, snapping away. John looked down and saw the massive ramp, the scattering men. There was an anti-aircraft gun in position and this opened fire, but nothing came remotely close.

'Another run, sir,' Langley suggested.

John sent the Mosquito into a steep climb while turning, still followed by his flight.

'You know what,' Langley said, 'we could drop a bomb right down that slot.'

'Not much good unless there is something down there, and we don't know that. Get your photos.'

'Bandits, two o'clock,' Lewis said.

John turned his head and saw the swarm of 210s just emerging from the thick cloud a few thousand feet above the English squadron. They were already very close, and he realized that in tactical terms they had been caught napping. 'OK,' he said.

'We are not here to fight. Take out who you have to, but let's go home.'

He climbed and was overtaken by a stream of red tracers. It was a long time since he had been that close to an enemy fighter. But as always he had not been hit and, following his instructions, he ignored the attack and continued to climb, only to hear Evans's voice shout, 'I'm hit.'

John looked over his shoulder, and Langley said, 'Holy shit! Look at that fellow!'

John had already levelled off preparatory to returning to help his friend, and now he saw what the sergeant meant. The fuselage of the 210 that had fired at him and missed, but had struck Evans on his tail, was covered in a mass of black bars, above which was the unmistakable marking of a wing-leader; the rank in the Luftwaffe being much higher than wing-commander in the RAF.

'That must be a hundred-plus kills,' Langley said. 'You don't reckon that could be your brother, sir?'

That's not possible, John thought. Max was at death's door only a few months ago. And yet . . .

'Sir?' Langley asked, as the Mosquito dropped down; Lewis was obeying orders and making for home with his precious photographs, while both Evans and his navigator had managed to bail out and were floating earthwards above their blazing machine.

John had switched wavelengths and could hear the German voices shouting a warning. And the Wing-Leader was also turning to climb for an engagement. 'Nine lives,' John said, speaking German. 'But this is your last.'

The Messerschmitt pilot had realized that he was not going to gain sufficient height in time, and levelled off, guns blazing. But he could not hit the Mosquito travelling at full speed, and now he was in John's sights. John loosed both rockets and saw his target explode in a ball of fire. Then he was soaring upwards again and turning for home.

The Whirlwind

John parked his bike and went to the door, to be welcomed as always by Clements and Rufus, with the usual exchange about the weather. But the butler could tell that his young master was not in the mood for humour.

Jolinda came down the stairs to greet him. 'Johnnie! I wasn't sure you'd make it.'

John kissed her. 'Special op, two days off.'

'Oh, hell. I'm on duty tomorrow.' She held his hand as they went through the drawing room, pausing for the obligatory salute to Karolina. 'But the op was a success?' She knew better than to ask what it was.

'Yes and no. We did what we were sent to do, but we lost Taffy Evans and his crew. I think they're all right, but they're prisoners of war.'

'Oh, shoot!' Jolinda had never met Evans, but she knew he had been John's wingman for the past few months. 'How did it happen? Another lucky shot?'

'No. Dad in the library?' He had seen the Rolls in the garage.

'Yes.' Jolinda's tone was watchful; she could tell that something even more serious than the loss of Evans had happened.

John continued into the library. 'Johnnie,' Mark said. 'We didn't know you were coming in tonight. Drink?'

'I'll get it,' Jolinda volunteered.

'I was given a special furlough to come home,' John said as he sat down.

Mark frowned. 'Problems?'

Jolinda opened her mouth and then changed her mind; whatever had happened, it was John's business to tell his father. She gave her husband his drink and poured one for herself.

'We lost Evans and his crew,' John said.

'Is he the one you call Taffy?' Helen asked. 'Oh, what a shame.'

Mark was studying his son. 'That isn't the end of it.'

John drank deeply. 'No,' he agreed. 'We were surprised. We were flying very low on what was basically a photo recce, and this squadron of 210s suddenly dropped out of the clouds. Their leader fired at me, but he missed, and struck Taffy instead.'

'That *is* bad luck,' Mark commented. 'Although of course we're glad he missed you.'

'The pilot had the markings of a wing-leader,' John said quietly. 'And more than a hundred bars on his fuselage.'

His father stared at him, as did the two women. 'That's not possible,' Mark said. 'The Germans themselves admitted that he had a broken back, two broken legs, and a broken arm. Six months ago. No one can have recovered from injuries like that in six months.'

'Maybe. But I saw the markings. So did Chris Langley.'

'Did you see his face?' Jolinda asked.

'Well, no. It all happened very fast, and he was wearing an oxygen mask.'

'Well,' Mark said. 'If he has recovered that quickly, he must have the constitution of an ox.'

'Or a Bayley,' Jolinda suggested.

'You have to say good luck to him.'

'Too late for that,' John said.

Again they all stared at him.

'I put two rockets into him. The plane exploded.'

'And . . .'

'He went up with it. There was no sign of a parachute. He wouldn't have had time.'

The room was silent; Mark looked into his empty glass. Jolinda took it from his fingers, but he shook his head.

'I had to do it, Dad,' John said.

'I know that.' Mark raised his voice. 'Clements!'

'Sir.'

'The Bollinger. We'll drink a toast to a very special gentleman.'

Jolinda lay with her nose close to John's shoulder. They had not had sex; much as they normally treasured these brief breaks together, she had understood that he was not in the mood this time. 'Is it over?' she asked.

He turned his head. 'There's a way to go yet. Maybe a long way.'

'I was thinking of your personal trauma.'

He put his arm round her to hold her against him. 'Can killing your own brother ever be over?'

'You said you hated him.'

'Yes, I did. And I did hate him, for being a traitor, for letting the family down, for being an enemy – and for what he did to you.'

'You don't know he had anything to do with that.'

He kissed her. 'It's easier to believe that he did.'

'Now,' Dr Eisner said. 'The great day, eh?'

'As you say, Herr Doctor.' Max looked at Hildegarde, standing on the other side of the bed, and she squeezed his hand. She knew that, for all the many dangerous and indeed life-threatening experiences he had endured in the course of the war, he was probably more apprehensive at this moment than ever before in his life.

'If you will assist us, Frau Bayley? Just to start things off.'

'Of course, Herr Doctor. I'll just put the chair here, shall I, in case we need it?'

'No, no,' the physiotherapist said. 'We do not wish to see that chair. Put it outside in the hall. We are never going to look at that chair again. Are we, Herr General?'

'If you say so, Herr Doctor.' Max looked at Hildegarde and winked. At least, she reflected, however apprehensive he might be, he was tackling the problem with his usual élan. She wheeled the chair into the corridor and returned to wait by the bed.

'Now, sir,' Eisner said, and peeled back the sheet. Hildegarde sighed; every day for the past month Max had undergone extensive physiotherapy, and the muscles had undoubtedly regained some strength, and yet every time she looked at those wasted legs protruding from beneath the night shirt she had a pang of despair. 'If you will sit up.'

Max pushed himself up, also looking down the bed at his legs.

'There is no discomfort?'

'Not right this minute.'

'Now, swing your legs out of bed.'

Max looked at Hildegarde.

'No, no,' Eisner said. 'Your wife is not to help you this morning. She is not to help you get out of bed ever again, Herr General. It must be your will, your decision. I just want you to sit on the edge of the bed.'

Max drew a long breath, gritted his teeth, and swung his legs out of the bed, to let them dangle.

'There you are,' Eisner said enthusiastically. 'You never know what you can do until you try. Now, Frau Bayley.'

Hildegarde brought the crutches from the wall against which they had been leaning.

'One in each armpit,' Eisner said, beckoning Hildegarde to assist him in placing the crutches. 'Now, for this morning, we will help you get to your feet. Don't attempt to move immediately. Just stand there, getting your balance, and getting used to the feel of the crutches. Frau Bayley?'

Hildegarde grasped one arm. Eisner took the other, and they gently lifted Max, most of his weight being taken by the crutches. Eisner made sure they were firmly placed on the carpet, then nodded. Taking another deep breath, Hildegarde released the arm and stepped away. Eisner did the same. Left to himself, Max swayed slightly.

'Just concentrate, Herr General,' Eisner said. 'You can do it.'

Again Max gritted his teeth, and slowly regained his balance.

'Excellent!' Eisner declared. 'Excellent! Frau Bayley?'

Hildegarde had been briefed as to what she should do. She crossed the room to stand against the wall, some ten feet away.

'Now, Herr General,' Eisner said. 'Go to your wife.'

Max took a deep breath and gazed at Hildegarde, who held up her arms for him, then moved the right-hand crutch forward, transferring his weight as he did so. A pause while he regained his balance, then he swung the left-hand crutch, but this movement was two vigorous. The crutch went out and he collapsed, prevented from falling full length by Hildegarde, who started forward to catch him. 'Max! My darling! Are you all right?'

Max was on his knees. 'If you mean apart from being crippled,' he said with bitter frustration, 'then yes, I am all right.'

'But that was splendid,' Eisner said. 'Splendid!'

'What? One step?'

The doctor helped him up, and with the aid of Hildegarde sat him in a chair. 'One step, on your first attempt? What more could you expect? One step today, two steps tomorrow, a hundred metres in a month, a thousand in two months. That is our programme.'

'So tell me when I am going to fly again.'

'Ah . . . well . . . let us get you walking first. Then we will think about the other things, reflexes, muscular response, mental agility. We must start at the beginning, Herr General. But we will get there in the end.'

Max looked at Hildegarde, who half turned her head. 'There is a car engine.'

'If it's Erika come back again . . .'

'I do not think,' Hildegarde remarked, 'after what happened the last time, that Erika means to come back at all.' She went to the window, looked down into the courtyard. 'Ooh! It is an official car.'

'Berlin,' Max growled. 'Sending to find out how soon I can report for duty. What do I tell them, Doctor?'

'That it may be a little while yet, but for a desk job, well . . . six weeks.'

'A desk job,' Max muttered.

Oriane appeared in the doorway. 'It's Field-Marshal Milch!' she squealed.

'What?' All three of them faced the door, like rabbits caught in a car's headlights, Hildegarde thought.

'Thank you, Countess.' Milch entered the room. 'Max, how good to see you. Hilde.' He embraced Hildegarde, then regarded the doctor without enthusiasm.

'Walter Eisner, Herr Field-Marshal. Physiotherapy.' Anxiously he extended his hand.

Milch's squeeze was perfunctory. 'I was told that General Bayley would be up and about by now.'

'Well, as you can see, Herr Field-Marshal, he is out of bed.'

'But not standing.'

'He was standing a few minutes ago. But . . . well . . . he is not yet used to his crutches.'

'When will he be fit for duty?'

'We were just discussing that very thing, sir. I would say not more than six weeks.'

'Six weeks,' Milch said, half to himself. 'Thank you, Dr Eisner. I will speak with you later.'

Eisner hesitated, but he understood that he had been dismissed, gave a bow, and sidled from the room.

'If you will excuse us,' Milch said.

Oriane was still hovering in the doorway. 'Of course, Herr Field-Marshal. Will you stay for lunch?'

'Thank you. It has been a long drive.'

Oriane looked at Hildegarde. 'Well,' Hildegarde said, 'I will leave you to it.'

'I wish you to stay,' Milch said. 'Would you close the door, please, Countess?'

Oriane gave a loud sniff but she left the room, closing the door behind her.

'I will fetch another chair,' Hildegarde volunteered.

'I can sit on the bed,' Milch said, and did so. 'How seriously do you take the medical mumbo-jumbo?'

'Eisner believes what he says,' Max said. 'However—'

'He cannot walk,' Hildegarde interjected.

'But he will, in time.'

'Yes, but . . .'

'A serious situation has arisen,' Milch said. 'Gunther Langholm is dead.'

'Oh, my God!' Hildegarde cried. 'How?'

Max said nothing, just stared at the Field-Marshal.

'He led a squadron to attack and disperse a flight of Mosquitoes, who were photographing one of our more secret installations in the Pas de Calais. He actually brought one of them down, but was then hit by another. Two rockets. His plane exploded before he could get out.'

He gave a brief smile, 'The British think it was you. Gunther had more than a hundred kills, and he was commanding the Wing. We have not corrected this misapprehension so far. The fact is that Gunther was almost as charismatic a figure as you, Max. His men worshipped him. Since his death, and with you out of action, morale has slumped. We need you to restore that morale.'

'You promised him a desk job,' Hildegarde said.

'And he will get it, in due course, but at this moment, his presence in the Flanders Wing is more important. There can be no doubt that the Allies are going to attempt to invade

Fortress Europe this summer, and all logical military opinion
holds that this invasion will take place across the narrowest
part of the English Channel. That is the Pas de Calais. It will
be the task of the Flanders Air Fleet to make such an invasion as difficult as possible, if not impossible. As you well
know, Max, air superiority is the decisive factor in battle
nowadays.'

'He cannot *walk*!' Hildegarde shouted.

'I believe that your very presence will make all the difference,' Milch said. 'Your re-emergence from the dead, eh? And
it will distress the Tommies and the Yanks. They think you
are dead. When they are faced with the fact that you are actually alive, well . . . They do not know that you cannot fly, as
yet. They will expect you to confront them at any moment.
Do you play chess?'

'I know the moves,' Max said, not meeting Hildegarde's
eye.

'Well, there is a saying in chess, and it applies to war as
well, that the threat is greater then the execution. Your presence in Flanders will constitute a threat which may cause them
to re-think their plans, just long enough for us to bring *our*
plans to fruition.'

Now at last Max looked at Hildegarde and saw the concern
in her face.

Milch had observed the look. 'There is something else I
have to say that might interest you,' he said. 'Captain
Mannheimer, who was Gunther's wingman on that day,
reported that the aircraft that shot him down had at least forty
swastikas painted on its fuselage. How many Mosquito pilots
can you think of, Max, who have more than forty kills to their
credit?'

Max's head slowly turned back, while Hildegarde clasped
both hands to her throat. 'I will be honoured, Herr Field-
Marshal, to resume command of the Flanders Fighter Fleet.'

Milch leaned forward to clasp his hand. 'I knew I could
rely on you. When will you be ready?'

'I can leave tomorrow, sir.'

'I would prefer you to be on your feet, if that is possible
in the near future.'

'Of course, sir. I will be on my feet a fortnight from today.'

Hildegarde opened her mouth and then closed it again.

'Excellent. Just to know you are coming should go a long way to restoring morale. The Fuehrer will be pleased. He thinks very highly of you, you know.'

'But he has sent no message of condolence or sympathy,' Hildegarde commented. 'In six months.'

'The Fuehrer is very busy,' Milch said severely. 'He spends nearly all his time at his East Prussian Headquarters at Rastenburg, directing operations against the Soviets. But he is constantly informed of what is happening on our other fronts and, as I say, he is a great admirer of your husband.' He stood up. 'Now, I would like to say hello to Little Max, and then to have lunch. I wish to be back in Berlin tonight, which means leaving Munich by four.' He gave one of his infectious grins. 'One of these days, when we can spare the machine, I will change my old 110 for a 210, eh, and be able to travel a bit faster. But right now, Max, you have priority. May I give you a hand, Hilde?'

Hildegarde looked at Max.

'I think, Herr Field-Marshal,' Max said, 'that as you have no time to waste, we should use the chair.'

'But how do you negotiate the stairs?' Milch snapped his fingers. 'Of course, that peculiar ramp thing you have fitted up, with its block and pulley arrangement. That is brilliant. When you retire from active service, we will employ you as an aircraft designer.'

'It was Hilde's idea,' Max said modestly.

'You understand,' she said that night in bed, 'that he has sweet-talked you into committing suicide?'

'Oh, come now, my darling. How can my life be in danger if I cannot fly?'

'You are going to tell me that when you are in command of all those aircraft you are not going to take one up?'

'I give you my word that I shall not get into an aircraft again, at least until . . .'

'Until when?'

'Until I feel strong enough to do so.'

'That is not acceptable.'

'What do you mean?'

'I would like you to promise that you will not fly again until *I* feel you're strong enough to do so.'

'Now really, Hilde, I am a general.'

'And I am a general's wife, and the mother of his child, who I need to have a father.'

The light had been switched off, and her face was no more than a blur. But Max had heard that tone often enough in the past. And he valued Hilde more even than his career. He took refuge in realities. 'But you will not be there,' he pointed out. 'So how will you know when I am fit to fly?'

'I will know,' she assured him. 'Because I *am* going to be there. Baby and I are coming with you.'

'The pilots are assembled for your address, Herr General,' Peltzer said.

Max looked through the open door, and frowned. 'I need them all here, Peltzer. Every pilot in the fleet.'

'I know that, Herr General. This is your fleet.'

Max looked through the door again, counting.

'There are forty-seven, Herr General,' Peltzer said.

'I have forty-seven pilots to defend north-west France? When last I was here I had forty-plus squadrons. How can forty-seven pilots adequately man the Kammhuber System?'

'The Kammhuber System was abandoned three months ago, sir. Losses have been very heavy. I have accumulated what we have into four squadrons. We are, of course, promised reinforcements.' He lowered his voice. 'We are always promised reinforcements.'

Max regarded him for a moment, then turned to the young woman in secretarial uniform, standing rigidly to attention behind her desk. 'Who is this?'

'Your secretary, Herr General. Fraulein Krantz.'

'Well, Fraulein Krantz, I have a first task for you. I want you to place a person-to-person call to the Air Ministry in Berlin, to Field-Marshal Milch. Use my name, and if there is any problem tell them it is a matter of national security.'

'Yes, Herr General.' She sat down and picked up her telephone.

'Do you still wish to address the pilots, Herr General?' Peltzer asked.

'Of course.'

'Ah . . .'

Max's smile was grim. 'I am going to lie, Peltzer. If I have to send those boys to their deaths, I want them to believe that it will be worthwhile.'

Peltzer gulped and followed him into the next room. 'Gentlemen!' he announced. 'Our new commanding officer: General Max Bayley.'

There was a storm of cheering. Looking over their faces, Max could not doubt that the welcome was genuine. It gave him a warm feeling in his heart, even if this could not quite combat the sickness in his stomach. He had entered the room on his crutches. Now, standing beside the desk, on which he could lean if necessary, he carefully laid them on the table. He had rehearsed this time and again over the past fortnight, with Hildegarde standing at his elbow to catch him if he fell. Now he was on his own, but he felt confident enough, as long as he did not have to move.

'Gentlemen,' he said. 'Thank you. You will observe that the suggestions that I am a total cripple have been somewhat exaggerated.'

There was a roar of laughter.

'Unfortunately,' Max went on, 'the quacks insist that I am not yet ready for combat flying, and as I expect instant and unquestioned obedience from you in response to my commands, it would be hypocritical of me not to obey the medical commands to which I am at this time subject. However, we are talking only of a week or two, and then I shall be personally leading you into battle. And as of this moment I am commanding you into battle, whether I am physically present or not. Colonel Peltzer has flown with me many times, and fully understands my tactics. He will carry them out in my name, and you will follow, in my name.' He did not look at Peltzer, but he could almost hear the Colonel gulp; he had always regarded as suicidal Max's tactics of flying straight at an enemy and forcing him either to collide or give way and present a target.

'Now, obviously,' Max went on, 'I would like there to be many more of you. Actually, there is no army commander in the history of warfare who has felt he had sufficient men. But they have always managed with what they had. And I can tell you that there are another two hundred replacement pilots due to arrive here in the near future, every one with a new 210.'

Again there was a burst of cheering; again he did not look at Peltzer.

'However,' he said, 'our business is to seek out and destroy any aircraft belonging to the RAF or the USAAF that enters our airspace. I know that this is an immense task as they possess far superior numbers, but it is a holding operation. I can tell you now that within a few weeks our new, unmanned rockets, the V1, will be ready for launching, and will inflict paralysing casualties on the enemy, which, unless he is bent on committing national suicide, must bring him to the conference table. And just in case he is at that level of desperation, then at this moment being tested, and soon to be in full production, there is an even larger and more powerful flying bomb, the V2, against which no enemy defences are capable of battling. So I tell you this. You are not only fighting for your homes and your loved ones, you are fighting for the continued honour and glory of the Third Reich, for the future of this great nation of ours. Thank you, and good hunting.'

He picked up his crutches to another storm of applause. Peltzer followed him outside. 'Was any of that true, sir?'

'Why, yes, Peltzer. The V1s are just about ready for launching, and the V2s are in an advanced state of testing. And who knows, we may well soon have an influx of new pilots, and new machines.'

'And will we really be able to stop the Allies invading, bring them to the conference table?'

Max looked at him. 'Why, no, Colonel. I do not believe we will.'

'But then . . .'

'We keep that opinion to ourselves, and when the time comes, we die, doing our duty to the Reich.'

Peltzer merely gulped.

'Well, gentlemen.' Hastings looked over his assembled pilots. 'I have to tell you that as from Monday, there will be no more leave, so enjoy this weekend. 'From then on we fly round the clock. We are using the new Typhoons, which, as you know, are specifically designed for ground attack and are very nearly as fast as ourselves, to destroy as required every bridge, every railway line and every ground installation in western France. Our task is to cover them from attack by enemy aircraft. However . . .' He smiled. 'That does not mean you should not do some strafing of your own should the opportunity present itself.'

'Does this mean the balloon is about to go up, sir?' someone asked.

'You are entitled to form your own opinions, but I would not discuss them with anyone. We have been given a task, and we will carry it out. I want every man back here by Sunday night. Dismissed. A word, John.'

John waited while the other pilots filed from the room, already chattering with excitement.

'Do you believe this news coming out of Germany?' Hastings asked.

'As a matter of fact, I do. I felt all along that if he really had been that badly injured, it was just too soon for him to be flying in combat again.'

'Langholm was one of their very best,' Hastings remarked.

'Oh, I know that. I'm pretty sure he was the beggar who shot me down over the Channel in May 1940.'

'And how do you feel about having to take on Max all over again?'

'If he turns up, sir, it will be a pleasure.'

Hastings considered for a moment, and then nodded. 'How does your father feel about it?'

'I haven't been in touch since the news was released.'

'But you'll be seeing him this weekend.'

'I'm looking forward to that. I gather they're having a bit of a time down in Sussex, and of course they're not allowed to leave the house – I mean to go anywhere.'

'So they'll be happy when we get the off.'

'Won't we all? Ah . . .'

Hastings shook his head. 'I can't give you the date, Johnnie, because I don't know it. It's locked up inside Eisenhower's brain at the moment. Not that I'd give you the date even if I did know it. But in view of our orders, I would say that it has to be pretty soon. I'll see you on Sunday night.'

'It'll be the first week in May,' Mark said.

John looked out of the window at the downs below the house. That so peaceful scene he remembered from his boyhood had been transformed into a vast military encampment, which stretched out of sight to left and right. To get home he had had to pass through six checkpoints, at each of which, for all his uniform of a senior RAF officer, his identity card and his pass were carefully inspected. 'Do you know something I don't?' he asked his father.

'Common sense. And a knowledge of tides. They'll want high water for the landings, and a full moon. Ergo, the first week in May.'

'And the weather?'

'Ah. That's the joker in the pack. But again, the first week in May has got to be as good a bet as any.' He turned back from the window and sat down. 'I suppose you're all geared to go?'

'We start Monday. Round-the-clock bombing.'

'So when will you be home again?' Jolinda asked.

'How long is a piece of string? If Dad is right, maybe three weeks. If he isn't, or the weather cuts in . . .'

'Shit!' she suddenly cried.

'You'll miss the Cresswells' party,' Helen commented.

'Helen,' Mark said patiently. 'We are none of us going to the Cresswells' party, unless the invasion is over and done with by then. We can't leave the property until then.'

'Oh, dear.'

'You were given the option of moving out of the mobil-ization zone three months ago,' he reminded her.

'Yes, but you weren't leaving.'

'Of course I wasn't leaving. This is my home. I'd far rather be here and unable to leave than stuck in some London hotel, and have nowhere that I'd want to go.'

Helen sniffed.

'Time for another drink,' Jolinda said, getting up. She knew they were merely skating about the subject they all wanted to talk about but that each was reluctant to bring up. 'Or would you rather switch to champagne?'

There was a moment's silence. Then Mark said, 'You know, that might be a good idea. Clements!'

'He's in the kitchen,' Jolinda said. 'I'll get it.'

'That girl certainly knows how to break the ice,' Mark commented as she left the room. 'What would we do without her?'

That produced another sniff from Helen, but he ignored her.

'You'll have to excuse me, Johnnie. He's the last human link I have with Karolina.'

'There is nothing to be excused about, Dad. He's a great

fighting pilot, and if he's flying again in what must be a pretty parlous physical state, he has more guts than the next man. And he's my brother.'

'But the next time you get him in your sights . . .'

'Oh, yes,' John said. 'I mean to finish the job.'

Max stood on the tarmac to watch his squadrons come home. *Squadrons*, he thought; *now there was a poor joke.*

'Twenty-seven, sir,' Fraulein Krantz stood at his shoulder, binoculars levelled, counting. 'Ah . . .'

'Yes?'

'I do not see Colonel Peltzer's markings, sir.'

Max took the glasses and levelled them. 'Because he's not there. Have the senior surviving officer come to me the moment he is down.'

'Yes, sir.' Krantz gazed at him, but said nothing more. Her face said it all. She had to know that the end, at least for the Luftwaffe in Flanders, was very close. But she did her duty with competent serenity, at least visibly.

He moved quite freely now, even on crutches, sat behind his desk, and heard Mannheimer's voice. A moment later there was a knock on the door. 'You wished to see me, Herr General?'

'I wish to know what happened today, Captain. Sit down.'

Mannheimer slumped into the chair before the desk. His uniform was sweat-stained and his face was haggard. 'As you know, sir, we were directed to intercept a squadron of Typhoons strafing railway bridges over the Seine. We gained them, and were engaging when we were attacked from above by a squadron of Mosquitoes. They were upon us before we could gain sufficient height, and . . . Colonel Peltzer went down almost immediately.'

'Did he get out?'

'I did not see him jump, sir. We lost eight planes.'

'And in return?'

'We got one, sir.'

'I see. Well, go and get some rest. I am promoting you Colonel.'

'Sir?'

Max gave a savage grin. 'Yes, I know. It is a bit hollow. But you deserve the rank. Thank you, Mannheimer.'

Mannheimer went to the door, and checked. 'Going by the markings on his machine, I would say that the Mosquitoes were led by your brother.'

'Who else?' Max agreed.

The door closed and Max was left staring at it. *He is going to win after all*, he thought. *In fact, he has already done so. But if only I could be up there to take him on, one last time.*

There was a tap on the door, and Krantz came in. 'Excuse me, Herr General, but the Field-Marshal is here.'

'What?' Max stood up so violently that he lost his balance. Krantz hurried round the desk to hold him up.

'Field-Marshal Rommel,' she whispered.

'Oh.' He got his crutches into place and stood to attention. 'Herr Field-Marshal? Heil Hitler!'

Erwin Rommel saluted with his baton. 'Heil Hitler!'

Max had not met him before. He was not a tall man, but was very solidly built, with rounded features in which there was a curious mixture of softness and granite. Now he nodded to Krantz, who hurriedly left the room, closing the door behind her. 'I am pleased to make your acquaintance, General Bayley. I have heard excellent reports of you.'

'Thank you, sir. Will you sit down?'

Rommel sat in the chair before the desk. 'How many squadrons have you got in the air at this moment?'

'I have no squadrons in the air at this moment, Herr Field-Marshal.'

Rommel frowned. 'I counted twenty-seven machines on the ground as I came in.'

'That is correct, sir.'

'That is the total force at your command?'

'Yes, sir.'

'But you are expecting replacements.'

'I have been expecting replacements, Herr Field-Marshal, for the past month. There do not seem to be any available.'

'That is absurd. I will get on to Berlin immediately. You realize that an invasion is imminent?'

'I was told it was imminent a month ago.'

'It was. And they apparently changed their minds, presumably because of the weather.'

Max looked out of the window at the heavy clouds over the airfield. 'It is not a lot better now.'

'Nevertheless, we are into June. Eisenhower is running out of time if he is going to get his moon-tide equation right this summer. I believe he may be going to chance his arm, regardless of the weather. And if he does, logic points to the Pas de Calais, which comes under your command in the air. Now, the only mistake we can make would be to let him create a bridgehead. No matter how many men, how many resources the Allies have at their command, they can only put a limited number ashore on the first day. Those men must be contained, and thrown back into the sea before they can establish themselves. My ground commanders understand this, and so must you. I know your resources are appallingly limited. As I have said, I intend to do something about this immediately, but there may not be time to make sufficient difference. The fact remains that once the battle commences, you must throw every man and every machine you possess into it. I do not expect you to attempt to combat the enemy air forces; they are too powerful and too numerous. Your task will be to assist in destroying the enemy on the beaches, destroying their landing craft, their ships, their people. It does not matter if you lose every plane and every man you possess, providing that first wave is driven back into the sea. If we can accomplish that, it is my belief that the invasion will be called off for this summer, and by next year all our new weapons will be in service. Do you understand me?'

Max swallowed. 'Yes, Herr Field-Marshal.'

Rommel stood up. 'Then I will wish you good fortune, Herr General. Heil Hitler!'

Max waited for the Field-Marshal's car to leave the station yard, then called for his own car, and was driven into Ostend. The house was on the beach and, being away from the port, was undamaged. The guard on the gate presented arms, and Max limped into the house itself.

Gerda the housemaid hurried forward in concern. 'Herr General?'

'I will be home for lunch, Gerda.'

'Yes, sir. Frau Bayley is on the beach.'

'Thank you. Open a bottle of champagne to drink with the meal.' He hobbled out of the back door to survey the beach and the sea beyond. It looked absolutely peaceful, although a brisk wind was whipping up the odd whitecap. But the wind was warm.

The tide was full, and there was almost no evidence of the many underwater obstacles that had been placed during the past few months. The little boy splashed happily in the shallows, watched by his mother, who sat on the sand a few yards above the water. She wore a black bathing costume, her hair was loose, and she looked absolutely beautiful. A good memory, he thought, to take with him into eternity.

She heard the crunch of his feet and the crutches on the sand, and turned, rising to her knees. 'Max!' She was as surprised as Gerda had been to see him home in the middle of the morning.

'My darling!' He laid down the crutches and carefully lowered himself to the sand beside her.

She gazed at him. 'What has happened?'

'Nothing – yet. But I have come to talk to you. Will you please just listen to what I have to say, and then do as I ask?'

She was frowning. She had never seen him so serious. 'Of course, if it is that important to you.'

'It is the most important thing in the world to me. This morning I received a visit from Field-Marshal Rommel.'

'I wondered when he was going to turn up. He's been just about everywhere else on the Atlantic Wall.'

'You promised not to interrupt.' He gave her the gist of what Rommel had said, then held up his finger as she would have spoken. 'There is no longer any use pretending that it may not happen, and if the Field-Marshal is right, and he usually is, it is going to happen right here. And it could be tomorrow. I wish you and Max to leave today.'

'And go where?'

'You will go to Bitterman. It is your home, and if anything should happen to me, just contact Milch and he will make sure that it *is* your home, and nobody else's.'

'But you intend to stay here.'

'My darling, this is my command.'

'And you are my husband.'

'And Little Max is your son, to whom you have a greater duty than to me.'

She stared at him, but he knew she would obey him. 'There is one thing more.'

Her mouth twisted. She knew what it was.

'I wish you to release me from my promise not to fly until I am fully recovered.'

'Max!'

'Release me!' His voice was hard. 'Or force me to concede that I am a coward.'

Hildegarde burst into tears.

'Well, gentlemen,' Group Captain Hastings said. 'I have just heard from Area Command. It is tonight.'

Every head turned to look out of the window at the lowering clouds.

'I know,' Hastings said. 'It is not ideal, but it is better than a couple of days ago, and the Met boys say it will stay this way for the next couple of days.'

'Two or three days?' someone commented. 'Isn't that chancing their arm?'

'Was there ever a war fought without chancing an arm or two? It's tomorrow or it's off again, with the tide-moon ratio becoming more and more unfavourable with every month. Right. Your targets are all road and rail communication to the south-east of Caen. Beginning here.' They crowded round, and he indicated the map. 'It is very important that you do not strafe north or west of that mark.'

'But isn't that a bridge?'

'That is the Orne River Bridge. Our people want that intact, and they are putting down an airborne Commando troop to seize it and hold it until ground forces can reach it. Your job is to prevent Jerry bringing up any heavy stuff to regain it.' He looked around their faces. 'You will maintain your attack until it is time to return here to re-arm. I'm afraid you may have to fly several sorties.'

'I take it we're allowed to take out any interference by the Luftwaffe?' Spencer inquired.

Hastings grinned. 'Our information is that there is no Luftwaffe left to interfere. Good luck, and good hunting, gentlemen.'

With the departure of Hildegarde and Little Max, Max had a camp bed made up in the office: the house by the sea, even in the brief couple of months they had lived there, held too many pleasant memories. Now he was on the spot for whatever might turn up, and he was awakened just after dawn on 6 June by an anxious Krantz. 'I have General Bayerlein on the telephone, Herr General.'

'At this hour?' But Bayerlein was Rommel's chief of staff. He swung his legs out of bed, and Krantz helped him to his feet and inserted his crutches into his armpits, then made sure he successfully crossed the floor to his desk, and the telephone extension. 'Bayley.'

'Good morning, General Bayley. Field-Marshal Rommel wished you informed that the enemy have landed. The invasion has begun.'

Max looked out of the window. It was already broad daylight, and although the beach and the sea were invisible from the airfield, he could see the twin spires of Ostend cathedral, and there was no suggestion of any bombardment or fighting over there, while the sky was empty of aircraft. Dunkirk, Calais and Boulogne were only a few miles south of where he was sitting. Any invasion would surely have been discernible, either audibly or visually, from Ostend. 'May I ask where you are calling from, General Bayerlein?'

'Is that important? I am in our headquarters in Rheims. What is important is that the Allies have several thousand ships in the Bay of the Seine, and are pouring men and materiel into Normandy.'

'Normandy? My God! We had supposed—'

'I know. We have been outwitted. We require every machine you have that will fly down here to strafe the beaches and help drive them back into the sea.'

Max still found it difficult to believe what he had been told. 'Are you sure this is not a diversion?'

'General Bayley, if the Allies can afford to use an estimated six thousand ships and five thousand aircraft as a diversion, then God help us all. How soon can you get there?'

'In an hour. Did you say five thousand aircraft?'

'That is correct. How many do you have?'

'Twenty-six.'

'My God!'

'No, make that twenty-seven,' Max said, the adrenaline bubbling in his veins.

'Well, their aircraft are more concerned with bombing and

strafing our rear areas than with patrolling the beaches. Come in low, and you stand a chance of getting through. One hour, General.'

Max hung up and looked at Krantz. 'Sound the alarm, and then help me dress.'

This usually took several minutes, owing to his slow movements. The young woman gulped, ran into the outer office to press the switch that had the siren blaring, then returned to help him into his clothes. 'Thank you,' he said as she knotted his tie. 'I know this is remiss of me, Krantz, but I have never asked your Christian name. I think I should know it now.'

Her cheeks were pink. 'It is Adelaide, sir.'

'Thank you. I will remember.'

He got his crutches into place and hobbled to the door.

'Will you be back for lunch, sir?'

He turned his head to look at her. 'Who knows, Adelaide? Do not wait for me.'

Mannheimer and his pilots were assembled, all staring at their commanding officer, wearing full flying kit. 'Herr General?'

'Gentlemen, the invasion has begun.'

All heads turned to look towards the sea, as he had done earlier.

'In the Bay of the Seine,' Max told them. 'There is a large enemy concentration. Our business is to clear the beaches. It is not to engage enemy aircraft. Therefore we are going to fly at two hundred metres to escape observation.'

'Yes, sir. But . . . you are going to lead us?'

'That is my intention.'

'Your aircraft . . .'

'Steiger!'

'It is being wheeled out now, Herr General.'

On his instructions, Max's aircraft had been kept fuelled and fully armed since his return, and in fact he had sat in it from time to time, both from nostalgia and a desire to familiarize his shattered body with the controls. Now he was lifted up and settled in the cockpit. Steiger himself adjusted the belts. 'Give them hell, Herr General.'

Max squeezed his hand, and a few moments later was airborne, swinging south, moving the plane from left to right as he tested his feet on the rudder bar. They still felt curiously disconnected from the rest of his body, but the messages from his brain were getting through. He felt a glow of exultation as he hurtled over the landscape, the sense of extreme speed accentuated by the rooftops streaking by beneath him, so close he felt they could almost be touched. Dunkirk, Calais, Boulogne, Dieppe . . . He gulped as he saw the enormous accumulation of ships in front of him. Above his head there was a constant procession of bombers, almost wingtip to wingtip, but as Bayerlein had promised, none of them noticed the small German squadron so far beneath them.

Le Havre and the huge Bay of the Seine opened in front of him. Once again he gulped. There were even more ships crammed into the huge inlet, and it seethed like a disturbed ant heap, with some fairly large vessels still manoeuvring into position while others, closer to the shore, unleashed a steady stream of packed landing craft. The beaches themselves were crowded with men and vehicles, some forming up, others heading inland. They were meeting with considerable resistance, but were steadily pushing at the high ground behind the shoreline.

Now the approaching aircraft had been seen, and the anti-aircraft batteries on the ships opened fire.

'Ignore them,' Max said. 'Our target is the beaches.'

A moment later he was swooping low over the surprised men, firing his machine-guns and rockets, watching them scatter, and many fall.

'Good shooting,' Spencer told his pilots as the bridge burst into flames and disintegrating stonework. 'One more run, at the next, three miles upriver. Then it's home to re-arm.'

But he had only just finished speaking when a voice broke in. 'F Squadron, abort your mission.'

'What?' Spencer shouted.

'You are required over the beaches, urgently. Our forces are under attack by enemy aircraft.'

'Shit!' Lewis said. 'I thought they didn't have any left.'

'So, apparently, did the brass. You heard the man. Follow me.'

Spencer swung his aircraft in a tight turn and headed north-west. John checked his instruments. Fuel was no problem, but they had been blazing away without restraint, and as the Group Captain had just said, it was almost time to go home to re-arm. This would have to be a quick battle.

'There they go,' Spencer said.

The houses of Caen were visible to their right, and they were flying over the small harbour of Ouistreham, where there was considerable fighting going on. In front of them was the German squadron, having completed one run and now turning back for another. Only one squadron, but it seemed to be having considerable effect on the beaches.

'Do you see what I see, sir?' Langley spoke as quietly as ever. As he was not flying the plane, and there was no navigation or photographing or bomb sighting to be done, he had been able to study the fast closing enemy, who had apparently only just sighted the approaching Mosquitoes, and were turning to meet them.

'It can't be,' John muttered.

'That's a hundred plus. And a wing-leader's marking. And we know Langholm is dead.'

John turned to make for Max's machine as the air became filled with chattering machine-guns and flying tracers. And now Max spotted him as well, again easily identifiable as he had the most kills of any of the British pilots. 'Bastard!' he said as the two machines hurtled at each other, closing at more than a mile every five seconds.

'No, no, Johnnie,' came the reply. 'You're the bastard.'

'Christ!' Langley said. 'He means to ram!'

John could remember those had been Max's tactics even as far back as the Battle of Britain, always relying on the opposing pilot giving way first. And usually it had been successful. But not today. The Messerschmitt was in his sights. He squeezed the trigger, saw an instant burst of smoke from his opponent. But in that instant the Mosquito shuddered violently, and there was a creaking sound. 'We're hit,' he told Langley unnecessarily. 'Get out.'

'Bit low for that, sir,' Langley replied. 'I think we're going in together.'

'How do you feel?' Spencer stood by the bed.

'Bloody awful,' John said. 'What have I got?'

'A broken shoulder. You deserve more. What is the point of having the fastest combat aircraft in the world and wasting it on an old-fashioned confrontation?'

'Did I get him?'

'He went down. As to what happened to him, well, like you, he was too low to bail out, but we think he made it behind German lines before crashing.'

And he was already half crippled, John thought.

'Your wife and father are here,' Spencer said. 'So I'll leave you to it.'

'Oh, you noodle,' Jolinda said. 'I hope you're satisfied.'

'I didn't win.' John pointed out.

'You didn't lose,' Mark reminded him.

'But if he's alive, I'll have to do it all over again.'

'I don't know about that. Now we're ashore in force and making progress, wouldn't you say that the end is in sight?'

'Not while Max is about,' John said.

Jolinda kissed him.

The ambulance came to a gentle halt at the steps of the schloss. Count Max, Oriane and Hildegarde were there to watch it, but only Hildegarde went down to be beside the stretcher as it was carefully taken from the rear of the vehicle. 'Oh, my darling,' she said.

Max squeezed her hand. 'Only a bullet wound this time. And a slight jarring to one leg. I came down in a potato field.'

'He isn't dead.'

'I know. They managed to fish him out of the drink. But I did hit him. That's the first time I have ever got a Mosquito. And the next time . . .'

She walked beside him, still holding his hand, as he was carried up the steps. 'Is there going to be a next time, Max? You know we didn't throw them back into the sea? They're coming closer every day. And you're out of action for at least three months . . .'

'I know it's a hopeless mess, my dearest. But we're going to *live* until we die right?'

'And go on killing, until we die?'

'We deliberately sowed the wind,' Max said. 'Now we can hear the whirlwind, as you say, coming ever closer. But we – you and I at least – are going to face it with a smile.'